CAPTAIN'S LOG:
WILLIAM SHATNER'S

PERSONAL ACCOUNT OF THE MAKING OF

CAPTAIN'S LOG:
WILLIAM SHATNER'S
PERSONAL ACCOUNT OF THE MAKING OF

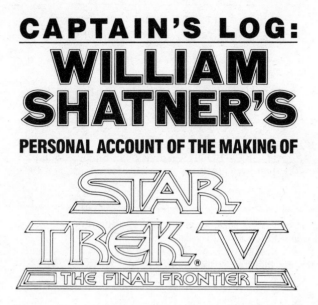

STAR TREK V
THE FINAL FRONTIER

AS TOLD BY
Lisabeth Shatner

POCKET BOOKS
New York   London   Toronto   Sydney   Tokyo

For the cast and crew of
Star Trek V: The Final Frontier

Another *Original* publication of POCKET BOOKS

POCKET BOOKS, a division of Simon & Schuster Inc.
1230 Avenue of the Americas, New York, NY 10020

ISBN: 0-671-68652-6

First Pocket Books trade paperback printing July 1989

10 9 8 7 6 5 4 3 2 1

POCKET and colophon are trademarks
of Simon & Schuster Inc.

Printed in the U.S.A.

CONTENTS

ACKNOWLEDGMENTS

Since so many people were part of the making of *Star Trek V,* it would be impossible to list them all individually. But I would like to express my deep gratitude for all the help and support that each member of the cast, crew, and studio has shown me. I would also like to give special thanks to Harve Bennett, who was so generous with his time, wisdom, and advice.

Other thanks go to Terry Erdmann, Tim Downs, and Robert Parker for their contributions to the interview chapter. To my editor, Dave Stern, I express my appreciation for his guidance. I would also like to thank Noela and Rueben Hueso for their patient help in transcribing my taped interviews. My friends and family, who were incredibly supportive throughout my experience, also deserve thanks. Special gratitude goes to Mary Donovan, Kathleen King, and Jason Hoffs, who were especially helpful when I needed it. Most of all, I'd like to thank my father for giving me this opportunity, and my stepmother, Marcy, whose idea it was in the first place.

CAPTAIN'S LOG:

WILLIAM SHATNER'S

PERSONAL ACCOUNT OF THE MAKING OF

INTRODUCTION

People are always asking me, "What's it like to be Captain Kirk's daughter?" The question seems strange, because it reminds me that they see my father differently than I do. To them, William Shatner is the legendary Captain Kirk, the brave leader of the *Enterprise* and its crew. To me, he's just dad. It's true—most dads don't phaser aliens for a living. But he is still my father: the man who comforted me when I was little and scared of the dark, who forbade me to see "The Exorcist" when I was twelve, and who told me to be home early when I was sixteen. So I am always a little shocked when someone asks him for an autograph or his picture, because I am reminded of the huge impact "Star Trek" has made on the American public. At those moments, I realize he is not just my father. He is Captain James T. Kirk of the starship *Enterprise* as well.

As a little girl, I felt confused because of this dichotomy. I knew my father "pretended" for a living, although the nature of his pretending remained a mystery. My confusion finally became apparent to everyone one evening when I walked into the den to say good night to my parents. They were watching, of all things, "Star Trek." On the screen, a giant, slimy-looking lizard, making hideous hissing noises, was chasing my father. I was terrified, and burst into tears, certain the monster was about to hurt my daddy. (The fact that he was sitting right there on the couch didn't count for much at the time.) He was then forced to leave Captain Kirk fighting the giant lizard in order to comfort me. He assured me the monster was only "pretend" and wouldn't harm him.

My awareness of his profession grew in stages. One particularly vivid memory I have is of a trip to Disneyland when I was about five. My parents, my older sister, Leslie, and I were all standing in front of the *Matterhorn.* Leslie and I were trying to convince my mother to let us go on the ride, when three teenage girls appeared next to us and began jumping up and down, pointing excitedly at my father. I couldn't understand their strange behavior, nor could I understand why my father became flustered and hustled us away from the ride. All I knew was that I was losing my chance to ride the *Matterhorn.*

He led us unwillingly towards the *Mad Hatter,* which I considered one of the most wimpy rides in the park. It didn't even rate a "C" ticket (those were the days when Disneyland still rated their rides by using alphabet letters. "C" was definitely for babies.) It was just about the last ride I wanted to go on, but my father insisted. So we suffered through the Cheshire Cat's grinning and the Rabbit's perpetual tardiness, convinced that the teenage girls would be gone when we got off. Our hearts sank when we saw them waiting for us at the exit.

We tried *It's a Small World* next. This attraction was a definite improvement. There were lots of dolls with sparkling costumes, and I even started humming the lyrics to the song. We emerged triumphant—the girls were nowhere to be seen. Our euphoria lasted approximately three minutes, until we spotted them following us again.

What started out as mildly annoying had now become infuriatingly intrusive. None of us were enjoying ourselves now (not even me), though we made one last attempt to escape on the *Skyline Tram.* No one would be crazy enough to follow a poor family of four up above the park—would they?

But as we were floating above the grounds I looked behind me, and saw the same three girls in the tram behind us, still laughing and pointing at us, oblivious to the fact that we felt more like hunted game than a family at Disneyland.

When we got off, my father finally had had enough. "If I give you my autograph, will you promise to leave us alone?" he asked. "Yes, yes!" they cried, still jumping up and down. He hastily scribbled his signature on an eagerly proffered sheet of paper, and the girls magically disappeared. We were finally left as before, still trying to convince my mother to let us ride the *Matterhorn*.

The incident at Disneyland stands out in my mind as my first confrontation with my father's fame. I knew he must have done something important to deserve such attention, although I wasn't quite sure what it was. I didn't fully comprehend the situation until I actually appeared on an episode of "Star Trek."

The episode, entitled "Miri," took place on a planet where no one survived past adolescence. There were several scenes which required a group of scruffy children to run around an abandoned schoolroom. I was going to be one of those children.

When we reached the studio, a lot of other children were waiting in a large room near the set. The place looked like a disaster area. Kids of all shapes and sizes were running about, shooting "pretend" guns at each other, playing marbles, or screaming loudly. The din was unbearable, and it frightened me so much I burst into tears. My bewildered mother tried to comfort me, but I was inconsolable. I didn't understand who all these people were or why we were all waiting in this large, noisy room. All I wanted to do was go home.

I calmed down once we entered the set and were directed to the costume room. This was the first time I realized we were supposed to be having fun. Someone handed me a box with a costume in it, and told me to put it on. Since Halloween was one of my favorite holidays, I opened the box eagerly—I was getting a chance to dress up, and it wasn't even Halloween! However, my excitement was somewhat lessened when I saw the costume. It was a beige, apron-like dress with the words "I Spy" printed on the left pocket. Even at the age of five, I considered myself too mature to wear such a silly costume. I spent the next hour with my left hand over the print.

My mother made matters worse when she asked the costumer if they had any green wigs left. She had seen a little girl walk by with a wig of long, green ratty hair and she wanted one for me. I breathed a sigh of relief when she was informed none were left.

In spite of my costume, I was beginning to enjoy the attention. Leslie, who was also appearing in the episode (and got a much better costume than I did), accompanied me to the make-up room to visit dad. When we walked into the room, he was sitting in the make-up chair, his back to us. We ran forward excitedly, relieved to see his familiar outline. When he turned towards us, I caught a glimpse of his arm and saw the skin on the inside of his elbow was covered with a long, bluish-red scab! I blanched, and my dad burst out laughing, and told us to touch the sore. It was made of rubber—at that moment, I realized everything was "pretend." Once I understood that, I relaxed.

Next, we were led onto the set, which looked like an ancient, cobwebbed version of the schoolrooms I knew. Leslie and I, along with the other kids from the waiting area, were carefully placed around the room. My father then appeared and bright, hot lights were turned on us. A make-up man came around and put dirt smudges on our faces, something which Leslie didn't appreciate very much. We stood around for a while, and I got pretty bored. An older boy was nice enough to give me a piece of Wrigley's spearmint gum, my favorite. We stood around some more.

Finally, my father started talking. I understood that his words belonged to the "pretend" realm, but what he was saying still didn't make much sense. "Look at your hands," he commanded. "They have blood on them." When no one moved, he stopped talking. "Well, look at them," he said, and all the kids looked down at their hands. I followed suit, but didn't see anything unusual. I wondered why he told me there was blood on my hands when there wasn't any.

The next scene didn't clear up my confusion. The nice boy

with the gum was told to pick me up and carry me towards my father, whereupon I was supposed to take a swipe at my father's face. I knew this part was "pretend." In fact, I couldn't keep a smile off my face every time I got close to hitting him. My father kept saying, "No, no you can't smile," every time I grinned. We had to do it four or five times before I finally could keep a straight face. I wasn't entirely sure why I was supposed to look as if I meant to hit him.

The last scene I was in occurred when Dr. McCoy overdosed on the antidote he had developed and Captain Kirk came running into the room where Dr. McCoy had collapsed. My father entered carrying me, and set me down next to the actress playing Janice Rand, who was kneeling on the floor. The scene took a long time to film. Eventually, I began looking around the room, and discovered I had a bird's eye view of the top of the actress's head. I was utterly fascinated by her hair, which was woven into a checkered pattern on top. I stared at that hair for a long time, wondering if it was possible to actually play checkers on it.

After my appearance on "Star Trek," I had pretty much figured out what my father did, although it didn't seem like such a huge deal at the time. After all, I "pretended" too, with my dolls at home, and games at school. It seemed natural to me that "pretending" continued into adulthood. When I overheard the occasional whisper that "her father is on TV," I ignored it. Who cared? I was more concerned whether I could read the green primer instead of the babyish red one, or whether the cute boy next to me looked at me that day or not.

I began awakening to the reality of the situation with my parents' divorce. Even at five years of age, I knew exactly what was going on. I stood on the front porch of our house, my arms entangled around my father's neck, begging him not to go. But he gently disengaged himself from my embrace, got in his car, and drove off. At that point, I realized part of him was gone forever. He appeared only once or twice a week after that to see me and my two sisters. Sunday was the most special day of all, when we got to spend the whole day with him. We

13

would usually do some kind of activity—horseback riding and ice skating were our favorites.

Matters got worse when we moved, and I unwillingly attended a new grade school. Everything there seemed strange and unfamiliar—much more attention was placed on my last name than at my old school. I distinctly remember one boy joking, "I'm going to marry you, divorce you, and take all your money." I smiled, but I didn't think it was so funny.

As my father's fame increased, I became more and more uncomfortable with the attention that accompanied it. I was desperate for acceptance at school, but my discomfort made me shy. My silence was interpreted as snobbery, and by the time I reached seventh grade, I felt like an outcast.

I retreated into the only two things which gave me pleasure—books and food. I read everything I could get my hands on, especially science fiction, fantasy, or mystery novels, usually accompanied by a chocolate bar. The fatter I got, the more miserable I got. I spent lunchtime sitting on the bleachers at the end of the playground, my nose buried in a book.

At this point in my life, my father's appearances took on a somewhat magical quality. He would appear on the weekends, and for a few hours, sweep me away from reality. He often took us traveling with him when he worked—Hawaii, Florida, Canada. And he was always doing something interesting. When we visited him on the set of "Barbary Coast" he was so well disguised that we didn't even recognize him. My sisters and I would watch proudly on the sidelines as he acted in a variety of TV shows, movies, and plays. And we met fascinating people when we were with him—actors, directors, or other show business people he had known through the years. When I watched him, I was struck by his energy, his talent, and the way he could make people laugh.

At this point in my life, I felt a strange ambivalence towards "Star Trek." I knew much of my father's success as an actor was because of the series, and for that I was grateful and proud. "Star Trek" had also made him the magical, famous father who could sweep me out of my misery. But it was also "Star Trek" that had set me apart in the first place, making me an outcast and the target for so much criticism. I often felt that I had no identity other than "Captain Kirk's daughter," and even joked that those words would be engraved on my tombstone.

I carried that ambivalence into high school, where it suddenly became very important that I establish my own identity. I did everything I could think of to accomplish that—joined the cheerleading squad, the modern dance group, and always did the best I could in school. By my senior year, I felt I had made some progress. I had my own friends and activities, and had done well enough in school to assure my entry into almost any college I wanted.

But just as I felt the noise about "Star Trek" subside in my own head, the outside world began to shout about it again. *Star Trek: The Motion Picture* was released, and was a tremendous success. But as proud and grateful as I was for the boost the film gave my father's career, I couldn't help but be frustrated by its success. Any hope I'd ever had of disassociating myself from "Star Trek" seemed gone.

By the time I got to college, my paranoia was in full swing. I would refrain from telling people my last name, so months would go by before anyone would discover who I really was. The fact was, I didn't know who I really was. I wanted so much to do something significant, something worthwhile, something that would prove I was a separate person. As my frustration grew, my resentment continued to build. Again, I tried a variety of things to distinguish myself, including a stint in Milan as a model. But even in Italy they knew about "Star Trek," and my nickname among my Italian counterparts soon became "Captain."

I returned home with the same sense of doom. During this period, my father had landed the series "T.J. Hooker," and was working at the furious pace that series television demands. I was hopeful that the series would give him—and me—some identification with something other than "Star Trek." The series was successful, but it seemed nothing could ever eclipse "Star Trek." I would consistently hear jokes on TV and radio about how weird it was "to see Captain Kirk in a police uniform."

During the filming of *Star Trek II: The Wrath of Khan,* he was so busy the only way to see him was to visit the set. During this time, I had reached a point of real crisis in my life. College was almost over, and I had only vague plans for my future. My love for books had given me a desire to write, but I dismissed these ideas as folly. What could I possibly do in life that would measure up to my father's success? My epitaph— "Captain Kirk's daughter lies here"—seemed predestined.

Since my father was so busy with the *Star Trek* movies and his series, it was difficult to discuss my concerns with him. And when I actually had the chance to talk to him, we would often butt heads. I had continued modeling for a short period after graduation, whereupon he assured me I was "bumbling my life." By the time he filmed *Star Trek III,* we were battling on a regular basis. The one and only time I visited him on the set of *Star Trek III* we fought until I was reduced to tears. I left the set sobbing and never returned.

At this point, I decided to go to law school. This pleased my father, and our battles soon subsided. But I was never really happy with the choice, and often found myself thinking up story ideas for movies and TV shows in the middle of class. During one particularly dreary lecture, I came up with an idea for a "T.J. Hooker" episode, which I then told to my father. He liked it, and suggested I present it to the producer of the show.

Arriving at the producer's office, I was so nervous I had to read directly from the typewritten page I had prepared. I was sure he was just listening politely as a way to please my father. To my surprise, he liked the idea and told me to go ahead and write the first draft. I was so excited when I left the office— finally, doing something I really wanted!

The producer and story editors liked the first draft, and gave me the go-ahead for the second draft. The episode was finally produced, which they entitled "Partners in Death." When I saw my name on the opening credits, I knew I had found something I really wanted to do.

But to this day I still wonder how much of it had to do with my father. I found myself in the same ambivalent position as before; grateful for the opportunity I knew never would have occurred but for my father, and wondering how much of it I really deserved. I wondered whether I'd ever be able to accomplish anything on my own.

After law school, my path became much clearer. I knew I wanted to give writing a try, so I got a part-time legal job and began scribbling in my spare time.

Just a few months later, my father asked me to work with him on this book. I was so excited I literally jumped up and down. It seemed my dream of writing a book was coming true. The irony of the subject matter did not escape me. "Star Trek!" It seemed as though my father's—in fact, my whole family's—fate was inextricably linked to the legend.

I carried my frustration into the initial stages of this project. I was sure everyone involved thought I was there for no other reason than my last name. But the only reaction I ever got from the crew was support and encouragement. Since many of them had entered the business through family connections, it didn't seem particularly unusual that I was doing the same. In fact, they urged me to make the most of my opportunity.

As time went on, I began to relax and really enjoy the people and the project. I was filled with admiration for these people who had stuck to their creative visions over the years and had actually made a living at doing so. One of the most valuable lessons I gained from this experience was that dreams really can come true if you work hard enough and believe in yourself. I had never really been surrounded by a group of people who taught this axiom so clearly.

The one person who demonstrated this lesson most distinctly was my father. Although I had often visited "Star Trek" and other sets, I had never had the opportunity to observe him in his work environment for any long period of time. I had always known how smart and talented he was, but I had never seen him put his abilities into action until this moment. Day after day he was called upon to make creative decisions involving the look of a scene, or an actor's performance, or even what God's image should be. Although he had many talented people surrounding him, the ultimate decision always remained his. He was forced to rely on the only source of creativity he knew—himself. Time and time again I was filled with admiration as he managed to make these decisions successfully. I felt grateful to be witnessing a project that involved such a creative director and crew.

And "Star Trek" began to look like the magical, wonderfully inventive show it really had been all these years. By the end of principal photography, I found myself in the new position of actually liking "Star Trek," free of any ambivalence or resentment.

The fact is, "Star Trek" always has been, and always will be, part of my life. The man in the command chair, making life and death decisions every day, exploring strange new worlds, seeking out new life and new civilizations (including giant lizards) is not only Captain Kirk—he's my father. And I am very grateful to have worked alongside him during the last few months, observing his talent, dedication, and enthusiasm during the making of *Star Trek V,* an enterprise that has made me proud to be Captain Kirk's daughter.

1

WILLIAM SHATNER'S JOURNEY

Whenever I see my father in his Starfleet uniform, it brings back memories of the "Star Trek" television episodes and films. But as I began work on this book, I realized I knew very little about my father's own memories of those days. How did he approach playing Captain Kirk for the first time? Indeed, what motivated him to become an actor in the first place? What were his early years like? When did he first want to become a director? These questions, and many more, piqued my curiosity. I sought the answers one day as we chatted in his office, waiting for a preproduction meeting on *Star Trek V* to begin. Behind the desk where he sat hung posters of each *Star Trek* movie, the color renderings of his face projecting strength and assurance behind each glass encasement. It seemed an appropriate setting to discuss the man behind the image—the man behind Captain Kirk.

My father explained that he was bitten by the acting bug as a young child. "When I was six, I was in a camp play in the Laurentian Mountains in Canada," he said. "I don't remember exactly what the play was about, but I do know it had something to do with Germany and children. I was a child whose dog was being taken from him. Another camper was playing the dog. Of course I didn't realize how meaningful the play was, but this was the late thirties, and the war was gathering at this point. So this play about this child and his dog must have struck a nerve in the audience, many of whom must have had relatives being killed, or incarcerated, or kicked out of the country at that very moment.

"In any case, I finished the play, and at the end I looked up and saw that everyone was crying. At that moment, I had a firm feeling of being able to get ahold of people's emotions. I think that was all the reinforcement I needed. So from that moment on, I wasn't interested in anything else except acting. That and sports. So I would box in camp and then do a play. Or I would miss football practice for rehearsals. But even at that point I knew how important acting was to me."

His desire to perform carried over into school. "I grew up in Montreal, and I would do fairy tale plays in a little theater after school hours. There was a radio show every Saturday morning that also did these fairy tales. I was always playing Prince Charming. So I did these plays and radio shows for four or five years, starting at age ten."

Although he was gaining rapid experience as a child actor, his parents regarded his acting as a hobby, something to be indulged, but never taken seriously. "My father thought it was a foolishness I would soon outgrow. He wanted me to go into his business—he was a clothing manufacturer in Montreal. And I, because my thoughts were led by him, thought that was the case—that this was merely some flight of fancy. These movies that I would go to as a kid in the neighborhood theaters and watch four or five times in an afternoon, or the ones I made my parents take me to on Saturday mornings, were just forms of amusement to them. None of us realized at that point—not even me—that these films were seeping into my skin, becoming an essential part of my being. My parents never took them seriously."

But he did. And every year he would continue doing the radio shows, weekly plays, and once a year a larger production such as *Ali Baba and the Forty Thieves*. By the time he reached high school, acting had become a regular part of his life. "When I reached high school, I started auditioning for amateur theater. I always got the parts I read for. The shock of being turned down when I later became a professional was profound.

The joy of acting at this point in my life was reinforced by my success. I always got good notices, people approved of me. I was successful as a child. So what acting gave me was far more than a sense of expression—it was everything a child needs.''

What about studying? ''I didn't study too much,'' he laughed. ''I always got by—somehow or other I passed—but just barely. I think my parents wanted me to become a professional, but in my environment that was every parent's desire for their child, in order that the child could stay alive and provide for himself. Most of the parents that I knew were immigrants, or first generation descendants of immigrants, and there was a hunger and a need and a drive in them. That's what my parents were. In those days, having your son hang about with these vagabonds was nothing to be proud of. These were the days when show business people were to be feared. They were the itinerant wanderers, the minstrels. So of course my parents didn't want that for me.''

In spite of his parents' admonitions ''to get serious,'' he continued to pursue his two loves—sports and acting. But not without a price. ''I played various sports, skiing and football for the school, and at the same time I was always doing plays. That dichotomy frequently got me into trouble when I would have to sacrifice one for the other. I remember one play, *Golden Boy,* by Clifford Odets, which was very much my story. In the play, the boy wanted to be a boxer and a violinist, just as I wanted to be an actor and an athlete. But both required a lot of attention. So I would miss football practice and be kicked off the team because I had missed practice for a play. Then I would do the play an injustice when I had to do something for the school in sports. Gradually, I realized I had to make a choice, and my choice was to be an actor.''

He continued to choose acting, even after he entered McGill University and was supposedly pursuing a degree in business. ''I scraped enough marks together to get into McGill, which was the most respected school in Montreal. Each year I barely made it through. I would fail at least one subject every summer and have to make it up in the fall. My grade point average was just above fifty percent the whole time—below fifty percent you failed and were kicked out of college. So I was getting fifty point five, things like that. It was terrible. I just about made it. But all that time, I was spending hours and hours in the drama department, acting.''

He became heavily involved in the school drama clubs, at one point heading all the radio, television, and theater groups. He wrote, directed and acted in the college reviews three out of the four years he attended the school. ''I remember we had a little room way down in the basement. Our review was called 'The Red and White Review' because those were the colors of McGill. And this became my little place—I would take girls down there—it was awful. More things went on in there than just writing 'The Red and White Review!' But it was a lot of fun and a lot of intrigue.''

Despite all the fun he was having, there was a serious undercurrent of disapproval forming in his family. His father had become increasingly concerned that his son was heading for a dead end. ''By this time, my father was getting worried. There was one fateful evening, in about my third year of college, when my father said, 'You have to start giving this up.' Before that, I had never entertained the thought of becoming a professional. But when I heard those words, out of my mouth I blurted, 'I want to do this for a living.' My father just became unglued—he lost his temper with me. We never really could talk sanely about it. So even though I was enjoying a reputation as a really good amateur actor in Montreal, I was a prophet without honor in my own family.

''My father always assumed I would take over his business one day. I would go down to this clothing factory and work for him on weekends and summers. After one hour there I would get very tired. It was so boring. Yet I could work eighteen hours a day on a musical. Dimly, I began to perceive that I didn't want to go into my father's business. But the thought of not going in, of doing something I wanted, didn't seem likely either. All I remember saying to him was, 'No, I want to try acting,' not even knowing how to begin.''

But he did begin. He took his first baby steps into the professional theater world by attaining an assistant manager position in a local summer stock theater. "I applied for an acting job at the Mountain Playhouse in Montreal after graduation. The woman who was running the theater had directed me in some university plays. She told me all the acting positions were taken, but there was an assistant manager job available. I grabbed the chance but I was a terrible manager. I proceeded to lose the money and the tickets. They even thought I had stolen some money at one point. I just couldn't keep track of it. So they fired me as an assistant manager and hired me as an actor. And when the summer was over, the producer of the play recommended me as an assistant manager to a theater in Ottawa, which is about 150 miles from Montreal. I don't know why he did this, but he did. So they took me on as an assistant manager and a bit player. The same thing happened. They saw I was a good actor and a bad assistant manager. So they fired me as manager and hired me as an actor."

It was in Ottawa where he had his first hard times. "I lived alone for the first time. I lived in a little garret in a house, and lived on a tiny amount of money. I couldn't make ends meet. I couldn't pay my rent, and eat, and do my laundry, and go to a movie once a week. So frequently I didn't do my laundry. I ate as little as possible, at Woolworths and the Five and Dime, places like that."

Did he ever regret the decision to act during those lean years? "I never wondered what I was doing, because I was doing well. I was getting good notices and a lot of experience. At this point my father gave me some money and said, 'If you think at some point you've made a mistake, you'll always have a place at home with me.' He was very, very kind, and in that last moment, very encouraging. But I never did go home, because soon after that Tyrone Guthrie, the leading director in the English theater, came to Canada to set up the Stratford Ontario Theater for Shakespeare. His assistant came to Ottawa to direct a play, where she spotted me and asked me to go to Stratford. I had already been asked to go as a spear carrier the year before, but since I was doing well in Ottawa, I turned it down. But this time, I got offered the juvenile roles. So I accepted and had my first experience with big-time Canadian actors, directors, and especially this world-class director, Tyrone Guthrie. He took me under his wing and was very encouraging. He even told me I could become an Olivier, whom Guthrie had directed while working in England.

"There were other encouraging things said about me at that time. There was one moment that is forever ingrained in my mind. Guthrie put on the play *Henry the Fifth,* in which I was to understudy Christopher Plummer. I was so excited about being in the play that I memorized the whole part of King Henry before I even got there, even though I was only the understudy and only had a minor role in the play. But one day Plummer got sick—later it turned out he had kidney stones—and I had to go on. Only they couldn't find me to tell me because I was out swimming or something that day. So finally at about four in the afternoon they found me and told me I was to go on. Now I had never rehearsed the play and never had rehearsed with any of the other actors. They had managed to round up a few of them to practice with me. They kept asking, 'Can you do it, can you do it?' and I answered 'Yes.'

"And I went on. I had gotten through all the difficult parts of the play and only had the flirtation scenes with the princess left. I relaxed, and I lost my concentration so I couldn't remember what the next line was. There was an actor there named Cherry who had a photographic memory. This Cherry fellow was promoted to my former role of Henry's brother when I was given Henry's role. So Cherry was on the stage with me when I went up on my lines. So I walked slowly up the stage, figuring I could make it look like some deep, meaningful moment. I put my arm around Cherry, leaned in close, and said, 'What's my line?' He wasn't used to playing the role, so he froze. And I said a little louder, 'What's my line?' but there was no response. I kept saying, 'What's my line? What's my line?' until I finally realized he wasn't going to tell me. So I walked slowly back up the stage until the line came to me, and I went on and finished.

"The funny thing was, when the play was over, the cast turned to me and applauded. The next day all the Canadian

24

papers were full of notices about how wonderful I had been, including that deep, meaningful moment between Henry and his brother. They thought it was a great interpretation of their relationship! Comments like that really kept me going. So I worked very hard, and stayed in Stratford for three summers, and went back to Toronto in the winter.''

But all this success didn't come without a price. It was in Stratford where he learned about loneliness. ''For those three years I was alone almost all the time. Either it was difficult to make friends, or, as I recall, the people in Toronto were so clannish that I couldn't break through. So I was mostly alone for three years. I learned all about how terrible, debilitating, and mind-numbing loneliness can be. Fear of that has always been with me.''

But it didn't last forever. ''While I was at Stratford, there was a girl there who would come and hang around backstage frequently, and we kind of found each other. I got married very early on, way before I was close to doing anything successful. At that point, Guthrie was doing *Tamberlaine,* which went to New York on a limited run. I got good notices in New York, and agents started to swarm all over me, asking me to stay on in New York. But Guthrie was going to the Edinburgh festival and I wanted to go with him. So I went to the festival first, and then with my new wife, I went to New York to try and break into the New York acting scene.''

The contacts he had made from *Tamberlaine* soon picked him up, and he was immediately thrust into the latter days of live television, where he worked constantly. ''Live television was exactly like the life of five years I had just led in Canada doing play after play. I imagine, looking back now, that it was unusual for somebody my age—who looked younger—to come in and read for a part and seem accomplished and experienced. The people directing in those years hadn't had much experience in the theater themselves. Many of them were fresh out of school or were stage managers and such. And here was this experienced actor coming in. So they hired me and I did a lot of work.''

It was live television which soon brought him to the attention of Hollywood, and he was offered a lucrative contract at MGM. Even though the contract offered him a much larger sum of money than he was used to earning, he turned it down so he could return to New York and appear in the Broadway play, *The World of Susie Wong*. Unfortunately, it turned out to be the worst experience of his young professional life. "It was supposed to be this poetic play about a young painter in Hong Kong. But Josh Logan, the prime director of that age, brought in a young girl for the lead that he had found for *South Pacific*. She had very little experience acting, so we disagreed a lot. Josh Logan stopped coming to the play because he couldn't stand the arguments. I found myself in the nightmare position of being locked by contract into a job I detested. It lasted for two years! But the experience forged and tempered me. These qualities helped my career along."

He soon found himself back on television. "I played a young lawyer in a pilot called 'The Defenders,' a father and son lawyer show. It was made into a series, and I was asked to play the lead, but I turned it down because in those days serious actors didn't do series. Other series were offered to me, but I turned them all down. Still, I was working both coasts, including a year in the play *A Shot in the Dark*, with Julie Harris and Walter Matthau. And there I learned to perfect my comedy timing. The precision of comedy timing was always something I admired and strived to do. Then I began to see that timing was so fundamental to everything; timing in how a line is read or written, timing in a scene, and all those scenes timed to make a full-fledged story.

"And of course, timing in a lifetime is important. Which is how I got 'Star Trek.' I had been offered a new series by one of the same people who did 'The Defenders,' Herb Brodkin, who had been a big name in live television and still was somebody at the beginning of filmed television. This new show was called 'For The People,' and it was a series about a district attorney—really the other side of 'The Defenders.' So I did that in New York for six months. At the end of the job, I got a call from Gene Roddenberry, who said he had made a science fiction pilot called 'Star Trek' which hadn't sold, and would I come back to Hollywood to see if I wanted to play the lead in a second pilot? So I went back to Hollywood and saw this pilot. I saw a lot of wonderful things in it. But I also saw that the people in it were playing it as though 'We're out in space, isn't this serious?' I thought if it was a naval vessel at sea, they'd be relaxed and familiar, not somewhat pedantic and self-important about being out in space. It seemed to me that they wouldn't be so serious about it. And the fact that I had come off all these years in comedy—I wanted it to be lighter rather than heavier. So I consciously thought of playing good-pal-the-Captain who, in time of need, would snap to and become the warrior. I broached this idea to Gene, and it seemed to strike a note. So the story was written, the pilot made, and ultimately it sold. The next thing I knew, I was to play Captain Kirk on a weekly basis.''

How did he approach that job? "It's always been my feeling that, when doing a series, you go in with great intentions," he said. "You're going to do a great character, you're going to do wonderful things with the writing. And by the second or third day, you're so tired, that all that falls by the wayside and you're just surviving. You come to work and you're tired, get a cup of coffee and are refreshed. Then you take a deep breath and you do the scene as best you can. Since you haven't read much of the script since the script wasn't ready, and is in the process of being changed anyway, you do immediate things. The only immediate things you can do are what you the person, the human being, would do in a given situation. So I always had Captain Kirk behave as William Shatner would, or rather, how the ideal William Shatner would behave in the face of danger, love, passion, or a social situation. So all of me is invested in him, because I had no other choice. I couldn't plan ahead because I didn't know what was coming next. I didn't know what the next day's work was frequently. I just didn't know where the character was going. So I played everything instinctively, immediately.''

Did he rely on certain stock responses as a way to get around the problem? "I tried not to rely on stock responses to play Captain Kirk," he said. "Besides, a stock response, done with immediacy, is no longer stock because an emotion in-stilled with freshness injects any stock response with newness. A response only becomes stock when you do it by rote. I always tried not to do anything by rote.

"Even though Captain Kirk found himself in a dramatic situation every week, the lovely part of 'Star Trek' was that many of the seventy-nine episodes were unique and different. We were in many situations which were not the standard police story of 'get the bad guy.' There were variations. I think that was a large reason for 'Star Trek's' popularity. I mean, in what series, movie, or dramatic literature, for example, does a hero have a woman's mind inside him, which was one of the episodes? How do you act as a man with a woman trapped inside your body? I took wild guesses. I had six days in which to play a woman in a man's body. I overdid it some. I'd do it differently now, with my ability to rethink it and to see on film what worked and didn't work. But I gave it the old college try. I tried not to simper, because Captain Kirk wouldn't simper, so I was a little tight-assed about it and delicate, that sort of thing.

"I guess the way I work as an actor—I say 'I guess' because I don't consciously have a methodology—is to ask, 'How entertaining can this be?' How many levels of expression are being said here in a 'hello,' for example? What is really being said in this 'hello'? The person the character is saying 'hello' to—how well does the character really know him? Does he really mean 'hello'? What has gone before that he is saying 'hello' in his own life? So that 'hello' can have many variations. And you can play more than one variation in the very 'hello.' And so, in the interests of not only my character, but in the pure idea of entertainment value, I have tried to keep as many balls in the air as possible when saying a line. That's how I approached playing Kirk."

Shaping the character of Captain Kirk was only part of the creative experience of "Star Trek." "Gene gave me a lot of leeway into a lot of creative areas, in terms of story, casting, and such. So I felt very good and very free starting off in the series, and as the show progressed, the relationships between the characters began to form. For example, it was during this time that Leonard found many of the Vulcan things that he did, sometimes almost by accident. The Vulcan neck pinch came about because of his feeling that Spock wouldn't use weapons. We were trapped in a boiler room of some kind when this problem came up. So he pinched our captor on the neck and we made believe the guy would fall. That began the Spock pinch. The Vulcan hand sign was another discovery of Leonard's. There was something vaguely ecclesiastical about it. It was a secret sign at the time of the temple, something like that. And I kept working on my original thought, of not taking my command too dramatically seriously.

"But we had a lot of fun. Frequently, we would break ourselves up over the military language, which sounded official but often didn't make sense. Sometimes we couldn't go on acting because we were laughing so hard. Also, I loved playing practical jokes. One of my favorite memories is of a joke I played on Leonard. He had acquired a bicycle while we were shooting. He was the only one who had one. He would leave this bike outside the stage door, so that when we broke for lunch, he could hop on his bike and be the first one to get to the commissary. He always got in line first and got his meal first, so afterwards he would have time to go back to his dressing room and rest. Everyone else had to walk, so by the time we got down there, got in line, and ate our meals, it was time to go back and shoot.

"So one day, I went to the prop department and got a chain and a lock and locked the bike to a post. So he came running out, found his bike locked, and sat there fuming while the rest of us went on to the commissary. Well, he got some wire cutters and some bolt cutters and cut the chain and lock off. He didn't know who did it. The following day, I went out and got his bike and put it in my dressing room. At the time, I was taking my dog, Morgan, to the studio and he would guard my dressing room for me. So lunch was called, and Leonard went running out, only this time he couldn't find his bike. He said, 'All right, now who took my bike?' And I said, 'Leonard, I don't know who took it, but I think I saw somebody put a bike in my dressing room.' So he ran to my dressing room, went to open the door, and this maddened Doberman barked at him. He reeled back, closed the door, and by that time we were in the commissary. So he really got upset. He knew I had something to do with it, but he couldn't prove it. The following day, I took his bike and hung it way up in the rafters of the stage, with a spotlight shining on it. He ran out at lunchtime, couldn't find the bike, and ran back in. He said, 'Bill, where did you put my bike?' I put my arm around his shoulders and said, 'Leonard, lift your eyes to the stars.' So he looked up and saw his bike. But he didn't laugh.

"But I did. And I had a lot of fun times like that on 'Star Trek.' I liked the show so much because it was science fiction. There was this fantastic milieu and laid directly on top of it was a real story, a very solid, dramatic story with basic human considerations. All the stories attempted to have those kinds of ideas in them. So when 'Star Trek' ran for three years, for the most part every day was a happy day. I loved coming to work. When one script wasn't so good, in a week's time it was over and we'd be on to another script which was better. I remember thinking, 'I've never been so happy as an actor and for such a long time.'

"I'd gone through some terrible experiences during *The World of Susie Wong*. And I had just spent a year doing *A Shot in the Dark,* and six months being uncomfortable in New York while shooting 'For The People.' But here I was, at home, doing wonderful stories with a good group of people, like the directors. We used the same ones a lot so they all kind of knew the show. And we had good people in the front offices like Gene Coon, who, after Gene Roddenberry, was the real heart behind 'Star Trek.' He was the producer from the first half of the first season to the second half of the second season. He had done a lot of television, but more importantly, he had been a military man. His laconic, abbreviated style of writing became an important part of 'Star Trek.'

"While it lasted, 'Star Trek' was creative, wonderful fun. But when it was over, it was just another show. It was over and I was on to the next thing. So when it began to come back, it was quite a shock. My first real encounter with its return from the dead was when I was doing a summer stock theater play back East. I had bought a truck and a camper to live in, in order to save money on hotels and airfare. I had hit some tough times and was trying to save as much as possible. So I was living in this camper, touring on the straw hat circuit, even though I had just come off this successful series.

"In order to have transportation when I was at a theater for a week, I would take the camper off the bed of the truck. Now these campers stand on four little thin legs when they're not being carted around. And so I would live in this shell, which had a bathroom and a kitchen and a bed, and then I would use the truck to get to the theater. This was during the time that the moon shots were being made, and the lunar module, which was landing on the moon, landed on four spindly legs like this cabin I was living in. So for all the world, I was living in what looked like a LEM, a Lunar Excursion Module I believe it was called.

"Early one morning as I was sleeping, there was a knock on the door of this little camper. I got out of bed and opened the screen door, and there was a child of about six or seven standing there. 'Are you Captain Kirk?' he asked. And I said, 'Yes, I am.' And he said, 'Is this your spaceship?' and I said, 'Yes, it is.' And he said, 'Could I see it?' and I said, 'Yes, you can.' So I brought him inside. I showed him the shower and said, 'This is where I beam up.' I showed him the stove, and said, 'These are my controls.' And I showed him the radio and said, 'This is how I talk to Mr. Spock. Now go away, little boy, and let me sleep.' And away he went . . . I believe there is a young man in New Jersey who will read this and now know that he did indeed see Captain Kirk aboard his spaceship on that day long ago."

But in spite of the laughter that the incident caused, and the huge success of "Star Trek" syndicated reruns, the next ten years proved frustrating for my father's career. "I was doing a lot of small films, a lot of television, even another series called 'Barbary Coast,' " he explained. "But somehow, even though I did a lot of work, none of it was distinguished. It just wasn't my fate to be asked to do the big material. The material I did, I did to the best of my ability. I invested it with what talent I had and did it as well as I could—but I was always scared, always apprehensive. I thought for a period of time there I'd stop acting and try to do something else, although I wasn't quite sure what else I could do. I still had the vision that my father had painted for me of being some itinerant actor who was unable to make a living. So it was with great joy that I heard *Star Trek: The Motion Picture* was going to be made. At last, I'd have the opportunity to do a big motion picture, the likes of which I hadn't been involved with in a long time. The idea that I might be saddled with identification problems didn't really bother me. The money was very good, the exposure was going to be very good, and the script seemed reasonably good at the time.''

Was it difficult to play Captain Kirk after a ten-year absence? ''I looked at a couple of old 'Star Treks' to see what I had been doing,'' he answered. ''But since Kirk had always been so much me, I thought if I could look somewhat decent and do my 'classical thing' I'd be able to reassemble the character. So I went into training. I ran, lifted weights, that sort of thing. But my real opportunity to grow and change with the character started with *Star Trek II*. As the character got older, we decided to play along with the aging process instead of acting like nothing had happened. That's how the eyeglasses and such got started. Then we realized that *Star Trek II* might beget *Star Trek III*, and that got very exciting.''

Although *Star Trek* grew increasingly successful, my father had no thought of directing one of the films at this point. ''Even though I had become progressively more involved in the stories during the series, and helped shape the stories for the movies, the idea of directing was a dim secret in the back of my mind, a fantasy that would never be realized. Until one day I learned that Leonard didn't want to do the next *Star Trek* movie. They cajoled him, and then finally, as he told me later, as some blind stab—as almost a joke because he would have done it without it—he said, 'All right, but if I do it, I want to direct.' They fought and fought about it. No one was going to give an unknown director a motion picture like this. So he said, 'Okay, I won't be in it,' which was something he really meant. That was the break. So he got to direct *Star Trek III* and ultimately *Star Trek IV*.

"Now somewhere along the line, Leonard's lawyers and my lawyers had gotten together and drawn up a favored nations clause, which meant everything he got, I got and vice versa. Well, in the beginning, I was commanding more money, so that any raises I was getting, Leonard would get also. So I made Leonard a great deal of money on my lawyers by bringing him up to the salary I was getting. We used to joke about that, how that clause had benefited him so much. But in the end, the fact that Leonard directed a picture, which meant that I would get to direct one, was by far the most important consequence of that clause. So for a long time though I thought he was the benefactor of the favored nations clause, I am far and away the recipient of that clause.

"So now, through an accident of fate, through a fellow actor, I have been given the opportunity to fulfill my dream. In addition, I saw the possibility somewhere along the line, almost unconsciously because it wasn't something I planned to do, of telling a story I cared about. It wasn't something someone just handed to me—I saw the opportunity to direct something that I cared about, that I helped fashion. And that is going to be the ultimate thrill. So to me, *Star Trek V* is the moment in my career for which I have been preparing all my life. I see everything I've done as preparation for this moment—the plays which taught me timing and discipline; television, which taught me about camera, story, and pace; and now film, which I hope will teach me many new things. And I know since I'm not a young kid, an opportunity like *Star Trek V* may not come again. So I am determined to enjoy every moment, both beneficial and excruciating. Because *Star Trek V* is the epitome of my career, my experiences, my hopes and dreams. It is the quintessential me."

2

CREATING THE STORY

My father loves to tell the stories. When my sisters and I were little, we would beg to hear his tales. Often, after dinner was over and we were sitting around the table contentedly, we would chant, "tell us a story, tell us a story," until he would finally relent. Sometimes he would relate one of the standard Grimm's fairy tales or another like it. But often he would just wing it and make up one of his own. For me, these were the best ones. Often we would be hanging on the edge of the table, waiting for him to finish. His enthusiasm and conviction had us convinced the story was real.

Over the years, he's been able to carry his storytelling abilities over to his career in several different ways. To him, acting has always been just another form of storytelling, since an actor is required to convey emotion and important information about the story all at the same time. But he's also worked as a scriptwriter. In fact, about thirty years ago, when my father was just starting to achieve some success as an actor, he was in a studio building completing work on a live television show. He got in the elevator to go home, and was surprised to find a well-known producer standing next to him. They exchanged greetings, whereupon my father said, "Oh—by the way, I have three scripts I wrote that I'd like to send you tomorrow." The producer nodded his assent, then got out of the elevator. My father scurried home in a panic since, of course, he had not written any of the scripts. He immediately scribbled his stories onto paper and sent them off to the producer. No one was more surprised than my father when the producer immediately bought all three.

Other attempts at writing, although sporadic, have met with similar success throughout the years. My father thought up many concepts for his series "T. J. Hooker," and other episodic television shows. He is constantly generating new ideas for television and film, and spends much time and energy developing them into scripts.

However, although he participated in the story process for the *Star Trek* movies, he never had the opportunity to flesh out an idea of his own. His contribution to the *Star Trek* films has remained that of consultant, suggesting possible plot or dialogue changes which would enhance each script. With *Star Trek V,* he finally got the opportunity to develop his own concept. After debating a myriad of possible story ideas, he picked a topic which had interested him for a long time.

"I had always found TV evangelists fascinating," he explained. "They are so sure God is speaking to them, that God is telling them what to do. I kept wondering why God would choose them and not other individuals. That became the basis of my concept for *Star Trek V.*

"I took the TV evangelist persona and created a holy man who thought God had spoken to him. He believed God had told him, 'I need many followers, and I need a vehicle to spread my word throughout the universe.' That vehicle he needed became a starship which the holy man would capture when it came to rescuing some hostages he had taken. I had this opening scene where this holy man converts someone through the power of his mind.

"Next, I introduced our three leading characters—Kirk, Spock, and McCoy—at Yosemite. It was only much later that I realized this rock climbing sequence was a mythological symbol of man's trying to achieve greater heights, which is of course what the whole story is about. In any case, Spock flies up to visit Kirk while he's climbing, then saves him as he slips and falls. McCoy watches the whole scene, and when Spock later brings Kirk back to the campfire from where McCoy has been watching, they discuss life and death, aging, whether Kirk was afraid, and so on as we introduce the themes of the movie.

"They are then informed that they have been assigned the mission to rescue the hostages that the holy man has captured, so their shore leave is canceled. When they are told who the holy man is, Spock realizes that he knew him from a Vulcan seminary. He informs Kirk that this man was so brilliant, that it is within the realm of possibility that he is indeed the Messiah, which causes the rest of the crew considerable shock and consternation. But they continue on their mission, nevertheless.

"When they arrive on the planet that the holy man has conquered, they try to reason with him. This reasoning escalates into fighting, and before it is over, the *Enterprise* is boarded by these primitives. There is a pitched battle down the corridors of the ship, where at one point the holy man is about to be killed. But Spock warns him of Kirk's plan to kill him, and the holy man escapes. As a result, he captures the ship, which makes Kirk furious with Spock. When Kirk asks Spock why he didn't kill the holy man, Spock answers, 'I knew he might be the Messiah, and in that moment, I couldn't kill him.' The holy man then throws Kirk, Spock, and McCoy into the brig together.

"Meanwhile, the rest of the crew is captured, and a relationship springs up between Scotty and Uhura. During this time, the holy man persuades the rest of the crew, other than Kirk, Spock, and McCoy, to go along with him to find God. Everybody is mesmerized and intrigued by the thought of finding God. Later, the holy man visits the brig to tell the three heroes what he's about to do. Then he tries to convince each of them he is right by using the power of his mind. He brings up how McCoy's father died, how McCoy had to kill him because he was suffering. Then he deals with Spock, and conjures up a vision of Spock's birth where he is rejected by his father and his mother.

"Then he tries to show Kirk the way. He does this by telling

Kirk no one ever loved him, that he's alone in the world, that all Kirk has ever cared for is the *Enterprise*. Then he heals a long-standing soreness in Kirk's knee, and Kirk is suitably impressed. Then Kirk is reminded of his son, who died because of him, and that stabs at another long-standing pain that has been bothering Kirk. The Holy Man promises surcease from this pain when they see God. Kirk, though, has no faith in anyone but himself and no belief but in his ship and his shipmates, even though all the rest, through one means or another, are mesmerized by the holy man.

"Finally, the *Enterprise* arrives at the planet where God supposedly resides, in the center of the universe. Kirk then decides to join with the rest of the crew, at least it seems like it. But Kirk, Spock, and McCoy are at odds. This pseudo-mutiny aboard the ship has set Kirk apart from the rest of the crew members. So agreeing, but also disagreeing, Kirk, Spock, McCoy, and the holy man are beamed down to the planet. It's like the drawings of Dante's *Inferno,* like a flaming hell. When God appears, he seems like God, surrounded by seraphim and cherubim. But gradually, in a conversation between God and the holy man, Kirk perceives that something is wrong, and begins to challenge God. God gets angrier and angrier, and begins to show his true colors, which are those of the devil. The cherubim and seraphim turn into the Furies as Kirk, Spock, and McCoy turn to flee, each at odds with the other. So they only try to save themselves.

"McCoy falls and is surrounded by these Furies. Then Spock is surrounded, too. Kirk is about to escape, when he realizes he can't. He turns around to save Spock, which he does, putting his life on the line. As a result of that, the rift between Kirk and Spock is healed, and they can escape. But they, too, decide to descend into hell to rescue McCoy from the river Styx. They rescue him, pursued by the frenzied minions of the devil. They get back to the ship, and are saved.

"So essentially that was my story: that man conceives of God in his own image, but those images change from generation to generation, therefore he appears in all these different guises as man-made Gods. But in essence, if the devil exists,

God exists by inference. This is the lesson that the *Star Trek* group learns. The lesson being that God is within our hearts, not something we conjure up, invent, and then worship.''

He brought this idea to the attention of Frank Mancuso, Chairman and CEO of Paramount, even before *Star Trek IV* had finished filming. Mr. Mancuso liked the idea, and gave him the go-ahead to develop it further. Next, my father had to choose a writer to flesh out his idea into a detailed story outline or "treatment" form.

"I had read Eric Von Lustbader's work—*Ninja* in particular impressed me—and it was so moody, so mysterious, I thought he would be perfect. I approached Mancuso and he said 'let's go with him,' so I flew to New York to meet him. He ended up being a great guy, and the studio entered into negotiations with him, but they couldn't agree on terms.''

Time passed without any more progress, and my father became frustrated. "I finally decided to do something about it, so I dictated the story myself and had it typed up. I presented it to the president of production at the time, Ned Tannen. I was very anxious about it, because this was the story I wanted to do. I felt like I had been searching for a philosophy, a way of thinking, and I wanted to express what my search had been like, and some of my thoughts, in dramatic form.''

Part of his intense desire to see his story produced grew out of a need to contribute his own ideas to "Star Trek." "I've spent my life doing other people's ideas and thoughts. I had here a rare, if not unique, opportunity to absolutely do what I wanted to do. The key to it was to convince the studio that my story would work. I knew that it was inherently very dramatic. But I also knew there would be some feeling against having a story about God in a popular film. I also knew they might object to it as being too heavy. But I handed it in, wanting the verdict very much to be in my favor. This was one of those rare opportunities in my career where I could taste how much I wanted something.''

In spite of his enthusiasm for the story, my father had to overcome many hurdles before he could move forward and see his vision become a reality. One, of course, was getting the

Paramount executives to approve his idea. But they were not the only ones my father had to convince to do the project. While he waited for their response, he grappled with an equally important problem: how to convince Harve Bennett, producer of *Star Treks II, III,* and *IV,* writer of *III,* and co-writer of *IV,* to come aboard for the fifth *Star Trek* adventure. "I knew Harve Bennett was a key element in making *Star Trek V,*" my father explained. "His experience on the other three movies, as well as his talents, were of primary importance. I knew I would have to convince him to join me if I was going to get this movie made."

My father viewed Harve Bennett as a key ingredient for many reasons. An enormously successful producer, Harve had worked at ABC and Universal on such shows as "Mod Squad," "Rich Man, Poor Man," "The Six Million Dollar Man," and "The Bionic Woman." His vast experience in the television series format had given him an ability to create quality products on budget and on time. For that reason, he was asked to come to Paramount and work in the television department where he produced the Emmy award winning miniseries "A Woman Called Golda." Shortly thereafter, he was unexpectedly given the chance to apply his talents to *Star Trek II,* whose progress had been slowed by the enormous expenses of *Star Trek: The Motion Picture.* He recounted the unusual experience which gave him his first opportunity to work on *Star Trek II:*

"I came to Paramount with no anticipation of doing feature pictures at all. I was here to do television. But the second week I was here I got a call. Now you have to remember that running the studio at the time was Barry Diller, who used to be my assistant at ABC, Michael Eisner, who used to be a counterpart of mine at ABC New York, and running the entire operation was the great immigrant, the last of the moguls, Charlie Bluhdorn, who built Gulf and Western, and bought Paramount.

"Barry calls me in and says, 'Will you come to a meeting in my office?' and I say 'Sure.' Now don't forget, Gary Nardino, who headed the television department, has brought me here.

And in the room is Gary Nardino, who is sitting way in the back, over in a corner somewhere, Michael Eisner, Barry Diller, and Charles Bluhdorn. Barry Diller says, 'I'd like you to meet Charlie Bluhdorn.' And Charlie Bluhdorn gets up and says, 'Hi, I've heard so much about you.' I said, 'I've heard a lot about you, too, Mr. Bluhdorn.' And he said, 'Call me Charlie,' and I said, 'Okay.' He said, 'Sit down, sit down.' Then he said, 'Did you see *Star Trek: The Motion Picture*?' What's flashing through my mind is 'yes, I've seen this movie'; this was the movie where Chris Bennett and Susan Bennett, age six and eight, in the only time in my memory say, 'dad, can we get some popcorn. I want to go to the toilet, dad.'

"So I said, 'Yes, I did.' He said, 'What did you think of it?' Well, I didn't know, but forty-seven paragraphs raced through my mind in one second and I finally, as I usually do, decided that the truth was the only thing I could say. So I said, 'Well, Charlie, I thought it was boring.' He suddenly turned on Michael Eisner and said, 'See, by you, bald is sexy.'

"So I knew I had said the right thing from his point of view. Then he says to me 'Can you make a better movie?' I said, 'Oh yeah. I could make a better movie, yeah sure.' He said, 'Could you make it for less than 45f——g million dollars?' I'm looking around the room and they're all . . . So I said, 'Charlie, where I come from I could make three movies for that,' which is actually true. He said, 'Okay—I believe it. Do it.' I say, 'Okay.' I look around and couldn't believe it was over. I don't know what's going on here except, you know, 'Thanks,' and 'We'll talk to you later.' I'm out the door at ten AM.

"At twelve-thirty PM there was a reception for Charlie at the commissary and I go in. I'm the new kid in town, I grab a tray and I go to the hors d'oeuvres. Into the commissary there come some ruffles and flourishes, and in walk Michael, Charles, and those guys. Charlie starts shaking hands at the cashier's desk and suddenly he stops and sees me across the entire length of the room. I'm at the first table with my tray and then I hear, 'Excuse me, excuse me,' and he crosses the room, cuts up the stairs, comes to the wall and says, 'Harve!' and he hugs me. That's the kind of man he was. He said, 'I believe in you. I trust you. You go make your movie and we'll make lots of movies together.' Meanwhile everyone in that room is looking at me and him.

"Then after *Star Trek II* was released, my secretary tells me I got a call from a guy named Charlie from what sounded like a car phone. She said 'You know a guy named Charlie that's got a car phone?' I say 'No,' then 'Oh—it's Charlie!' I get on the phone. 'Charlie, are you in your car?' 'No, I'm in my airplane in the Dominican Republic. I just wanted you to know I saw *Star Trek II* and the grosses are going to be huge. You kept your word, didn't you, kid? You told me you'd do it and you did. So we're gonna make a lot of movies together.' I said 'Gee, Charlie, this is really nice.' He said, 'Well, I'll see you next week. Bye!' I said 'bye' and hung up. I never saw him again. He never came out to LA. And within the year he died. In his airplane, so they say."

His mentor may have disappeared, but Harve was grateful for the opportunity Mr. Bluhdorn had given him. With *Star Trek II,* Harve found a way to distill the essence of "Star Trek" and apply it in heavy doses, breathing new life into the ailing franchise.

"I think 'Star Trek' makes people who watch it feel smart," he said. "And the reasons for that are so justifiable—look at television. What's on television that appeals to anyone of intellect? You don't have to be a big intellect to recognize that 'Star Trek' deals with ideas. And [a] family, [of characters]. I mean, my God, Roddenberry did stuff in the sixties that, ironically, only one other show that I know of was doing, and that was 'Mod Squad'! But 'Mod Squad' was doing it at a gut level, and 'Star Trek' was doing it at a concert level, an opera level. It was doing racism, chauvinism, disarmament, world peace, all that stuff. It was doing it in such a visionary way that none of the reactionary people in the world caught on to the fact that it was progressive propaganda for a better world, because it was, after all, out there in the twenty-third century.

"In those days, in order to succeed with a series, you had to deliver 20 million people. 'Star Trek' never did that so it got canceled. But it delivered fifteen, fourteen, ten. Well, that was enough to support it in syndication during the seventies. You could find your favorite 'Star Trek' on every channel off network. Great. All the same people who loved it stayed with it. *Star Trek: The Motion Picture* almost killed it. It depressed the syndication, it depressed everything. So if I have made a contribution, it was to have resuscitated a beached whale.

"I saved the whale by going to the second element so vital to the material, which is the characters. The family—the love and loyalty of these people to each other—and the outstanding, irrevocable star appeal of Spock, Kirk, and McCoy, all so different, and yet all so beloved. A leading man, an android, and a curmudgeon. Not bad!"

Harve applied this formula to the next three *Star Trek* movies, and was instrumental in the success of each. "On *Star Trek II* I had a writer whom I selected. He did a nice job on the first draft and then got kind of lost. When Nick [Meyer] came in as director, he had read the draft that had been written, and that I had privately made a lot of changes on. He liked the material and had a lot of other great ideas. What happened was, Nick and I did what we subsequently did on *Star Trek IV:* we did a ghost write and divided it into sections. I wrote a draft and sent him pages and he rewrote and sent back pages. We did this for about two weeks, that was *Star Trek II.*" (Harve and Nick lost the Writer's Guild arbitration for screen credit on *Star Trek II.* However, they received credit on *Star Trek IV.*)

"On *Star Trek III,* I said, 'Look, it's got to be faster and more efficient. I'll do it myself.' So I was sole writer on *Star Trek III. Star Trek III* was the easiest writing job I ever had. The reason for that is, since it was so direct a continuation of *Star Trek II,* the outline was already in place. I knew exactly what I had to do and I did it in six weeks. So we got ahead of schedule and that was all easy, but in a strange way I was right back to episodic television. I was writing a miniseries, if you will. If you'll analyze the films, you'll readily see that they could be classified as episodes one, two, three, and four of the series that I am producing."

But it was precisely Harve's sense of continuity—his ability to see *Star Trek* as a progression—that was so important. His experience on *II, III,* and *IV* had given him an opportunity to analyze the appealing personality traits of each character, something which had proved so instrumental in the success of each film. His familiarity with "Star Trek" lore, the progression of the movies, and his strong sense of story structure were invaluable. My father knew *Star Trek V* would prove impossible without Harve Bennett's help.

However, in spite of his tremendous success rate with each *Star Trek* movie, Harve hesitated about doing *Star Trek V.* In fact, he really wanted nothing to do with *Star Trek* at that point.

"I was not anxious to do *Star Trek V,*" he explained. "My reasons were [that] I had been emotionally beat up by Leonard Nimoy. I respect him for what he has done, but in the transition between *III* and *IV,* Leonard had come to regard me as in his way, with regard to the auteurship of the film. I was not only the man who said 'No,' but the man who was conspiring to . . . you know. So that on one occasion, it got really mean on the stage—mean from him to me. I was smarting—'Who needs this sh-t?'—was foremost on my mind. Plus the fact, if you keep doing the same material, whether it's a series or big pictures, you're still doing a series."

My father had his work cut out for him. He had to convince Harve that *Star Trek V* would be creative, stimulating, and most of all, fun. But how to approach him? "I asked Harve to meet me, so we could discuss *Star Trek V.* I asked him if he would come to the Equestrian Center so I could talk to him," my father revealed. "But Harve said, 'No, not on your turf.' It struck me as a strange phrase, but as I got to know Harve, I knew him as a man who interprets symbols, and has a sense of strategy. I suspect that was what he was thinking at the time. I, of course, didn't care where the meeting took place. So I met him at his house."

I asked Harve what he had been thinking at the time. He related his feelings about the meeting: "I said, 'Bill, if I'm to consider doing this, there have got to be some things that we have to talk about. You have to know where I'm coming from, and I have to know where you're coming from.' He said, 'Terrific. Why don't you come out and have lunch with me at the Equestrian Center?' I said, 'No way.' And he said, 'I don't understand.' I said, 'One of the things I want to talk to you about is very personal. And it's going to be on my turf, not yours.' He said, 'Where do you want me?' And I said, 'Come to my house.' Now, Leonard Nimoy had never put foot in my house except for a party once. All my meetings with Bill as star had been at his house. I was convinced I wouldn't do this movie if no one was going to come to my house! Bill said 'What time?' and he was there.

"We spent four marvelous hours, at my bar, hanging out. Just letting it hang. I told him quite frankly all the things I would never live through again. And he made certain promises, certain emotional promises, to me. He's never broken a promise about anything. I said, 'if this isn't fun, I'm out of here. If you accept me as your producer, you accept me as the man who is going to say "no," to you, and you accept what I think about the story.' "

My father was willing to do what Harve asked. "I went to his turf because it didn't matter to me. All I wanted to do was convince him that I needed him, that he would have a good time making a movie with me. I spoke at great length with him. I spoke from my heart about my enthusiasm for the story, the various aspects of how to tell the story, and my desire and my need for him. Mainly that, actually—my need for him. As I spoke, I saw him looking more and more interested."

He had managed to convince Harve to do the movie, but another hurdle presented itself: Harve had reservations about my father's story. "I told him I didn't like the current story very much, the one that had been written without any participation by me," Harve said. "I told him, 'I don't want to find God. That doesn't interest me at all.' I thought there had to be a better way to tell the story." In fact, Harve was not the only one with doubts. Unknown to my father at the time, the studio was not convinced the story would work. David Nicksay, senior vice-president in charge of production, was given the job of supervising the movie's progress. He explained why the executives were concerned:

"There was no question it was an ambitious story. The ambition on a creative level, of attempting to tackle the subject matter of the story, was really a big bite. It was not an automatically simple set of problems to solve. I think the concern was, 'Can that be solved in a way that works within a framework of the history of *Star Trek*?' You know, are we suddenly making a Eugene O'Neill drama out of a very successful series of movies that were accessible to the movie-going public?"

The concerns having been voiced, the challenge became how to accommodate them without killing the integrity of the story. There had to be a way of adding humor and lightness without sacrificing some of the larger philosophical issues. In order to find out if the story would work, the next step was to prepare an outline for a first draft. But the entire story needed to be analyzed, reworked in a way that would satisfy all those involved. It fell to my father and Harve to try and accomplish this task.

"For the first three weeks of preparation, Harve and I remained locked in his room for hours at a time, talking about how we felt about various aspects of the story," my father said. "The death of McCoy's father reflects my father's death. How we felt about God, and the search for God, whether God exists, what is the accepted Western form or not—all these various things. We reached deep into each other's lives. We did a psychological judgment of each other that I think was probably unlike anything that had come before between a director and a producer. We became very good friends as a result of this intensive time spent together."

They also made some major decisions during this period. The primary one concerned the concept of God itself. Harve was adamant the idea of searching for God would not work. He explained why: "Basically what Bill was saying—and he was saying it loudly, and in some cases, publicly—was 'We're going to see God!' And I said, 'Now, Bill, if you reduce this to its absurdity, which is a *TV Guide* log line, "Tonight on STAR

TREK: The Cast and Crew Go To See God," everyone will say, "What, are you crazy?" ' We then had a long session in which I introduced him to a concept which I have long lived by that is so simple, but took a long time to quantify. It's a concept called suspense versus surprise. If I have one rigid rule it is to simply ask myself that question.

"Now, a story consists of multiples of that question. Every moment they change but the generality of it does not. You are either telling a suspense story or a surprise story. The best illustration of this I learned from a book, not on writing, but on film editing. It said the essence of film editing is contained in the following problem: Given—master scene is of Laurel and Hardy walking down a street. Hardy slips and falls in the shot. Laurel looks back. That's shot one. Shot two: Insert, banana peel. There are three possible ways to put the insert in. One is, don't put it in. Then everyone says, 'What's that? Why did he fall?' And you never know. The second is, Laurel and Hardy walk down the street. Cut to banana peel. Cut back to scene. This is called suspense. Tell the audience in advance something is about to happen. Will it happen—yes, or no? It doesn't matter. Third possibility: Shot of Laurel and Hardy, Hardy falls, cut to banana peel. That explains the surprise.

"Now, I explained that whole story to Bill. I said to him, 'When I read that, light bulbs went on all over, and I realized everything I was doing—whether editing film, whether I was writing film, whether I was talking story—has to do with what the audience knows and what it doesn't know. And that in some cases you have to make these choices.'

"I said to him, 'They're Going To See God' makes this a story of neither suspense nor of surprise. A little bit of suspense because you're asking: 'What will God look like?' But the problem is, God will never match the expectation. From the beginning the audience will say: 'Show me. Prove it to me. What's this going to be?' You cannot tell the story this way. The moment, 'We're going to see God' does not come at the beginning, it comes at the end. We talked and we agreed and he recognized that difference. So the moment now became Kirk saying, 'Wait a minute, how do you know you're going to get through the Great Barrier?' And Sybok [the Holy Man] says, 'The Vision.' And Kirk says, 'What vision?' And Sybok says, ' "The vision given to me by God. He waits for me on the other side." ' Kirk says, 'You are mad.' That's the same thing I was saying people would say to Bill: 'Bill, you can't go and see God. You're mad.' But if Kirk says at the end, 'You're crazy. You can't go to see God,' then the audience is on our side. And that's how the story changed.''

Once Harve convinced my father when the search for God occurred, they then had to address what the crew would actually find once they got there. Again, Harve was firm that my father's original concept of searching for God—who actually turns out to be the devil—was going too far. My father explained the concern:

''My story said 'God' and 'The devil,' or 'The Devil,' which implied there was a God. It was then decided that it shouldn't actually be the devil and God, but an alien acting like them. It was a huge change, and I believe it came from Harve. It lightened up the story. The reason we did it was there was a great deal of fear from the studio and from Harve about offending people. I acknowledged that it could offend people. The original holy man was a messenger of God. He was a man who thought he was the Messiah. He came bearing the word of God, and took us to God, who was in fact, really the devil. So when the angels changed, they changed into the Furies. And the Furies pursued us around the rocks and the fire. When that original change was made, to make it not God, but an alien who acted like God and the devil, then it changed the whole feel of the story.''

Once this change had been made, the story was almost automatically lightened in tone. The next step was to find places to add humor, to stay with the laughter which had earmarked the recent *Star Trek* movies. But before my father and Harve went any farther, the third hurdle presented itself: to find a writer for the screenplay.

Harve made the initial investigation:

''Writing a screenplay is like writing a blueprint. It has a special skill to it,'' he explained. ''There are actors who can act, and actors who can play charades. Screenwriting is like doing a charade. It's a sign language. You have to be so economical, because an audience in a dark room will not sit, and they will turn off on you if you say, 'It was a languorous, slow evening. The man walked mysteriously across the carpet.' They just want you to cut to the chase.

"Knowing that, we wanted Nick (Meyer) to write it. He was the only clear-cut choice that Bill and I would have instantly done. But he was off doing other things. So we went the traditional route: we read. We must have read fifty, a hundred scripts. Then one caught my eye. I said, 'Bill, I think this is the guy—read this.' And he read the script, called *Flashback*, which brought David Loughery to Paramount. We thought it was marvelous. It had a quality, nothing space age, just a quality of understanding characters, an ability to trip you up so you get fed up with a character, who would then say something outrageously, cynically funny. I said, 'this is the guy.' And Bill said, 'but it doesn't sound like *Star Trek*.' So I said, 'Let's see *Dreamscape*,' which is a picture David had written, and David hated and I thought was boring. I thought the script was 'Ugh,' but Bill saw the poetry in *Dreamscape* that he did not see in *Flashback*. So he went with the choice.''

My father was surprised at how quickly they had found a writer. "Based on Harve and the studio's recommendation, the search for a writer was telescoped. I was shocked at how short a period of time it had taken. So David Loughery joined our circle of two, which then became three."

No one was more surprised at their choice than David, a young writer who had recently tasted some success at Paramount. "I'm not exactly sure how I got hired to write the script, but I'll give you my version," he told me. "I had just sold an original screenplay to Paramount. On the merits of that script, the studio offered me an overall deal which I accepted. Lindsay Doran, one of the executives, asked if I had any interest in writing the next *Star Trek* movie, and I said 'Sure,' figuring that it would be the last I ever heard of it. I thought I was an unlikely choice to go where no man had gone before because, with the exception of *Dreamscape*, all of my scripts had been contemporary pieces, mostly comedies. But a week later they put me together with Harve Bennett and we hit it off immediately.

"At the time Harve was less than sure he wanted to produce another *Star Trek* movie. He'd made the last three which formed a complete trilogy and didn't want to get involved with the next one unless it was something special. Bill had written his own outline called *Act of Love* and it was my understanding that, although the studio liked it, they thought it might be too dark, too heavy. Because of the huge success of *Star Trek IV,* they wanted the next movie to be full of humor."

It was precisely because of his humor that David appealed so much to Harve and my father. "David is hilarious," my father explained, "one of the funniest people I've ever met. He is forever coming up with one-liners, each one topping the next. His humor proved invaluable in the coming weeks, as we thrashed out an approach for an outline which preceded the first draft."

They made an unlikely team: Captain Kirk, Commander of the Starship *Enterprise*; Harve Bennett, veteran writer and producer; and David Loughery, young, wise-cracking writer. Unlikely, perhaps, but it proved to be a fortunate collision of talents. Together they pounded out an approach to the story which they felt satisfied all requirements, especially where humor was concerned.

"A major thrust at this point was that we had to lighten up here, because the commercial aspect of *IV* was the humor," my father explained. "So we began to look for areas of humor at every opportunity, even in the midst of this heavy story. So Harve, David, and I sketched out scenes of humor. There's one precious moment where Harve and I began to say, 'What if?' How do we get from the shuttle into the town of Paradise? Now we've got this group of people at the water, how do we now get the horses? And he and I began to sketch out the idea of Uhura doing a naked dance. Well, we became so unglued by the thought that I was literally on the floor laughing. Harve was hysterical with laughter, and David was looking at us with a peculiar laugh saying, 'All right, guys, let's get serious. What

49

are we going to do?' With the same voice Harve and I said, 'We're not kidding, that's what we should do.' And of course we maneuvered it so she would do the dance not quite naked. And all the time David thought we were kidding. Not only kidding, but that we had gone off on some terrible turn and were having ourselves a drunken time.''

They had many sessions like that. So many, in fact, that David commented, "we had so much fun in those early sessions, laughing and carrying on, that the people in the outer office must've wondered what we'd been smoking.'' But the sessions had a serious thrust in spite of laughter and fun they generated. They were still seeking a way to piece the story together, to make the progression of events occur in such a way as to make sense when the final search for God began. In order to accomplish this goal, they relied on some basic structural devices.

The primary tool they used became the element of surprise. ''The objective for *V* became: How do you tell a serious story that says, 'We're going to see God,' reverse it, and say, 'We're going on an adventure but we're not telling you where,' and it has to be funny?'' Harve asked. ''We did this by putting God at the end, as a surprise objective, in a bizarre series of plot twists and turns.

''For example, if you count how many surprises there are, you'll see it's the most surprising of all our material. You can count them: Kirk slips, starts to fall—you can't believe what you're seeing. It's as surprising as killing Spock. He's going to die! That's number one. Then there's the whole surprise that the *Enterprise* doesn't work. There's the surprise of having to rescue the hostages and have them turn on the crew. Then there's the surprise of Spock saying, 'I know this Vulcan' and Kirk saying, 'You mean he's your *brother* brother?' Big surprise! Just when you think Kirk's done in, we come to help him. And who's 'we'? The Klingons. Big surprise, and so forth. If there is a single pattern to all the discussions and all the contributions we made in this room for so long, it was 'That's expected—let's do something different.' So the thrust became, 'We can't just say we're going to see God; we've gotta go there by means of a maze of twists and turns.' And by the time we get there we say, 'That's what it was all about. That's the logic of this story.' And that's structurally what we achieved.''

In addition to adding an element of surprise, the Klingons also provided another important structural function to the writers. My father explained the use of these seemingly "black hats": "The Klingons were always regarded as an added threat. We kept them alive throughout the story—almost mathematically mapped it out—so that the element of tension would be there. Otherwise it would become, 'Are they going to see God, or aren't they—yes or no, yes or no,' like Ping-Pong balls. This way the elements of the unknown were kept alive, adding more tension and interest to the story. And, of course, they became an interesting way to resolve the final problem of how to get Kirk back on the ship.''

However, in spite of making some of these major changes from the original story, they still kept some of the initial concepts my father had envisioned. The holy man, whom they called Zar, still was a relatively dark and violent character, who rode a unicorn throughout his interplanetary adventures. This unicorn was an extension of Zar's violent nature, to the point where my father had envisioned a battle scene where the unicorn had speared an unfortunate soldier, who lay writhing and screaming in agony upon the unicorn's horn while Zar rode on in triumph. The journey to see God still took the *Enterprise* crew to the center of the universe, where Kirk was still the sole protestor against Zar's claim that God existed on the planet below. While the rest of the crew agreed to accompany Zar down to the God planet, Kirk made an independent decision that his duty was to seek out possible new life forms, "to boldly go where no man has gone before." It was Kirk's sense of duty—rather than his belief in Zar—that led him to investigate the planet along with the others. The end of the story still had Kirk as the sole fighter against the enraged alien until he is finally rescued by the Klingons.

Once Harve, David, and my father had agreed on the structural format of the story, they presented it, in outline form, to the studio executives. Satisfied that the outline addressed their initial concerns with the story, the studio gave the go-ahead for a first draft. David began writing the story into a screenplay format; however, before he had progressed very far, they hit the next hurdle. Gene Roddenberry, who was executive consultant on the movie and therefore retained the right to read and comment on the story and subsequent script drafts, had some strong objections to the outline. The fact that writing had commenced without his first giving his input had distressed him immensely. David immediately suspended any writing until they heard from Gene.

I had the opportunity to ask Gene about his feelings on the proposed outline. Sitting in his office, surrounded by "Star Trek" memorabilia from the old series and the new (hanging from the walls were Spock's lute from the old series, and a poster of the new generation cast as well as one of the original cast), Gene gave his views on the story:

"I thought it was very unwise to do a story which seemed to be talking about God because there are so many versions about what God is or isn't," he said. "And living in a time in which you have Tammy Bakker and the young lady who got screwed—not that that's an unusual happening in any religion—I think the public was beginning to see that many religions are nothing but flim flammery, dedicated to getting as many bucks as possible. And I didn't want *Star Trek* to be associated with any one of them.

"The original story I saw was, 'The *Enterprise* Meets God.' And my point was that it had to be even more obvious [that the 'God' is actually an alien]. I didn't object to it being an alien claiming to be God, but there was too much in it that an audience could have thought was really God or really the devil, and I very strongly resist believing in either. I do not perceive this as a universe that's divided between good and evil. I see it as a universe that is divided between many ideas of what is.

"I wasn't alone in it. I talked to Isaac Asimov, Arthur C. Clark, and Ray Bradbury, and they all said the same thing: It wouldn't be good for *Star Trek,* the *Star Trek* image, or the *Star Trek* property, to make it appear we were really dealing in religion. I had kept *Star Trek* away from religion for—what was it—eighteen years. I had refused to put in a chaplain representing the principal faiths. It seemed obvious to me that not only are there more than just three faiths on earth—in this nation we kind of divide it between three main ones—but that is not what the world is divided into. There's all sorts of Asians and everything else. So I thought, 'If you're going to have chaplains, you've got to have at least a couple dozen chaplains to represent that many faiths. And then since we're in a galactic Federation and every one of those eight planets possibly having twenty or thirty religions, too, then everyone on the ship would need a chaplain.' So as long as we weren't talking about religion [in the *Star Trek V* story], I had no objection.

". . . [But] I had some objection to McCoy and the others believing it was God. McCoy was saying, 'Hallelujah, I'm with ya, I'm with ya!' and only Kirk and Spock understood the difference. I said, 'Hey, these are people that have been with you for twenty years, through thick and thin, through a variety of things, and I don't really think you serve them well by having them fall on their face and say, "I believe, I believe." ' [So] I suggested he [Sybok] better have some power over them if you were going to have someone like McCoy say 'I believe.' You'd better have some reason to do it.

". . . [Also], unicorns are a fantasy thing that are very heavy in fantasy fiction. And I just cautioned that they could make it look like science fantasy rather than science fiction. In science fiction, you try to approximate what the general scientific view will be; fantasy you have 'people riding up in unicorns all through the galaxy. In science fiction, you know that's un-likely, at the very least. What I felt, for example, if they were going to put the acoutrements of heaven [in the story], how come you're just going to pick the ones common to western civilization in one small planet, such as unicorns, heavenly music, and earth-like flowers, and so on? If you're going to do that, you have to make it clear that it's how this particular group sees it. Another group from another place might see it a different way."

Was he upset that they had proceeded to first draft without getting his input first? "Yes, very," he responded to the question. "I created *Star Trek*. I don't take anything away from Leonard or Bill or anyone, but I'm the guy who did it. How dare they start something without listening to my comments, whether they follow them or not? And I've never insisted they follow them. If I had strong objections to the story, I would have stated them. The only objections I ever had are stated: 'Don't let it get into religion.'

". . . My attitude on these things is, anytime they ask me to help them creatively, I'll help them out. But since I'm not producing the films, I don't go over to their office and say, 'Let me see that sheet and let me see if I agree with the way you put it,' since I would object if someone did that to me. . . . I presume I'll be satisfied [with the final story] because your father is a good dramatist. I've seen that over the years. I have to see what is cut together before I say, 'Yes! I'm completely satisfied—or ninety percent satisfied.' But I don't intend to discuss that with the audience because we all stick together. And if he does a great job, I'll tell him he did a great job. And if he didn't do that great of a job, I'll still say I'm happy. I think he'll do a great job, though."

After receiving Gene's memo in which he made these objections clear, father was surprised and disappointed that Gene so adamantly protested the story. "We all respect what input Gene has given us through the years," my father explained, "so of course we were distressed and disappointed that he didn't approve of some of its elements. We had worked hard to try and please everyone."

In spite of the disappointment Gene's memo generated, my father recognized the value of some of Gene's comments. "Gene's job was to read and comment on the story. After we read his objections, we still wanted to do the idea. But what his comments did do was force us to reevaluate some things. And we realized that certain things needed to be reworked.

"During this time period, the studio had been trying to negotiate with Leonard for the movie. But they dragged their heels, so Leonard accepted a directing job on *The Good*

Mother. Also, the Writer's Guild strike was impeding our progress. So next thing we knew, starting date was pushed back another six months. Our favorite refrain became, 'We have a year,' since we had been allowed this additional time waiting for Leonard to become available again and for the strike to end. So when we got Gene's comments, we looked at each other and said, 'We have a year!' And we started looking for places in the story that needed to be reworked."

One of the first things they addressed was the character of Zar himself. "I had shaped the holy man as a person capable of great passion—capable of killing," my father explained. "And I had based him on historical precedent. But once we decided that this was no longer the Messiah, but someone who was mistaken, and once we decided that there was a similarity between Zar and Khan from *Star Trek II*, we tried to tread the line of making him less evil and more tortured. So any killing act no longer made sense, because he became good. In fact, he now has a line that says, 'Bloodshed is not what I wanted.' "

Harve likened the newly developed character—whom they renamed Sybok—to Timothy Leary. "We began working with the figure of a renegade Vulcan," he explained. "Why a Vulcan? Because we all liked the idea of a Vulcan laughing to open the picture—another surprise. And that fit very nicely into known Vulcan doctrine. We all knew that four thousand years ago Vulcans were pagans. And we all knew the name Timothy Leary came into our consciousness a lot. We said, 'Hey, wait a minute, here's a guy that teaches at Harvard. He's one of the respected folks in his field, and he says, "I've got it, I've got it—let's drop acid! You guys are old-fashioned. You should try it, it works." ' Timothy Leary went to perdition and back, and altered his state. He had a cult—all that stuff. Well, that became our figure. We wanted a Timothy Leary who was not tainted. Who at the last minute could say, 'If I get through the Barrier, will you believe me then?' Because if we don't have that moment, then everybody's been had because he's a nut. Personally, for me, one of the great moments in the picture is right before the cathedral forms.

Everyone is standing around, and they see nothing is going to happen, and Kirk can hardly even speak to the *Enterprise*. And Spock says to Sybok, 'Sybok—Perhaps . . .' I think you feel for Sybok. I think the audience will. It sets up his one moment of victory, followed by his moment of total defeat, which is, yeah, there was somebody, but you wouldn't want to live with him.

"One of the great struggles in the story was leaning too far one way or the other with Sybok. He at first was like the Ayatollah. Then we all reacted to the fact that he couldn't be such a heavy. Then in another series of events he became so wonderful. In order to justify that the crew would listen to him, we had to make him so wonderful to silence the criticism from various sources. So now he came out, 'I'm terrific.' And what happened? Kirk became the fool because he's the only one not listening. And we had to go back and play the game of is-he-or-isn't-he?"

Once they struck a balance with Sybok's character, there still remained the problem of how his convincing the crew to go with him could happen so easily. As Gene commented, it didn't make much sense that these loyal crew members would simply abandon their captain just because someone told them they should. In order to justify the crew's abandonment, it was necessary to show that Sybok had some strange power over their minds. Thus came about the mind melding power which could release a sufferer from the painful memories of the past.

"Gene's position was that, in the twenty-third century, the concept of God is ridiculous," Harve explained. "If there were a concept of God," he argued, "then at least it would have to be a rational one. You couldn't expect to say, 'I'm going to see God' and expect to have such sophisticated people accept that. He then suggested he would have no trouble with it, if it was some form of bizarre mind control. We felt that mind control was available to us in a much simpler form. He [Sybok] was a Vulcan. So if you took the concept that this was a renegade Vulcan and a pagan Vulcan, and was using the mind meld for his own purposes, then what you had was a Rasputin, a devil. That finally came to bear with Leonard's notes on the script, which said, 'A mind meld isn't a bad idea, but only as it was practiced without control, years ago. . . . It would no longer be possible to do that on Vulcan. It would have been forbidden.' Great—outlawed. So that's what's in the picture, an ancient practice now forbidden.''

This change in Sybok's personality and methods also spawned another development. ''Once we changed his character we also had to get rid of the unicorn, since the unicorn was an extension of his violent nature,'' my father explained. ''Also, since I don't go to many movies, I was unaware of how many unicorns had been used in some of these science fiction films. David loved the unicorn and had suggested a wonderful shot where, as the shuttle leaves, the unicorn looks after it as it takes off. So there was this shot of the unicorn watching the space ship leave. And the picture of the unicorn and spaceship stuck in my mind so that I fell in love with it. It was hard for me to give up the unicorn idea until I looked at some of these movies and saw that the unicorn had indeed been used so many times. As it turns out, it worked for the story because I had in mind shots where the unicorn spears a soldier and the soldier writhes on the spear. Those shots would no longer work once the image of Sybok had changed.''

Defining Sybok's mode of travel brought up yet another point needing clarification: where exactly did Sybok want to go? My father had always envisioned Sybok's destination as the center of the universe. ''I wanted the destination to be in the center of the universe, since that's where I had envisioned God residing,'' he said. ''Then it was pointed out to me that this is not God, whereupon I responded that we wanted it to appear as though God were there. But Gene pointed out that in the twenty-third century, only eleven percent of the galaxy will have been discovered, and that there will have been no way for us to have discovered the center of the universe by then. Not only that, but there's no center of the universe. So we got a scientist in to explain that there's no center of the universe.''

That scientist was Charles Beichman, who is an astronomer at Cal Tech and Jet Propulsion Laboratories (JPL). I had the opportunity to ask him about his experience when he visited the Paramount lot one day. We sat on a bench near the front gate of the studio as he told me what his role in *Star Trek V* had been. "Harve called up some people he knew at JPL and said he had a script that needed some advice on astronomy, on what sort of places the *Enterprise* could be going," he explained. "Bill had this idea of going to the center of the universe, and the idea was to find out where that was. Whether you take a left or a right, and how you program it into the computers. So the people at JPL looked at me and said, 'You know something about astronomy.' So they asked me to come down and talk about some possible where's and why's and how's and get something that will look at least coherent and believable within the overall confines of the whole *Star Trek* idea.

"It was a lot of fun for me. I had a number of sessions with Bill, Harve, and David Loughery. The first part was simply to try and give some overall sense of cosmology. What are the hierarchies within the universe? There's our solar system, there's the galaxy, there's groups of galaxies, then finally when you put all those groups of galaxies together, there's the universe. The concept cosmologically of there being a center of the universe doesn't really work because it's infinite and expanding. It doesn't have a center. So we went back and forth on that.

"Plus, if you go back and look through all the series and movies, *Star Trek* had, in fact, never left our galaxy. If you try and say where in the history of the exploration of the universe the *Enterprise* is, the *Enterprise* is in fact four or five hundred years from now, and the level that people have gotten to in exploring is basically ten or twenty percent of our individual galaxy. In fact, they have never left the galaxy. So what becomes a place that they might go which is distant, far, and dangerous in the context of where they are in the exploration of the galaxy would be the center—which is a very interesting place astronomically—it has huge explosions going on and such.

"If you draw a picture of the galaxy it looks like a dinner

plate, and there is a center to it. The idea at that point was, 'Okay, let's have the destination be the center. That's where the God planet is, that's where the beast has been trapped.' It's probably the most powerful place in the galaxy, because of all the energy being released there. For example, our sun gives off a certain amount of energy in a volume consistent with the solar system. At the center of the galaxy, the amount of energy coming out is the equivalent of a million suns in the same volume. So it makes it a very interesting place to send the *Enterprise*. It's the sort of place that if you had a creature with delusions of grandeur he might put himself. So that became the logical thrust of where the *Enterprise* could be going in a manner consistent with everything that had gone on in the past.''

Part of Charles' role was to conjecture what Sybok and the *Enterprise* crew would find once they reached the center. ''We think there are barriers around the center itself. There are giant clouds, stars forming, pulsars going off. There's all sorts of violent activity,'' Charles explained. This information was consistent with the theory that my father, Harve, and David had created of a Great Barrier that stood between the *Enterprise* and the God planet. Charles verified this theory with his astronomical information. ''They had the Barrier idea already partially formed,'' he explained, ''but what was less clear was where in the universe was it, and what was it a Barrier from and to. That was a lot of the stuff we worked out together.''

But what lay beyond the Great Barrier was more fiction than science. ''There's no reason why there oughtn't to be other planets with atmospheres where one can breathe. The fact that it is very close to the center of the galaxy, which is probably a more violent place than you might like to walk around unprotected, is probably a certain amount of poetic license. But you just say that whoever it was that trapped the creature on the planet also built a little energy Barrier so that there was just the perfect amount of sunlight, and it all looked sort of like Southern California. You can work it out if you have to. That sort of thing I think you just let the movies get away with.''

Once Charles had helped define where the journey was to

take place, my father felt that most of the controversial issues in the outline had been addressed. "I felt like we had made a tremendous amount of progress by the end of the first draft," he commented. "We had tried to take all the critiques, incorporate the valid points, and utilize the scientific information we'd been given. The first draft was the result of an incredibly intensive thought process. We were very happy with the results."

Unfortunately, however, not everyone felt the same way. Gene again communicated his concerns, which were similar to his initial objections to the story. Although concerned about Gene's reaction, there was little my father could do. He was committed to doing a project entitled *Voice of the Planet,* which filmed near Mount Everest. He left for the Himalayas, leaving the project in Harve and David's capable hands. They assured him that they would make every attempt possible to fix the script while he was gone. What he didn't expect, however, was that they would change the very foundation of the story.

In his absence, Harve and David screened *Lost Horizon,* and then wrote a draft which was heavily influenced by the movie. Instead of looking for God, Sybok was now looking for the equivalent of Shangri-la, which they entitled Sha Ka Rhee. (They got the name from Sean Connery, whom they felt should play Sybok. Unfortunately, he accepted *Indiana Jones and the Last Crusade* before Paramount could close a deal with him. So they lost the actor, but kept the name.) Upon his return, my father was dismayed at the change that had taken place.

"The idea of Shangri-la was totally a surprise to me," he said. "I came off of *Voice of the Planet* with Harve and David assuring me how much I was going to love the draft they had written. I took it home on a weekend and read it, and as I finished it I had tears in my eyes because I was so hurt. We had worked all that time with the idea of searching for God, and now suddenly David and Harve had changed the whole concept to Shangri-la. Shangri-la is a place to escape the world. A place where no one ever grew old. It wasn't even a concept about Eden—it's a whole other idea, Shangri-la, the place of great peace. And Sybok was leading us there. It was a totally different story.

"I spent two days in their office, with the whole group around, and I had to fight, to struggle for two whole days to convince them their approach was wrong. The producer and the writer were aligned against me, and I fought and fought and fought. Finally, I was able to separate Harve and David. I was doing it like a policeman; I separated Harve from David. I said, '*Star Trek* isn't running away. *Star Trek*'s concepts aren't about running away. We don't run to peace. We fight. We try and do things.' And that got Harve. It broke the unified front slightly. And then I moved in on David, and gradually, gradually, gradually over the two days I got them back to the original concept of God. After it was all over, Nilo Rodis, the art director, said, 'They didn't count on a passionate director.' It was true. I felt so strongly that the original concept would work that I was willing to fight for it."

Harve and David admitted they had taken a wrong turn. "*Lost Horizon* is a kind of heaven on earth," Harve explained. "Some of the allusions it was providing us were not the home of creation, the home of the Almighty. They were rather a safe harbor. We were getting our metaphors mixed up. So we pulled back from that."

What did remain from that draft, however, was the concept of Sha Ka Rhee, the ultimate place of knowledge. They decided that Sybok would now be searching for this place, and then announce at the end that it was God that had given him the vision of Sha Ka Rhee. This approach was the final phase of a solution for which they had been looking.

"The original concept was that Sybok was looking for God, who turns out to be the devil," my father explained. "Then we changed it to him going somewhere—the audience didn't know where—and at the end he announces he's going to see God, who is really an alien. After the Shangri-la draft, we finally came to the solution that Sybok is going to Sha Ka Rhee, and then announces at the end that God gave him this vision. It was a compromise position that worked out well for everyone, although we never really answer where he has gotten the vision.

"In my original story, he got the vision by going through the Great Barrier and actually seeing God, who was really the devil, although Sybok didn't know it at the time. Then, as the story changed, we discussed how Sybok got the visions. We didn't want to say that he had gone through the Great Barrier already, because we needed to keep the suspense element of the Great Barrier's danger alive. So we had to explain how he got the vision without going through the Great Barrier. We've never quite answered it. The off-screen thought is, in the same way a searchlight reaches out, he had gotten too close to the Great Barrier during his travels and the alien placed the thoughts in his mind."

After they had more or less solved the Sha Ka Rhee dilemma, the script continued to undergo several drafts, each an attempt to fine-tune basic structural inconsistencies which needed to be addressed. Soon after, one became glaringly apparent. The scene where Spock refuses to shoot Sybok cried out for a deeper motivation that would explain Spock's behavior. At the time, the only explanation given was that Spock knew this Vulcan in seminary school. It seemed an inadequate reason why loyal Spock would refrain from defending his ship and his Captain. Harve, David, and my father began searching for the background story which would make the scene realistic.

"We originally said that this Vulcan would be someone that Spock knew," Harve explained. "But at one point I said, 'Ah, it has to be more than that—it's his brother.' 'Get out of here!' they both said. 'Why his brother?' I'll tell you why I said it and why I fought for it: because none of us could solve the problem of why Spock wouldn't kill him. Why wouldn't Spock fire in defense of his ship and his Captain? The answer is that there had to be something else operating there. Just because he was another Vulcan wasn't sufficient. Spock would have found a way. He would have used a phaser, or the neck pinch—something. So I thought there was only one way. He has to hesitate because he has an emotional attachment. And for him to have an emotional attachment, you have to put a label right on his forehead that says 'instant understanding' hence, brother.''

My father was less than convinced Harve had found a solution. ''At first I didn't agree with Harve that the brother idea was necessary,'' he said. ''I thought Spock would resist shooting Sybok on philosophical grounds. It made it a less immediate reason for not shooting him, but it was more powerful. But I said to Harve, 'show me.' We then came up with a draft which worked, and Gene sent us a conciliatory memo in which he indicated a growing acceptance for most of our new ideas, including Sha Ka Rhee, the mind meld power, and the brother idea. But at that point, we had gotten some notes back from Leonard saying he felt the connection between Sybok and Spock was not strong enough to warrant Spock's behavior. So then began the arduous process of working out the details of their bond in a sufficient enough manner to make the story believable.''

I sat in on many of the story meetings where they struggled with the details of the Sybok-Spock relationship. Most of the efforts were devoted to creating a background story for the two young Vulcans: why Sybok left Vulcan in the first place, young Spock's feelings upon his older brother's departure, and Spock's struggle to conform to Vulcan society once his only ally had deserted him. No answers were easy, and they spent many hours tossing ideas back and forth. Here is an excerpt from an actual story conference between Harve, David, and my father in which they were striving to reconcile these concepts:

HARVE: A straightlaced, puritanical father has a natural son who is a WASP. Then he adopts a Puerto Rican, who wants to be a WASP. The natural kid says, ''Pops is full of it'' and the adopted kid says, ''Isn't that what we do here?''

DAVID: I think a lot of people go through life with a book that says, ''How to Be a Human Being.'' They do this, get a wife, kids, house, but do nothing for whatever is human. Spock's doing that.

BILL: Let's go even further. Sybok's mother is dead and Sarek marries Amanda. That's very interesting. She died under what circumstances? And why did Sarek, this cold, puritanical Vulcan, marry a Jew?

DAVID: Well, the show commented on that. But for our purposes, that doesn't work. We don't need duality.

HARVE: What was Amanda's relationship with Sybok?

BILL: Good. We have a number of elements. How did Sybok's mother die? Amanda's relationship with Sarek? Spock's relationship with Amanda?

HARVE: Larry can go older or younger.

DAVID: If he's younger, he's a bastard.

HARVE: Right, but that's a weakness because Spock has always been treated as a bastard.

DAVID: He's gotta be older.

HARVE: That's my gut, too.

BILL: We don't even have to say anything. Let's say they are contemporaries. One year is meaningless at twenty-five, let alone fifty. And they separated early. So nonrecognition of Spock works.

DAVID: I think we have to play it he's not sure.

BILL: But first time we see him, Spock can't say anything because he doesn't recognize him.

A publicity photo—in the days before ''Star Trek.''

A moment of quiet in the office.

The cast reads through the script at my father's house.

Dodie Shepard puts the final touches on Sybok's costume.

Who better to play the Admiral than "Star Trek"'s own leader, Harve Bennett?

Harve and my father share a laugh in between takes as David Loughery looks on.

Actor Larry Luckinbill pretends he's talking to "God."

My father practices his climbing technique on the Paramount lot.

His real climb at Glacier Point, a shot which never appeared in the movie.

Leonard Nimoy is suspended in flying apparatus as my father climbs the simulated wall of El Capitan.

Movie magic: Spock flies into frame as Kirk ascends the mountain.

Harve Bennett and Ralph Winter watch as the climbing sequence is filmed.

George Takei and Walter Koenig discuss their first scene with the director before shooting begins. That's script supervisor Marlon Tumen in the back.

Even Vulcans wear sunglasses.

Sybok leads his army toward Paradise.

I protect my father from the blazing sun at Ridgecrest.

HARVE: I think it's interesting Sybok is older . . . but it's not inconceivable Sybok has aged well. Also Spock's gone through radiation, everything.

BILL: And directing three pictures!

DAVID: The strange thing is, if Sybok is older, the influence Amanda would have had on him.

HARVE: But there are solutions to that.

DAVID: I always felt they met at summers or holidays or something.

BILL: It's better the other way—they were joined at the hip when young, then cast asunder. They were brothers—intellectual, emotional, spiritual—it all happened together. Until the split. What was the split? The adventure Sybok wanted to go on and Spock's need for approval of mommy and daddy.

DAVID: In a way, Sybok chose Amanda's way and Spock chose Sarek's.

BILL: Then Sarek says, "Stop feeding this to my beloved Spock," and Sybok decides to leave.

DAVID: Or both say they're leaving and Sarek says, "No you're not, are you, Spock?"

BILL: Good. Then Sarek says to Spock, "If you go, you're no son of mine."

HARVE: That's an interesting scene.

BILL: That scene of confrontation has to be a collision, a peak moment. That's what we have to build toward.

DAVID: But we have to be careful because the scene with the gun has to be a surprise. So my feeling is, I still think in that scene Spock has to retain a stoicism, a false confidence in his own ability to not surrender to his brother.

BILL: What we're forcing is a scene of confrontation while the others stand around. It has to be constrained.

HARVE: The scene you're looking for comes after the fun of Kirk saying "I've got to sit down." And then the moving part of the scene happens when Spock says, "Okay, okay, I've done something wrong." One question from McCoy can trigger Spock's speech.

BILL: Maybe we should shove all the moments prior into the observation room.

DAVID: The key to Sybok is . . . even if Spock would initially reject him, Sybok would understand the need to have Spock reject him. To me, Sybok reacts with a sense of humor. He understands the frailty of the people he's working with. He can't convert Spock right there and he knows it. But he understands why Spock rejects him.

BILL: I can see why Sybok goes towards Spock but Spock stops him.

HARVE: Larry Luckenbill used one word. Sybok reminded him of a very good priest in that a quintessential priest controls with such power by grasping one thing about you that controls you.

DAVID: It's the gift of any con man. If he says, "Bill, you're very intelligent," you think, "This guy is okay."

BILL: Yeah, I went to a selling seminar once and they said that. You can sell anybody anything if you can get their key.

Which is what writers do. They can sell a scene if they get that character's key.

After many similar conferences, they decided that the "key" to the relationship was the bond the two brothers felt as boys. Spock, ashamed and self-conscious of his half-breed status, longed to accompany his renegade brother on his journey to find Sha Ka Rhee. But Sybok is banished because of his heretical beliefs, and refuses to take Spock with him since Spock, in his need to become accepted by his father as a true Vulcan, has chosen the logical path of his Vulcan upbringing. When the two brothers are reunited, Sybok is able to conjure up Spock's painful memories of his rejection by both his parents, since he never really was accepted by either one. In bringing back this sorrowful reminder, Sybok is able to release Spock's pain, thus allowing Spock another chance to join his brother in the search for Sha Ka Rhee.

It took weeks to work out this solution, and all three were pleased with the results. What they didn't count on, however, was the strenuous objections that Leonard Nimoy would voice when he read the next draft of the script. Leonard adamantly opposed the story for two reasons: one, he felt that Spock had already reconciled the pain of his half-breed status in prior movies, and releasing him from this non-existent pain was an insufficient reason for him to join his brother in the present. Two, even if Spock was released from some kind of pain, he still would not desert his Captain in light of the extreme loyalty Kirk had demonstrated to him in previous films, i.e. going back to the Genesis planet at the risk of losing his command on the slim chance Spock might still be alive. Leonard believed that the current ending of the film, in which Kirk alone refuses to cooperate with Sybok, betrayed the character of Spock by not demonstrating the loyalty that Spock would most certainly feel for Kirk. He voiced his opinion in a memo which he sent to my father.

My father was distressed by Leonard's reaction. "Leonard's opinion has always been extremely important and we made every effort to give his views credence. Of course I was upset by this reaction, since we had worked so hard to please him. To make matters worse, we found out that DeForest Kelly was ill and had to be in the hospital for a time. There was a danger that he wouldn't be well enough in time to do the film. Plus, we were having some budget disputes with the front office and it was becoming clear that some cuts—probably in the special effects departments—would have to be made. I found all this out on the same day, a Thursday. That day became forever ingrained in my memory as Black Thursday.''

Once the shock of Black Thursday wore off, they needed to take some immediate action to remedy the situation. The first thing my father, Harve, and David attempted to do was incorporate some of Leonard's ideas into the script. Until this point, the script had Sybok successfully convincing Spock to join him by performing a mind meld, showing Spock a scene of his birth and then relieving Spock of the pain which the mind meld causes. They augmented this scene by adding a sequence in which Spock tells Kirk that Sybok has failed to convince him since he has already reconciled this pain. Then Sybok unexpectedly performs another mind meld in which he and Spock become young boys, Spock begging the youthful Sybok to take him on the search for Sha Ka Rhee. Young Sybok refuses, telling the boy Spock that it is impossible, since Spock has chosen the Vulcan way. The mind meld ends, and the adult Sybok says, ''That was your pain—you begged to come with me as a boy. Come with me now.'' By adding this scene, my father hoped that Spock's reasons for accompanying Sybok willingly would become clear to Leonard.

But Leonard didn't buy it. ''Leonard told me, 'under no circumstances would Spock betray his Captain,' which made sense, but left us with some major structural problems. If we changed the script so that Spock also refuses to accompany Sybok, what happens to the ending where Kirk is the sole protestor? And if Spock refuses to go with Sybok, we can't have McCoy agreeing to go alone. He would have to stay with Kirk and Spock. So this finely-wrought script, which we worked on all these months, was in danger of disintegrating before my eyes.

"This was very hard for me to deal with. As a lead actor, I was used to getting my own way. I found myself in the very unusual position of battling my own nature since I was being forced to compromise. And I found that some of the joy of the experience was diminishing with all the problems I was beginning to face: Leonard's objections, DeForest's illness, budget disputes. It all became very apparent to me one day as I visited the special effects make-up artist, Kenny Myers, to check on the Vulcan ear molds. He showed me a pair of baby Vulcan ears, which we were going to use for the infant Spock. Then he said, 'I heard the baby was sick.' My immediate reaction was, 'What—now one of the twins we're using to play the infant Spock is sick? What else is going to go wrong?' And Kenny said, 'No, your daughter Leslie's son.' I felt an immediate, momentary relief that it was only my grandson that was sick! That's when I knew the stress was beginning to get to me.

"I stuck to my guns, hoping I could convince Leonard he was wrong. But he remained firm, so we changed it. So in the final draft, Spock refuses to accompany Sybok, even after the second mind meld. And when Spock refuses, McCoy refuses also. Then Kirk, Spock, and McCoy all decide their duty is 'to go where no man has gone before,' so they agree to accompany Sybok down to the planet. But we still kept an element of the older versions, which is that Kirk still ends up on the God planet alone, being chased by the alien until he is rescued by the Klingons."

Although the new approach helped allay some of Leonard's fears, he still felt some story elements about the ending were incomplete. During this period, I was able to talk to him about his concerns.

"What I'm still wrestling with—or trying to be helpful with—is the thematic line of the whole story," he explained. "I don't think it's clear yet in the end what Sybok is really doing and what is this thing that is leading him on. What is the relationship between them and how did it affect us? and so on. There is a thematic issue here which is unresolved. Also a dramatic issue is unresolved. It's resolved in pyrotechnics, but

69

I don't think it's resolved in a way which touches us. Not about the brothers necessarily, but about what's happened to this person; what was obsessing him, what was driving him? There should be something like, 'There but for the grace of God go I,' or 'I won't make the same mistake he made,' something about mankind, something we should learn. . . . There's a line I pointed out where the writer has said editorially 'Sybok has an extraordinary revelation' and I said 'The writer may have said that, but I don't get that, because Sybok doesn't reveal that to us. He doesn't say "Run!" or "I've been a fool!" or something.' It may be clear in Bill's vision, he may have an image in his head that tells us that story, but I don't see it."

Time was running out. "We have a year!" became the standard joke, since the clock was now ticking away the weeks before principal photography began. No longer having the luxury of time to argue, they took Leonard's words to heart. In the climactic scene where Sybok realizes what he has found is not God, but a horrible alien, they added Sybok's lines: "This is my doing—my vanity. Save yourselves!" By including these lines, they hoped it would become clear that Sybok's ego allowed him to think God had actually spoken to him alone, and it was this ego which has proven his undoing.

The idea that God does not speak to one man alone was a thought which they wanted to explain further. At the ending party scene, they decided McCoy would say to Spock, "Has it occurred to you that something larger placed that Barrier there not to keep us out, but to keep that thing in?" Spock then responds, "I'll only say this: we have yet to reach the final frontier." Kirk then approaches them and asks what they're thinking. When they tell him, he says, "Maybe God isn't out there, maybe he's here, in the human heart." In Kirk's line was the crux of the entire movie, the idea that my father had been struggling for over a year to make clear. The irony of it was that it almost didn't get in the film.

"Harve, David, and I struggled for weeks to get that final scene right," he said. "We had two important ideas to get across in that scene: the idea of family, which Kirk, Spock, and McCoy realize they are to each other, and the idea that God resides within the human heart. We would switch the lines around in different orders, different scenes, anything we could do to make it flow and make sense. At one point, we decided to take 'God is in the human heart' out of the movie, because Harve and David didn't think it was as crucial a line as some of the others. But I knew that line contained the idea of the entire movie. So I insisted, and they finally agreed. So my philosophy—that God is within the human heart, and all of us being human, have God—was finally made clear.''

As the starting date for the film drew closer, it seemed as though they had solved their major problems. Gene had responded positively to the later drafts, and most of Leonard's objections had been incorporated into the script. To everyone's relief, DeForest was pronounced well enough to participate in the film. It seemed as though everything was going smoothly at last. But there was one more hurdle to overcome: the budget. In the final days before principal photography began, the studio handed down a pronouncement: the film was over budget and they would have to make some cuts. The most obvious place to begin the process was in the special effects, since this was by far the most expensive area. That meant the ending, which relied heavily on optical effects, was the first to be hit. This did not sit well with my father.

''My original concept for the movie had the characters descending into the equivalent of hell,'' he said. ''The angels surrounding 'God' turn into horrible gargoyle-type figures and chase Kirk, Spock, and McCoy into a burning chasm. I loved the idea of the cherubim turning into ugly, twisted monsters, but I was quickly told my idea was much too expensive. So we changed the gargoyles into Rockmen. That is, as Kirk, Spock, and McCoy are running away, these huge, twisted shapes break free from the rocks surrounding them and pursue the characters. I had in mind six Rockmen, six hulking, strange creatures—terrifying!

''But each of those Rockmen were incredibly expensive. We had to make a latex suit in which a man could fit, and the latex had to look like rock. The estimate for all six was something

71

like $300,000. It was way too extravagant. So the first thing I was told was that I could only have one Rockman. One! So here I had gone from this fantastic image of floating cherubim turning into flying gargoyles, then to six, hulking Rockmen, now down to one Rockman. It was one of the first lessons I had in the realization that the movie in my head was going to be different from the one in reality. But I basically had no choice, so we went with it. And one Rockman was all I got.''

But in spite of the compromises he had made, my father had accomplished an incredible achievement. He had taken an idea which had bubbled and percolated in his head for months and typed it into black and white reality. He had convinced an unwilling Harve Bennett to produce and co-write the film. Together with Harve and David Loughery, he shaped the story into a form which pleased a skeptical studio and finally quieted Gene Roddenberry's initial objections. He learned to compromise, to accept Leonard Nimoy's input, and acknowledge that some of his ideas were too costly for the reality of filmmaking. But most of all, he realized that his passion, his dream for *Star Trek V* had indeed become a reality. And as he completed his work on the story, he knew the best was yet to come.

3

PREPRODUCTION

During his story sessions with Harve and David, my father would often give descriptions of places they were in the process of discussing. "Paradise is a futuristic ghost town," he would say. Or, "The observation room is like a nautical men's club." But as the story sessions grew to a close, it came time to face the inevitable: what exactly were those places going to look like? Who was going to design the look of the film—the sets, the costumes, the lighting. And who was going to carry these ideas to fruition? How much money did they have, and would it be enough to do his vision of the film justice?

From the beginning, my father had some strong ideas about what he wanted. "I knew I wanted a very special look for *Star Trek V*," he said. "I wanted to make it different than the other *Star Trek* movies, grittier, more realistic. I would constantly describe my ideas to Harve and David, but I knew my descriptions weren't doing them justice. Then one day they said to me, 'Bill, this is Nilo Rodis, your art director. He's the man that will sketch out your ideas.' So I began a detailed process of literally visualizing the movie from beginning to end, using Nilo's talents as my guide."

Nilo was certainly up to the task. His unusual background had given him the training, imagination, and creativity to do the job right. Raised in the Philippines, Nilo emigrated to

73

America in order to study industrial design. After school, he began his career designing cars, although he soon left the field because "gasoline was not in [his] blood." He then moved on to the military, where he was designing tanks, when Lucasfilm found him. "They asked me to come and design *Return of the Jedi,*" he said. "I looked at them and said, 'What's that?' They said, 'It's the sequel to *Star Wars,*' and I said, 'What's that?' I had never seen these films before."

Even though art directing for film had never been one of his goals, his unfamiliarity with show business didn't seem to hurt his career much. He stayed at Lucasfilm for ten years. Soon afterward, he was offered a job on *Star Trek III,* and subsequently, on *Star Trek IV.* I asked him what his secret to success was. He explained that designing for movies worked on the same principle for him as designing cars or tanks. "You ask a person what they want. Then you either try to simplify it or make it more complex but you are always asking, 'What do you want to accomplish with this scene?' He then recommended watching a film without the sound. "I always do it in airplanes since there's nothing else to do," he laughed. "And you realize that you can communicate visually. One movie that did this was *Big.* Another one was *Mask.* You can communicate without words. So that's what I do, concentrate on the visuals. I transfer the script from words to pictures, so we can all see what the picture will do for us."

His approach worked so well on the prior two *Star Trek* movies that he was asked to repeat his success with *V.* One of the first things he did after coming on board was listen to my father tell him the whole story, a marathon session which lasted an entire day. He then went home and began sketching some of the scenes. The process continued for several weeks, until he'd succeeded in sketching out almost every scene in the movie. My father was thrilled with the results. "Rarely in a career do you have the chance to tell someone something and have it turn out better than you imagined," he said. "Nilo invariably brought back sketches which not only embodied my ideas, but amplified on them. He saw what I saw, and added his own vision, which really gave the movie almost an epic quality.''

Together, they visualized some fantastically complicated, visually distinctive shots. Two of my father's favorites were nicknamed ''The Powers of Ten'' and ''The Bierstadt Shots.'' He explained their significance: ''Nilo and I envisioned the shuttle's entry into the God planet as a magical, fantastical journey. I had seen some paintings by an artist named Bierstadt, who came out of the Hudson River School of painting. These paintings were of mysterious mountains, shrouded in dark, misty clouds—eerie yet inspiring. I knew I wanted that look for the movie, so Nilo and I spent some time discussing what it should be and we came up with some great ideas. We called this 'The Bierstadt Shot.' Another great shot we envisioned took place in the very first scene of the film, as Sybok is laughing and the camera moves into the sun. It moves further and further away until it's in the galaxy, then turns around and does a move into the earth, the image getting magnified larger and larger by powers of ten, until it reaches America, then California, then finally into a hand on a granite rock. And we called that shot 'The Powers of Ten' shot.

''But the moment that really epitomized Nilo's talents to me came when we were sketching ideas for the God planet sequence. Even though we had worked out the entry to the planet with 'The Bierstadt Shot,' it was still unclear how the whole drama of God appearing would unfold. I knew I wanted the beginning of the scene to include a Michelangelo-esque God. So Nilo began to sketch a face within a column, and people standing around it. When I saw the face and our relationship to it, I said, 'It's the eyes. The whole thing has to be the eyes.' And when he drew the sequences where we push into God's eyes, I knew we had found the solution to what God would look like.''

But these epic style shots could not be filmed by ordinary means. In order to create such special visual effects, it was necessary to hire a company which specialized in this type of work. But who?

''We asked several companies to all do the same thing,'' my

father said. "We wanted them to show us their idea of what a column of light with a figure inside it would look like. Each company did a test and came up with their own version of the effect. But we were distressed that no one seemed to be getting the idea right. One very well-known company merely put a figure inside a beam of light! Just when I was thinking the whole idea wouldn't work, I was told about a man named Bran Ferren who worked out in Long Island. So we all traveled out to see him and find out what kind of test he had run. When we got there, he told me that he hadn't filmed any tests, but that he had a lot of things to show me. So he took us into his workshop, and I saw a four-cubic-foot, plate glass container of water with a centrifuge. He put a light on the water, and then put chemicals in the water, and we saw what he was going to do. If you photographed this whirlwind, it looked like a vortex. In that moment, I realized he was a creative genius, so we gave him the job."

Bran, best known for his work on *Altered States,* then began to estimate how much all the optical shots would cost. "Our estimate was 5 million dollars," my father said, "which is obviously a tremendous amount of money. But we were so excited by the idea of shots like the God column, 'The Powers of Ten' and 'The Bierstadt Shot' that we were willing to spend that much. So we were eagerly anticipating the results of Bran's bid because we felt certain he was the right man for the job."

While waiting for Bran to get back to them, they continued to spend time resketching and refining the storyboards. As the storyboarding sessions grew increasingly focused, it became clear that the sketched characters needed life breathed into them. It was time to begin casting the film.

From the beginning, my father had envisioned Sean Connery in the role of Sybok. Not only did he have tremendous respect for Connery's acting talents, but he knew that Connery's presence in the film would draw in large foreign box office business. Since *Star Trek* movies have traditionally done poorly overseas, this would have been a great bonus. Unfortunately, my father was deeply disappointed to learn that

Connery had just accepted another part for the same time period when *Star Trek V* would be filming, and would be unavailable.

My father then began looking at other foreign actors which might bring in overseas business. "We considered several people," he said, "and were especially intrigued by one well-known Swedish actor who I consider very talented. But when we found out how expensive he was, that idea quickly flew out the window."

They had to go back to the drawing board. "Harve and I each drew up a list of possible candidates for the role. I then began the long process of looking at film that each of these actors had done. No one really caught my eye, until one day I was watching a tape of a show on LBJ [Lyndon Baines Johnson] that had played on PBS. The actor playing LBJ had tremendous energy and vitality. As I watched the show progress, I knew we had found our man."

The actor who had done such a dynamic job of portraying LBJ was Larry Luckinbill. Once he agreed to play Sybok, a major hurdle had been overcome. Storyboarding the film would now proceed much more smoothly.

But there were many other, smaller roles that had to be cast as well. Because a director is so busy during preproduction, he needs help finding the appropriate actors to audition for these roles. For *Star Trek V,* my father called upon casting director Bill Shepard to help him.

Bill, who had formerly worked at Disney for thirteen years, explained his job to me: "The responsibility of the casting director is to present the best possible actors to the director and producers for the film, always taking into account the size of the part, the budget, and availability of actors. After looking at the roles he has to fill, the casting director meets with the director and producers, and suggests actors. Interviews, auditions, viewing films and videotapes follow. Based on their readings for me, the actors then read for the director and producer. The director has the final selection of actors."

Bill undertook this process for *Star Trek V.* He auditioned actors for all the necessary parts, then brought the ones he felt were most appropriate for the roles to my father. The actors then read again, sometimes coming back two or three times before a final decision was made.

My father made his choices based on images that had formed in his mind before and during the script writing and story-boarding sessions. "We read Rex Holman for the part of J'onn. His face was so wonderfully lean, so gaunt, that it lent itself perfectly to the image we had of J'onn," my father said. "The same thing happened with Charlie Cooper, who plays General Korrd. Originally I was going to cast George Murdock, the actor who plays 'God,' as Korrd, but when Charlie walked into the room I knew I had to make a change. He read extremely well, and he looked so much like the Korrd that we had envisioned—like an old, Russian general—I gave him the part. I then recast George as 'God.' It was a rather strange way of finding the right roles, but it worked out perfectly. . . . Todd Bryant and Spice Williams worked the same way. They were physically right for the Klingons and were obviously talented enough to do the roles justice. And they could speak Klingon, of course! As far as the part of Talbot, I had always imagined David Warner playing Talbot because I think he is such a fine actor. He didn't read for the part. I just talked to him and assured him I'd keep his character alive throughout the movie. I was thrilled when he accepted the role."

While Harve and my father were casting the role of Caithlin Dar, I had the opportunity to sit in on some of the readings. The audition would begin with Bill Shepard bringing in one of several girls who were waiting outside my father or Harve's office. Because Caithlin was supposed to be young and exotically beautiful, each girl that walked in was lovelier than the next. The actresses would then read the scene where Caithlin enters the bar in Paradise City to find Talbot and Korrd getting drunk. If they liked the reading, my father would make some suggestions on how the actress could alter her performance, and he would ask her to read the scene again.

Over a series of days, Bill brought in several groups of girls, which my father eventually narrowed down to a much smaller number. Bill then brought these girls back and had them repeat the reading until my father finally picked a beautiful Chinese girl named Cynthia Gouw. "Her beauty and poise really sold her," my father said. "She looked right for the part, and Harve and I both felt she could do the role justice."

Once the problem of who would be playing the parts was solved, the next important issue was what they would look like when they were performing their roles. Although Nilo was originally responsible only for sketching the storyboards, he slowly found himself involved in this area as well. "The same thing happened when I was working for Lucas," he told me. "My storyboarding segued into costuming. Before I could completely visualize the scenes, I had to put people in them. They had to be wearing something. So I started putting costumes in the sketches."

He soon found himself heavily involved in the costuming process. "When Nilo and I would discuss a scene, I would be visualizing a face," my father explained. "But Nilo visualized the whole thing. So he dressed J'onn, the Klingons, and the girl. He basically had dressed everyone before filming began. His ideas were wonderful. The new characters were wearing gritty, real costumes that still had a futuristic sense. And the returning characters had a military, yet casual flair to their costumes that managed to retain continuity with the prior movies. I was very pleased with his work."

Nilo explained that he and my father worked together so well because they developed a mode of communication that didn't require words. "Sometimes people will have a code. You don't have to over-explain something to them. I have that rapport with Bill. He would say, 'You know what I mean?' And I would say, 'Yes.' Even though verbally he didn't describe it, we were looking at the same picture. That's sort of magic when that happens because you have a bead on what the director's thinking. Bill and I were on the same frequency."

Once they had agreed on a basic look, the next step was to hire a costume designer to realize and expand on their ideas. My father went through a long, intensive screening process, interviewing many people for the job. "We brought in several ladies, all of whom had sketches of what they thought a *Star Trek* soldier should look like. All the designs were too feminine, lacking the feeling of bold masculinity and simplicity I wanted to capture. At this point, the obvious finally occurred to me. 'Why don't we use Nilo as the costume designer as well?' So I went to Harve and asked to have Nilo as costume designer, having no idea he had already done this on *Jedi*. Harve said, 'Okay,' and that was that.

"I knew Nilo was the right person to design all the men's costumes, but I was a little worried about Caithlin. So I had Nilo draw up a series of sketches. Her costume had to be filmy, but it also had to look like she could travel in it. I knew we would have to disguise her in the first shot, so that also became a requirement. And when she was on the bridge, it wouldn't look right to have her in something too revealing. So we had to work through all these problems and he came up with some great suggestions—the hooded cape, for example. I was very pleased with the results."

In addition to designing, part of Nilo's "new" job was to ensure that the costumes were made on time and on budget. But he couldn't do this vast job alone. In order to implement his designs, it was necessary to hire a costume supervisor, whose role it would be to oversee the making of the costumes, organize the fittings, hire wardrobe personnel to dress the actors, and keep track of the large wardrobe once filming began. But who? Again they went through a screening process, finally settling on a small, spunky lady with a pixyish grin and an iron sense of discipline. Her name was Dodie Shepard.

Dodie had her work cut out for her. To start, she had to hire pattern makers and cutters to begin shaping the costumes for the new characters. Once the costumes had been assembled, she organized fittings for the actors, where each costume was nipped and tucked to the exact size. Sometimes the actors were required to come back two or three times to make sure every fold, tuck, or pleat was just right. My father's input also came into play here.

"I had quite a lot of interaction with Bill at this time," she explained, "to see if we were really on the direction he wanted to go, because we all have these visions, our own inside pictures of what's going on in our heads. We can talk about it until the cows come home, but then it finally gets to be show-and-tell time. So we would set up appointments for him to come over and see where we were going. He was beautifully patient about sitting there while we got maybe five or ten or fifteen looks set up for him, to say 'this is where we are going to go,' and if he didn't like it then 'let's pull this out and put this in,' or 'throw the whole thing out and start all over again.' We were very fortunate because my vision of a particular costume was usually very similar to what he was talking about. So there wasn't a conflict going on there, where he saw burlap and I was picturing something else.''

Assembling the new characters' costumes was not the only responsibility weighing on Dodie's shoulders. She was also responsible for outfitting all the background players in appropriate twenty-third-century gear. Since creating and fitting a costume from scratch is expensive, she dressed these extras from racks of already existing costumes. These racks of clothing were, for the most part, found at Western Costume, a legendary entity which has housed the costumes for scores of motion picture classics. Located down the street from Paramount, Western Costume has been a landmark for decades, one of the few remainders from Hollywood's memorable past. (Unfortunately, the large building with its racks upon racks of costumes will soon be sold. *Star Trek V* has had the dubious honor of being one of the last movies to utilize the great treasures still inside its walls.)

Dodie spent a great deal of time within this huge storehouse, looking for appropriate items. Guided by input from Nilo, she sifted through the racks of clothing in hopes of finding something useful. ''The process was a matter of touching, feeling, saying, 'This is a good base,' then adding to, or cutting from, the already existing costume.'' In this manner, she and Nilo managed to dress the various extras, and add color and texture to the overall look of the film.

But their job was by no means finished. They still had to contend with the *Enterprise* crew's costumes. For the location scenes, Nilo wanted a different look than the ordinary costumes provided. He then designed a new brown field uniform, which the crew would wear in combat situations, most notably during the Paradise City battle scenes. He also designed the Yosemite camping clothes, paying special attention to Spock's bomber jacket, since he wanted it to look functional, yet futuristic.

Initially, my father had wanted to redesign the entire crew's apparel. However, the cost was so prohibitive that they were forced to utilize some of the costumes from the preceding films. But it was no small task to gather the former gear together. Joe Markham, who was my father's dresser on "T.J. Hooker," *Star Trek II, III,* and *IV,* and who was later hired as one of the wardrobe personnel on *V,* explained the variety of costumes left over from the previous *Star Trek* films: "In Starfleet, there are four different uniforms that we have seen the *Enterprise* officers—the regular crew—in," he explained. "There is the regular Class A jacket uniform, the standard dress uniform. Then there is the leather dress jacket worn with a Class A shirt. It serves a different function. It's less formal, but still a dress uniform. We've also seen a different field jacket, one worn in combat situations. And now, of course, we have the new brown field uniforms, which are worn for combat situations.

"For the enlisted men, there are two different uniforms, in some cases three. There is a dress jumpsuit in red, which is their Class A dress uniform. We have two variants on it: one with black collars and cuffs, which is the normal style, and one with bright red collars and cuffs for trainees. There are also new field uniforms in brown for lower officers, almost identical to the command officers' field uniforms, but these have royal blue trimming and shirts.

"We also have three different maintenance uniforms: white for the engineers, orange for disaster workers, and gray for ship maintenance. But that's just the beginning. There are also special uniforms for security guards, special service personnel, medical personnel, prison guards, and Federation employees."

With such a large number of costumes involved, certain

problems inevitably arise. Of course, it is crucial that someone keep track of all the clothing. In addition, since scenes involving the same location are usually filmed together, a movie is rarely shot in sequential order. This means, for example, that an exterior shot of an officer going into a building is filmed at a different time than the shot of him actually in the building.

For such reasons, it is extremely important that someone is taking note of the costume details from scene to scene. One small slip can mean that the two scenes will be mismatched, and therefore unusable. In order to ensure this would not happen, Dodie hired Danny Bronson and Sue Moore, whose responsibility would be to help keep track of the costumes, dress the actors, and, most importantly, take note of such costume details. Danny and Sue noted their observations in a large notebook referred to as "The Bible," which had spaces for scene numbers, descriptions of the costumes, and polaroid photos.

The importance of costuming and its impact upon an audience soon became glaringly apparent to my father and the rest of the team. One morning, Harve found out that someone had stolen almost $60,000 worth of costumes from a wardrobe trailer the previous evening. And this was not the first time something like this had happened.

"Approximately a year ago some people came in through the wardrobe roof on a Saturday," Harve revealed. "They broke through and took selected uniforms, largely from the first series. Security staked the place out on the following night, Sunday. They came back! They caught them red-handed. And they recovered ninety percent of what they had originally taken on Saturday. They were Beverly Hills rich kids—*Star Trek* fans. Security had gotten a tip that they were coming back from some other Trekkies, who were so jealous that these other people had real stuff, they turned them in. Now, this past week, [someone] cut through a fence, came into the studio—cut through the fence, with wire cutters and a lock cutter, and broke a master lock which can't be broken by a gun—and got into an unmarked trailer. Nobody except insiders knew it was there. No one has found them, but our cops are working on the assumption that it's a repeat." David Loughery, renowned for his practical jokes, then sent Harve a ransom note for the missing wardrobe, which Harve assumed was real. He then spent the next several hours discussing the note with the police, until he was informed it was a fake. However, the whereabouts of the costumes remained a mystery.

In spite of the theft, the costume department continued its busy preparations, headed by Dodie and Nilo. However, this was not the only department in which Nilo was involved. He also contributed ideas for special effects make-up. He and my father spent many hours discussing how the aliens on Nimbus Three should look, and what the many faces of God should be. Once they had solidified some of their ideas, they began to interview people for the job of special effects make-up artist.

"We saw a lot of people, and we asked each of them to draw up their own sketches of these aliens. They were all very competent, but then in walked this vivacious, good-natured guy named Kenny Myers. Not only were his sketches on the money, but his personality gave me the impression he would infuse his work with energy and enthusiasm. So Kenny became our special effects make-up man."

Kenny maintains a studio about thirty miles outside Los Angeles, where my father would travel regularly to discuss what aliens and God heads should look like. I had the opportunity to visit Kenny there where, surrounded by kilns, head molds, and ghoulish masks from horror movies he had previously worked on, we talked about how he created the alien make-ups for *Star Trek V.*

"Bill and I talked extensively about the designs," he explained. "We would have a discussion, and then I would sketch out our ideas. We created characters we nicknamed things like Apeface, Wrinkles, Dark Eyes, Lost Soul, Corn Row, and Leatherface.

"Once we got a design locked in, my group and I would take a life cast of an actor, usually someone I have chosen because of his facial structure. The cast is made with dental alginae, the same stuff that dental impressions are made of. From that, we produce as many head molds as we need. I would then run this head mold by your father to make sure he saw the same things in it that I saw. Then, with clay, we would sculpt the character right on the head mold. We would then cut up the sculpture and transfer the pieces to a mold of the corresponding section of that person's face. So say we've cut the chin off the sculpture. We then transfer that chin section to a mold of that person's chin. We would do that for each section of the person's face.

"It's a very complicated process, because you have to know how it's going to lay down on the person's face before you cut the sculpture up. So say you have a character with huge cheeks and a little chin. And you know by experience that the edges have to overlap in a certain way when you apply the pieces to the actor's face. So you can't just take the cheeks and the chin and apply them as one piece, because you won't be able to blend the edges properly. This means you have to cut the cheeks separately from each other, and separately from the chin.

"Once you have these separate pieces, which are now lying on individual molds, you make a relief copy of each section. This is done by making another mold on top of the clay sculpture. Once that dries, we lift off the relief mold, and scrape away the clay underneath. Now we are left with the original mold and a relief mold, with a space in between them. This space is injected with latex, and this three-layer 'sandwich' is then cooked. Once it's finished cooking, we lift off the relief and remove the latex piece underneath. This is the actual piece which will be applied to the actor's face using medical adhesive."

This complicated process was used to create the "A" make-ups, the ones that would be seen up close by the camera. Other make-ups, called "mid-ranges" were to be seen farther away, and didn't require cutting the sculptures into separate pieces. These make-ups were created to merely slip over the actor's head in one piece. For the location scenes, my father envisioned many mid-range make-ups in the background, augmented by six to eight "A" make-ups near the camera. At four hours per "A" make-up, sometimes using two artists per make-up, the estimation was that three make-up trailers would be needed on the Paradise location.

But this was not all Kenny had to do. He also was responsible for creating the God heads from sketches he and my father had designed. In addition, he had to create a realistic looking Rockman, a process which involved an extensive amount of work. First, they decided that the Rockman should consist of a latex suit, inside which an actor would fit. In order to create this suit, Kenny and his crew had to make an entire body cast of the man playing the Rockman. The suit was then made in much the same way the make-ups were, including the clay sculpting, relief mold, and latex injection processes. The finished suit was then wired so that the special effects team could add fire-breathing apparatus.

The entire process for all these make-ups was long, difficult, and extremely uncomfortable for the actors. One actor, on whom Kenny was practicing an "A" make-up, said it felt like a warm loaf of bread being applied to his face. His comment inspired another thought: Did anyone ever freak out after enduring a long day under such uncomfortable circumstances?

Kenny said that, indeed, sometimes problems did arise. "Actors will sometimes say anything to get a job," he said. "I'm pretty good at eliminating those who'll have a problem just by asking them a series of questions, like if they are claustrophobic or such. Occasionally, one will get by you. They'll say they're fine, but once you get them in the chair, they start shaking."

He also went on to explain that any alcohol ingested into the system before applying the make-up can cause a problem. "Once the alcohol is in the bloodstream and it starts leaving, like when you are sobering up, it will suck the alcohol from the adhesive glue which is holding the appliances in place. So all that is left on the skin is the resin, which is almost impossible to get off. One time I had a guy come in drunk because he had tied one on the night before. It took us five hours to put his make-up on, and four hours to take it off. And he was screaming the whole time. Other times you get actors who can't stand it anymore and just rip the make-up right off. It's not too much fun to watch whole patches of someone's skin come off."

While Kenny was busily sculpting space age faces, my father was also heavily involved in designing the sets, a process which had been underway since his first storyboarding sessions with Nilo.

"When I started doing conceptualizations, along the way I had to describe the interiors," Nilo said. "But I also had to describe the exteriors, so I started visualizing the town, the bar, and other sets. And along the way, I developed a library of what things would look like."

After going over these rough concepts, Nilo and my father had to take the next obvious step: they had to find someone to design and build these sets. "We knew we needed someone with not only tremendous creative ability, but organizational and technical skill as well," my father said. "These sets needed to be as colorful, fantastical, and futuristic as possible, but still retain an air of realism about them as well. We also knew that we didn't have all the money in the world, so whoever got the job would have to know how to be economical and efficient, since many of the sets would have to be built at the same time."

It was quite a tall order. But it turned out they didn't have to go very far to fill it. "I had seen the sets for the new 'Star Trek: The Next Generation' series, and had been very impressed with them," my father said. When he met Herman Zimmerman, the man who served as production designer for the show, he was equally impressed. Herman's intelligence and creativity convinced my father he should get the job.

Once Herman had been hired, his first step was to sit down with my father and Nilo to discuss the sketches they had made for the various sets. "Bill, like most directors, knows what he likes when he sees it," Herman said, "but doesn't always know how to express it by drawing it, which is why Nilo was so valuable to him and valuable to me. [Nilo would] tell me what Bill was after and a lot of what we learned about in the sketches is what we didn't want, not always what we did want.''

Nilo agreed. ''When Herman came aboard, he started designing along the lines I had been thinking. So Herman became my boss, because an art director answers to a production designer. That's the way it works. The production designer literally controls the visual integrity and how you put it together, whereas my [input] was mostly blue sky on white paper. I had no concern for [practicalities]—what set on what stage because we only have X amount of ceiling, or a set is only this wide. I disregarded all that. I went for the blue sky idea and Herman made it real by looking into the parameters: how much he would spend, and coordination of massive amounts of work. So when Herman came in, I had to be realistic about my ideas, so they changed because we had to achieve a certain look within a certain time. And he was very good at that.''

Almost immediately, Herman became one of the busiest men on the production team. Not only was he responsible for designing the various sets—among them the Klingon bridge, a Nimbus Three barroom, an *Enterprise* bridge, ship bowels, turbo shaft, and a shuttlecraft—but he had to coordinate the building of all of them as well. ''We had to calculate when we should have our sets ready based on the shooting schedule; looking ahead and seeing how many weeks it would be to shuttle bay, or how many weeks it would be to another set,'' Herman said. ''Then we gave the studio a list of our requirements: like we needed stage 4 to start work, then we needed stage 7 or stage 18 and how long we would have those, because you get charged on a daily basis by the studio for the construction time as well as the shooting time. The studio also schedules those stages after we strike the set and get everything off the stage, but that's all part of what production is all about. It's not necessarily creative, but very necessary to getting the job done.''

At one point, Herman was building five sets all at the same time. Of course, he wasn't doing the job all by himself. The art department, headed by Michael Okuda, would first draft

Herman's designs. Once they had his ideas down on paper, Herman would then hire a foreman to oversee building on each particular stage.

It was also necessary to hire someone to "dress" the completed bare sets. For *Star Trek V,* this task fell to John Dwyer, an extremely talented set dresser who worked on the original "Star Trek" series, *Star Trek IV,* and "Star Trek: The Next Generation." John worked hand and glove with Herman to create the most convincing and imaginative look possible for all the sets.

Although Herman shouldered an incredible amount of responsibility for the construction of the sets at Paramount, he also faced a tremendous challenge with the building of the Paradise City location. Before Herman could begin directing his foremen to build the city, however, it was necessary to find the proper location. This task fell to Tim Downs, a young, energetic man who, despite his age, had been in the location scouting business for fourteen years.

"My assignment was to find a place in the desert where the movie company could hole up in a hotel and not have to move, even though they needed three different locations: one, the opening scene where Sybok first meets J'onn; two, the establishing sequences of the God planet; and three, the town of Paradise itself. I went through the script to break it down and get a picture of each scene in my head. Since I've been scouting for fourteen years, I had a working knowledge of the Mojave desert. I remembered Ridgecrest, which was centrally located between several sites that I thought might interest them. The way I sold them on using the Ridgecrest locations was to go up there and do some really good photography with my camera. Nilo had made some sketches of what the location should look like, so everyone had a preconceived notion of what they wanted. My thought was to try and fulfill these ideas. So I tried to match the sketches with my photographs. I shot some pictures through a filter to get the same purple color Nilo had drawn for the God planet. Then, for the opening scene, I took a picture of a car stirring up dust. I created a forty-foot plume of dust, so Bill could see how his original concept of Sybok entering in a cloud of dust could work. I realized they had some fantastic images already conceived. The closer I could get to fulfilling them in reality, the happier everyone would be.''

As it turned out, my father was thrilled. ''There was one magical moment when Tim came back from his scouting trip and came into a meeting with the Ridgecrest photos. He brought them in with a flourish and set them down beside the eight-by-ten sketch of the God planet that Nilo had made. Everyone gasped. The two images, the photo and the sketch, matched almost exactly.''

The next step was for the rest of the team to make a scouting trip to the site. Upon seeing it, everyone agreed that they had found the right place. ''Ridgecrest was perfect,'' my father said, ''it had Owens Dry Lake bed, which was a dry, vast expanse perfect for the Paradise City location. It had Trona Peaks, these strangely majestical, twisted formations that would work perfectly for the God planet, and it had Cuddy Back, which had the arid feel I wanted for Sybok's opening shot. We were very lucky to get three locations for the price of one, which was a key consideration when taking into account travel time and costs. But my biggest thrill happened when I saw Trona Peaks, which has one immensely tall, twisted pinnacle. The sun was coming up right behind it, giving off rays of sunlight which made the peak look mysterious and majestical. It was nine AM, and I looked at my watch and thought to myself, 'I'm coming back here and shooting the same shot at nine AM when filming starts.' It was one of the most thrilling moments of the entire production, seeing that shot. I laughed aloud with joy.''

But that was not all the laughing they did on that scouting trip. ''One of the biggest laughs I've had in recent years occurred out in Owen's Dry Lake bed, which we were scouting as a possible location for Paradise City,'' my father said. ''It was unbearably hot, with dry, desert winds blowing and undulating heat waves obstructing our vision. The ground was so dry it was cracked everywhere, like in those pictures you see of drought-ridden land. So there's a group of us out there in the middle of nowhere, standing on this dry, cracked land, when suddenly we notice that one small chunk of dirt has been kicked up out of the ground. David Loughery goes over to this chunk of dirt, picks it up, and packs it back down into the ground, saying 'At last, I finished the puzzle!' We all became totally unglued, since this was the most perfect, most hilarious description of what the land looked like.

"But that wasn't the only funny thing that happened. One morning we were all going to eat breakfast at a restaurant. We're walking inside, when suddenly this big, burly guy dressed in overalls appears out of nowhere and asks me for my autograph. I say, 'Do you have a piece of paper?' and he hands me his business card. I was so surprised that he had a card that I looked down at it. On it was his name, and underneath his name was printed the word 'Sawyer.' I said, 'Sawyer! What's that?' I had never heard of this word before. And he said, 'I play the saw for a living.' And I said, 'C'mon!' but he said, 'No, it's true. I play in a saw band.' I was so intrigued by this I said, 'I'll only give you an autograph if you play your saw for us.' Well, it turned out he had his saw with him, in the back of his truck. So while he got his saw, we went inside and sat down. And he came in, and serenaded us with the song 'Memories' on his saw while we ate. We were trying to be inconspicuous, because we didn't want everyone in Ridgecrest to know *Star Trek* was coming there to film a movie. But the next thing we know, the entire restaurant is staring at us. Here is this guy in overalls, playing 'Memories' on the saw, at eight AM in Ridgecrest. The most hilarious thing of all was, at a later point, Harve, David, and I were discussing the kind of music that should be playing during Uhura's dance on the sand dune. Harve was so enthused with the sawyer, we seriously considered using it. So we almost had a saw playing in the background of that scene!"

Once this interesting and eventful location scout had persuaded them to settle on Ridgecrest, Herman could progress with the design and building of Paradise. "The design of the city escaped me for a long time," he said. "I had many other things to do and I left it to almost the last thing. I didn't have an idea in my head as to what it was going to look like, but I have several resource books, *Architecture Without Architects* is one. It's an example of cities all over the world and their houses or structures that were made without plans . . . I came across a picture of a desert fortress in Morocco that was basically on a wheel. Everything radiated out from the center. Our town in the desert had to radiate out from the saloon to the main gate and it just seemed very appropriate. So I showed a photo blow-up of that city to Bill and he liked it . . . in about three days we designed the whole thing and it was pretty much built the way it was drawn.''

The building of the city involved tremendous man power and construction costs. The original budget for the city was $500,000 and took five weeks to build which, according to Herman, ''was something of a minor miracle.'' The actual construction went smoothly, except for the intense heat which, for the first week, was over 100 degrees. During various phases of construction, Herman would bring photographs of the city's evolution to my father, who would inevitably become excited at the progress Herman was making. ''One of the most intense, mind-boggling experiences I'm having on this film is continually watching my dreams become reality,'' he said to me one day after viewing some of these polaroids. ''I've thought about how Paradise City would look so many times in my imagination. So every time I see these pictures it's an even greater thrill than the last. I have to continually remind myself that this is not a dream anymore.''

As Paradise City and the other sets neared completion, my father's attention turned to other details. While Herman had been busy building sets, and Nilo had been busy storyboarding and designing costumes, the prop department had been busy constructing the various props needed to make an outer space adventure complete. The department, headed by Greg Jein, would take sketches that Nilo drew and from them, make prototypes of foam rubber or other material. Greg would then run these prototypes by my father to make sure he was on the right track. ''As with every department on this film, I was struck by the imagination and efficiency that Greg and the rest of the prop crew demonstrated," he said. "I almost always okayed their samples since they were usually dead on." His pleasure with the props became evident one day when Greg brought a box full of samples to get his approval. My father then spent the next hour sifting through the box, firing phasers at people or fiddling with the light switches on Scotty's engineering tools. He looked like a kid gone crazy at Christmastime. When I asked what a strange, waffle-like prop was supposed to be for, he put it on top of his head and said, "Beats me. I think it's something McCoy would use." His comment sent everyone in the room into gales of laughter.

Even though there were many amusing moments during this period, an undertone of seriousness lay behind almost every discussion. The starting date for the film was quickly approaching, and the final push to get everything finished was on. As the sets neared completion, my father would walk around on each stage with Nilo, discussing each shot in minute detail, often redrafting the storyboards to comply with his new ideas. At this point, he also began detailed discussions with the film's cinematographer, Andy Lazlo.

"I wanted a bold, colorful look for *Star Trek V*," my father said. "I have read this book, *Painting with Light*, which had given me a lot of ideas. Then I started looking at films in order to find a cinematographer. One film, *Streets of Fire*, really impressed me. It had a lot of interesting lighting effects that I felt could be utilized for *Star Trek V* . . . I had always been a little concerned about picking the right man, since I had heard some horror stories about cinematographers and directors fighting over the look of a film. I knew I didn't want that to happen, because I had some very definite ideas of what I wanted. But when Andy walked in, the first thing he said was 'It is my job to make the picture fit your vision.' He had also read *Painting with Light* and we talked about that. Based on my conversation with him and *Streets of Fire*, I asked Andy if he would do the picture."

Known in recent years for his work on such films as *Innerspace, Remo Williams, First Blood*, and *Poltergeist Two*, as well as *Streets of Fire*, Andy spent many hours discussing lighting effects with my father. They would go through the script and pinpoint potential problem areas, considering issues such as whether the God planet should be shot with a blue tone or a magenta, what the colors of Nimbus Three should be, whether the lighting on the bridge should be bright and homey, or dark and moody, like a battleship.

"The preliminary discussions with Andy were crucial," my father said. "I knew he was aware of my thinking about colorful, dramatic lighting, but we needed to thrash out all the details and make certain we were communicating on the same plane."

In the midst of resolving these major artistic issues in his discussions with Andy, a host of technical problems soon cropped up to confront him. Most of them concerned the filming of the God planet sequence.

When they had first presented their ideas about the sequence to Bran, he informed them it could be done in one of two ways. Either he could create the effect optically, which would require him to "paint" the images on the film, or they could film the effect live, which was less expensive but involved more unknown elements. Since money is always an object when creating a film, they chose the latter.

This choice suited their budgetary constraints, but created a host of new considerations for my father. "Having acted all my life, I had never been confronted by such technical details before," he said. "Filming the God sequence live was exciting, but meant that I was going to have to deal with an unknown situation. For example, filming Sybok, Spock, Kirk, and McCoy next to the column of light involved several elements. We would have to prefilm George Murdock, who was playing God, and then Bran would insert this image into the column of light. Once on the stage, that image of George in the column would then be projected onto a piece of equipment known as a beam splitter, which is resting next to the camera. This beam splitter would act as a mirror to reflect the image from Bran's projector onto the stage. The process works great, but presented a couple of problems. One, the actors are saying their lines to something they can't see. Two, the process only works for shots of the actors standing next to the image. If you want to get an over-the-shoulder shot of God, or an over-the-shoulder shot of the actors, you have to use different processes known as rear or front screen projection. That means, for example, that if you want a shot of all the actors looking at God, and you want the shot to be over their shoulders onto God, you have to literally project the image of God onto a large screen on the stage. Only then can you film the actors looking at this image.''

Using the beam splitting process meant preplanning the God sequence in minute detail, down to every move the actors made since the projected image would have to match these movements. In addition, the shots involving the rear and front screen projection process also had to be carefully planned, right down to the eye level at which George Murdock was looking, since his film would be shot months ahead of the actual God planet sequence. All this was very complicated, and caused my father some anxiety. ''I had planned out each shot very carefully, but there was still the element of the unknown involved. Would I match all the movements correctly? Would the performances of the actors and the images correspond convincingly? These questions would pop up in my mind throughout the day, making me wonder if I had made all the right decisions. As much as I was looking forward to the actual filming, I felt a sense of anxiety about it as well.''

To make matters worse, there were other unsolved problems which needed to be addressed. The opening shot of the movie, where Sybok rides towards the camera in a cloud of smoke, seemed easy enough to film, but was actually presenting some problems. In order to achieve the dust cloud look, the special effects team, headed by Mike Woods, had been running some tests of a rider with a canister of smoke attached to his back. The idea was for the canister to emit the smoke as the rider approached camera, thereby creating the dust cloud effect. However, the canister would only emit a steady stream of smoke behind the horse, and no dust cloud was ever created. In addition, they had also wired Sybok's cape so that it would stand away from his body while he was riding towards camera.

But when my father saw the cape, it looked bulky and unrealistic.

They also had to worry about how to create and maintain a steady haze of smoke during the Nimbus Three location scenes. My father was afraid that any method they used—burning tires was one that was suggested—would not prevent the dust from dissipating into the air if any wind started blowing. Another problem was the "horse" Sybok was riding. No one knew what color a Nimbosian horse (the former unicorn) was supposed to be, or at what height his horn should rest on his forehead. They went through several tests, first painting the horses gold and placing the horn high up between their foreheads. After seeing the tests on film, it became apparent the gold color didn't register well. The horses also balked at seeing the shadow of something strange between their eyes.

But that wasn't all. One of the Yosemite shots presented problems as well. My father had originally envisioned Spock catching Kirk by the foot and then carrying him, still hanging upside down, over part of Yosemite Valley and finally to the campsite where McCoy was waiting. In order to achieve even a semblance of this effect, it would be necessary to wire both Leonard Nimoy and my father into harnesses which would then support their weight, making it appear as though they were flying. Some tests were then run to see if the wires would show on screen or not. My father then watched many tests of poor, unwitting young men being hung upside down in wired harnesses, only to find that in every test the wiring was glaringly apparent. There was also the concern that even if they could hide the wires, the set required to film such a sequence would create too much environmental damage.

Although these were all pressing problems, they paled in comparison to the black cloud fast approaching the unsuspecting team. The studio had estimated the film's cost at approximately $30 million. The executives had given the assignment of keeping the film on budget to Ralph Winter, associate producer of *Star Trek III*, executive producer of *IV*, and executive producer on *V*, and to Ralph's co-producer, Mel

Efros. They were certainly up to the task. Ralph started his career making industrial videos, and soon familiarized himself with all the inner workings of the film industry. By the time he reached associate producer status on *Star Trek III,* he knew the breakdown of all costs associated with a motion picture. Together with Mel, who also had extensive experience with production costs, they were able to make a realistic budget projection for *Star Trek V,* which they estimated at slightly over thirty million dollars.

What the studio hadn't counted on, however, was my father's grand vision, or as Harve was fond of saying, "his appetite." With the visual effects, stunts, and complex optical shots he had envisioned, the budget grew to enormous proportions. The problem became clear when they received Bran's bid for all the visual effects.

"We had put in a number for the visual effects," Ralph said, "$4 million, which was a little more than *Star Trek IV,* but it was basically trying to hold the line and still enticing Bran to do it. But the first pass, with all the things Bill wanted, was $5, $6 million. So it was like fifty percent greater than it needed to be. So now we're at $31 million. Then the figures started to come in from Bran, which were a little surprising, on the high side, as well. Now we can't very well go in and tell them it was really more like $33 million. We would have been shot. We were already on death row once we were over the thirty number."

The concern over the high figures resulted in some emergency measures. A meeting was called for all key personnel, the objective being to cut excess fat from the budget wherever possible. The first casualties were the optical effects.

"I sat in the room with Harve, Ralph, Mel, Bran, Nilo, David, and Herman, and watched the total decimation of some of the ideas I had been dreaming of for months," my father said. "The first to go were the most expensive. 'The Powers of Ten,' and 'The Bierstadt Shot' were among the first, since they each cost something like $350,000. Next was a shot I had envisioned for Kirk's opening climb. I wanted to see him climbing El Capitan and then pull farther and farther back until he becomes a dot. That was another $350,000 gone. And the last shot of the movie, where Kirk, McCoy, and Spock are singing around the campfire, also changed dramatically. Originally, I had wanted to pull back farther and farther away from the campfire until you could barely see them, then tilt the camera up through a Bierstadt-like setting to the stars beyond. I was told that a shot like that, without any dissolves to break up the pull back, would be impossible to film within reasonable budgetary constraints. So that, too, was thrown out the window.''

But the massacre was by no means finished. The next to go were any production costs that seemed like padding including any unnecessary location time, personnel, or effects. ''In order to meet the cut-off point, we finally had to eliminate a day out of the location budget,'' my father said. ''This meant I wouldn't be able to complete all the shots I wanted out on location. I was very, very disappointed by this because I really wanted to give the movie that look of reality that can best be achieved on location. Also gone were some of the 'A' make-ups for the aliens, since they required not only an actor, but several more artists as well, all of whom had to be housed, fed, and paid for the days on location. And, something that really hurt, we had to cut down on the number of extras for the Paradise City battle scenes. I had dreamed for so long of shots where hordes of soldiers pour into the City, that it was very hard for me to accept this particular cut. I felt like this grand, epic movie I had envisioned had suddenly been reduced to an ordinary film. When I walked out of the meeting, it took me a while to realize that the movie in my head would not be the movie on the screen. It was my first big lesson as a director.''

As Nilo put it, my father was ''shredded'' after that day ended. But he had no time to dwell on his misfortunes. The starting date for the film was only a few weeks away, and it was now time to film the insert shots that would later be incorporated into the movie. These shots included the scenes with George Murdock and the evil Sybok sequences. In addition, they also had to prepare the segment where Kirk's superior officer commands him to go to Nimbus Three, as well as the commercial which would be playing on the screen when Caithlin first makes her entrance into the Nimbus Three barroom. These minor, although crucial segments, composed the first day of filming on *Star Trek V*.

My father approached the task with a sense of excitement. "I dream in films—I've always wanted to make a film. I've thought of the episodic television that I've done as short stories in a progression towards a novel. The absolute miracle of being able to direct a large motion picture is now a reality. People are asking me 'What do we do now? Where do we go?' . . . All the years of listening to people who knew what they were doing, and people who didn't know what they were doing, are coming out of my pores. I know things I didn't realize I knew. My enthusiasm, without my knowing it, seems to—at least that's what I'm told—be communicated to the people around me. The whole thing becomes a joyful experience instead of a humdrum one. There is tremendous excitement in getting a good shot to which everyone has contributed."

The efforts of this contribution were obvious from the very first shot of the Nimbosian salesman pitching seemingly lush, irrigated lots to an unsuspecting public. Associate producer Brooke Breton had arranged all details: the costume, a strange green plaid; the fish, protruding eyeballs and green fins; the background landscape, lush and beautiful. Everything went smoothly, the crew breaking into applause when my father yelled, "cut!" They then spent a short time filming the Klingon commander's message, and the passport photos of the hostages, film which would be shown to Kirk on the view screen before he arrives on Nimbus Three.

Unfortunately, the second half of the day did not run as smoothly. Next on the agenda was the filming of the Federation Commander ordering Kirk on the hostage mission. Casting the role of the Commander had not been necessary. Who was a more appropriate choice than the leader of the past three missions, Harve Bennett?

He laughed when I asked him if he had been nervous that

day. "I was simply trying to be faithful to the material," he answered, "which is to say, I had the difficult job of being superior to Bill Shatner, to the homeric hero. No easy task! The way to do that was to be stern, authoritative, and listen to my director." Harve's reading went smoothly, but the newly-assembled crew was faced with some annoying technical problems. The graphic display playing next to Harve was being projected by a beam splitter. This meant that the film for the graphics had to match the length of time required for Harve's speech. Unfortunately, the graphics film would continually run short of the written material, so Harve and the rest of the crew were subject to several frustrating delays.

"I was telling myself, 'My God, my director feels no one around him knows what he's doing,' " Harve said. "The irony was, on the day of the shakedown crew, the producer was the actor. I was just patient, though, and had a good time."

But the experience had shaken my father. "It was the first day, and already we were having problems," he said. "It made me wonder what I was in for once the real filming began."

To make matters worse, filming George Murdock and Larry Luckinbill's sequences didn't prove any easier. Those shots required precise measurements of movement and tremendous discomfort for the actors. "We had to film each of their speeches several times, each one at a different exposure since we wanted to gradually white out the faces inside the column," my father said. "This was very difficult for them, since they had to maintain a consistent performance level in each take. Also, we needed to move the camera progressively closer to George's eyes, because we needed to add a shooting flame optical at a later date. So poor George had these hot, white lights shining in his eyes. We also weren't entirely sure where his eye level was supposed to be, since we hadn't filmed the rest of the sequence yet. It was technically a very complex set of events."

Because of the excitement and tension the day generated, my father had forgotten one seemingly minor detail. When filming Larry as the evil Sybok, he had forgotten to tell him to look camera right instead of camera left. It was an important omission, because on camera, right and left are opposite of what they are on screen. This meant that Larry was looking the wrong way.

When this fact was pointed out to my father, he couldn't believe he had made such an elementary mistake. "My first day, and already I've made my first mistake!" he lamented. "I can't believe I did that. Camera right and camera left are one of the first things you learn about in film, and after all these years, I forgot it." He had to smile at his error, especially when it was decided that no one would really notice the mistake and there was no need to reshoot the entire sequence.

But the incident left him wondering. Would he make another, perhaps more crucial, mistake in the days to come? And how would he be able to accomplish all the shots he had envisioned for location, considering the shortened shooting schedule and the cuts in make-up and extras? As wonderful and exciting a prospect that shooting the movie presented, it was also a cause for much anxiety and tension.

"I want so much for this movie to be a success," he told me the day before we left for location. "I want it all to turn out the way I see it in my head. But location presents many unknowns: the weather, transportation, equipment breakdowns. Anything could happen. I just hope we can accomplish what we've set out to do."

As we left for Yosemite, everyone fervently wished the same.

4

IT'S LOCATION,
NOT VACATION

October 11, 1988.

As my father flew toward the Fresno airport, he was looking forward to the start of principal photography with mixed emotions. Thrilled at the prospect of actually watching his dreams come alive, he was eager to tackle the many creative challenges the upcoming days would bring. But other, less pleasant thoughts filled his head as well.

The weather, always a critical factor on location, was an even larger concern during this time of year, when only a few days might separate mellow fall and harsh winter. His worst nightmare already seemed to be coming true as ominous, black rain clouds filled the horizon when the team landed at the airport. The threatening implications of these clouds silenced everyone; no one spoke during the entire ride to Yosemite.

I asked my father how he felt about the possibility of foul weather conditions interfering with production. "I keep trying to release myself by telling myself certain elements are beyond my control," he said as he stared at the sky with a furrowed brow. "But that left me as soon as I saw the rain clouds. I thought, 'this is the only chance we have to get this.' At that moment I realized how much my preparation was subject to the whims of nature and the unpredictability of human personalities."

That kind of unpredictability had already proven itself a

102

force with which to be reckoned. Just a few short weeks before production was to begin, the Teamsters Union, ordinarily responsible for driving the trucks and overseeing their care, had decided to strike. This had forced Mel Efros and his production coordinator, Val Mickaelian, to do some quick rearranging. The film's transportation had been organized several weeks earlier by Paramount's transportation department. When the strike occurred, the transportation department then gave the production team a nonunion transportation coordinator. This coordinator was supposed to bring on nonunion drivers to replace the Teamsters and oversee the equipment on location.

The problem was, every experienced nonunion driver had been snatched up by the studios as soon as the strike began. This meant that new drivers, most of them totally unfamiliar with entertainment industry procedures, would be handling the many trucks needed for such a large location crew. The problem was unavoidable, and caused some concern among the *Star Trek V* production personnel.

To complicate matters further, there was the constant, lurking threat of the Teamsters' reprisals in the air. Allegedly responsible for violent retributions of anyone crossing their picket lines, the Teamsters' actions were another unknown element in the sea of unpredictability. Union reprisals were of such a great concern on *Star Trek V* that the nonunion drivers crept out of the Paramount lot in the dead of night to escape detection. Even so, the drivers were followed onto the highway by masked men, waving their fists and shouting threats. Mel was so convinced the Teamsters were planning some kind of sabotage on the way up to Yosemite that he arranged for a police escort to travel alongside the convoy.

Despite all those precautions, however, one incident did occur. Someone blew up one of the camera trucks while it was still on the Paramount lot. No one was hurt, but it didn't help to alleviate anyone's worries that similar incidents might occur on location.

The possibility of weather or transportation problems seemed very real to my father as he and the crew wound their way closer to Yosemite's front gates. But in spite of the many concerns, he had a strange feeling that all was well. "Even though there were some very real possible problems staring me right in the face, I knew that it would all turn out right. I just had a very strong feeling that we were going to get everything we needed without any major mishaps," he said. Apparently, somebody upstairs agreed with him.

As the vans wound around the final bend of the road, the dark, moody clouds dissipated, revealing shafts of bright sunlight that illuminated the browns, golds, and reds of the trees. At the park gates, El Capitan, a proud sentinel guarding the entrance to the park with its stern, granite walls, stood to greet us. The crew watched in awe as we passed underneath this most famous of Yosemite landmarks. It seemed that *Star Trek V* might be blessed with good luck after all.

The mood grew even more light-hearted with the news that all trucks had reached the valley unscathed. With so much good fortune, it seemed a celebration was in order. Once everyone was settled, Harve and Ralph organized a small gathering to celebrate the beginning of the movie. In a suite overlooking the beautiful Ahwanee Hotel grounds, the cast and crew toasted the new *Star Trek* adventure. Almost everyone was there: Leonard Nimoy, who was scheduled to film his scenes on El Capitan the next morning; George Takei and Walter Koenig, who would film their walk through "Mount Rushmore" at Glacier Point in Yosemite Valley; and, of course, the team which would make it all happen. Herman, Nilo, Ralph, Mel, Brooke, Val, Harve, my father, and others lifted their champagne glasses and toasted the film's success.

The first day of actual filming dawned clear, bright, and cold. As my father opened his door to leave, he noticed someone had written a note and left it for him outside his door. He picked it up and read it. The note was from Leonard, wishing him luck and success with his vision. Deeply touched, he left his room to join the others, feeling as though the day had already gotten off to a good start. His euphoric mood grew even stronger when he arrived at the location site, an outcropping off a mountain road overlooking the entire valley floor.

As he surveyed the majestic surroundings, the morning sunlight reflecting clouds of steam from his breath, he turned to the task ahead. The objective for the day was to film Kirk's climbing sequences up El Capitan, including Spock's sudden appearance in the shot, courtesy of his flying jet boots. But before he could get started, a visit to the make-up trailer was in order. As he had done on the original "Star Trek" television series and four other films, he climbed into the trailer and sat in the make-up chair, where he would be transformed into Captain Kirk.

Except for the special effects make-up, most of the make-up jobs on the movie were done by Wes Dawn and his nephew, Jeff, who both came from a dynasty of make-up artists. Their association with *Star Trek* extends back to Jeff's father, Robert, who had actually done the make-up work on "Where No Man Has Gone Before," the pilot that brought my father to "Star Trek." Since both were so familiar with the process, the application of the make-up was actually fairly painless. Wes concentrated on his straight "beauty make-up," which probably took no more than fifteen minutes to apply. Jeff's duties centered more around the appliance make-ups, the primary example of which was Leonard and his Vulcan look.

Leonard was already sitting cooperatively in his chair when my father arrived. First, Jeff had glued latex ear tips over Leonard's ears, which he then covered with make-up to match the rest of Leonard's base. In order to make his eyebrows appear to arch upwards, Leonard had shaved off half of his eyebrows, which were then replaced with fake Vulcan eyebrow ends that pointed up instead of down. While this process was going on, he and my father joked and laughed themselves silly.

I was reminded of the many times I'd watched my father in his make-up chair during the original series. He would often laugh hysterically at a joke that Leonard or some other cast member would make. Although it was many years later, some parts of "Star Trek" still seemed exactly the same.

Next, both actors moved farther down the trailer, where hair experts Donna Barrett Gilbert and Hazel Catmull waited expectantly with their combs, pins, and sprays. For my father, this next step meant sitting patiently while Donna combed and sprayed his hair into place. Combined with his make-up job, the total amount of time he had to spend in the trailer was about thirty minutes.

Leonard's make-up and hair would take at least an hour and a half to complete, so my father left his old friend in the competent hands of Wes, Jeff, Donna, and Hazel and stepped outside. The time had come for him to inspect the set and begin his first day as director of *Star Trek V*.

He approached the area where the first shot, Captain Kirk climbing up El Capitan, would take place. Although the sequence was short, without much dialogue, it had taken weeks of planning and coordination with several groups of people in order to prepare for it properly.

The filming of this shot had actually begun some weeks before, when a small crew, known as "second unit," was dispatched to Yosemite to begin filming Kirk's climbing sequence using a double in place of my father. The second unit team was headed by Bob Carmichael, who led a brave and energetic crew up steep mountainsides as they filmed various climbing manuevers. They also filmed many beautiful shots of the valley which would be used in the opening sequence of the film.

The second unit's job was made especially difficult because of environmental concerns surrounding the use of national parkland. One of the Yosemite forest rangers later explained the concerns to me: "The main [condition for the film permit] was that the impact of the filming operation on the routine use of the park by park visitors was minimized," he said. "And everything must occur safely . . . We try to tell people if they are doing something wrong which violates the Code of Federal Regulations, the body of law set up to protect the natural features of the park." The second unit was in fact cautioned at one point for disturbing some branches, which then sent shock waves of concern down to the team in Los Angeles. It was only a minor incident, but it pointed out the delicacy with which the entire production had to proceed.

Once the first unit arrived at Yosemite, it was their task to match the action to what Bob Carmichael and his crew had already filmed. Of course, prior to filming, the team had realized it would be much too dangerous to actually suspend my father and Leonard from the real El Capitan in order to match the second unit shots. The problem was cleverly solved by erecting a fake mountain on the location site.

Prior to filming, this "mountain" was constructed on the Paramount lot, where an entire warehouse is devoted to creating reproductions of various wall types. Fiberglass was poured into the desired mold (they have every mold imaginable, including brick, cement, and stucco) and then painted to match the actual El Capitan wall. This fake wall was painted by Jimmy Betts, who was able to match the colors of the actual mountain almost exactly. The finished wall also came complete with hand holds, hidden in a crack that matched the actual crack on the face of El Capitan. My father would use these hand holds to maintain his balance while reciting his dialogue.

Constructing the fake wall had not been the only preparation necessary for the sequence. Even though my father would only be climbing a few feet up the fake wall, he wanted his ascent to look realistic. This meant he needed to familiarize himself with the techniques and vocabulary associated with mountain climbing. In the weeks before principal photography began, he received a series of lessons on the subject from an experienced mountain climber. In between meetings at Paramount, my father would climb on a wooden replica of the simulated El Capitan wall erected on the studio lot, his teacher giving instructions as he went farther and farther up the wall.

As I watched these lessons proceed, I was comforted by the fact that he was safely harnessed by ropes. I was thankful not to be present at another lesson in which my father climbed over 100 feet, without any harness, up a real mountain about an hour's drive outside Los Angeles.

I asked him why he needed to climb a real mountain when he had a fake one in his own backyard. "I just kept going. I had two instructors who were real gung-ho, and they kept encouraging me, telling me that climbing a mountain was like skiing—if you get scared, you lose the edge. After I had climbed almost 100 feet, I looked down. Now I'm real scared of heights and I thought, 'I don't have to do this. What am I doing?' But like it says in the movie: I climbed it because it was there.''

After that experience, climbing the fake wall at Yosemite seemed like child's play. The first few takes of him ascending the wall went fairly smoothly, although there was always the concern they would take too long and lose the sunlight before they had finished filming the scheduled footage for the day.

"As director, I knew I had to keep a pace going, especially considering time had already been cut out of the location schedule and every moment that went by was precious. But as an actor, I knew I had to make my lines count, and look like I meant what I said. The two roles would occasionally conflict, when I would realize I was rushing my lines and not giving them enough import. I knew I had to be very careful of this, especially after the sound man, David Ronne, came up to me and said, 'I don't mean to be critical, but you sound like you're rushing.' I realized, of course, he was right. I was rushing, in my effort to move ahead as quickly as possible. I vowed to be more conscious of that after that moment.''

In spite of his desire to press on as quickly as possible, the next scenes involved a complicated special effect which required a certain amount of time to set up correctly. In order to make Spock appear as though he was flying, the physical special effects department, headed by Mike Woods, had to construct a special "flying suit" for Leonard. This suit was actually a fiberglass mold of Leonard's body from the chest to the thighs, which was then fitted with a hollow pipe which was attached to the abdominal portion of the mold. While Leonard wore the suit, this pipe would then be connected to another pipe of corresponding size which would protrude from the fake wall. If shot from behind, it would then appear as though Leonard was floating in space. All of this work, of course, was done weeks before the actual filming began, even though the actual on-screen time was mere seconds. It seemed ironic that to achieve one seemingly simple shot required weeks of advance preparation, not to mention the time on location to get

Leonard into the suit and attached to the wall. He suffered the associated indignities with grace and humor, and actually spent most of the time smiling.

Leonard was equally cooperative in achieving his close-ups, one of which required a technique similar to the other flying shot, only this time he would appear to dive after Kirk as Kirk slips and falls. Instead of being attached by the waist to a pipe protruding from the fake wall, this time Leonard was attached at his waist to a metal bar, which was bent away from his body. This bar was then flipped upside down, which then, of course, flipped Leonard upside down as well. Since the camera was placed at his head level, the viewer could see his jet boots pop into frame as soon as Leonard's head disappeared. The overall effect was one of Leonard diving after my father. Leonard was very accommodating in achieving the shot, even though it required a certain degree of tolerance for the uncomfortable equipment. He didn't blanch once, even while he was hanging upside down.

He was equally cooperative in obtaining the shots where it appears as though he is floating next to Kirk while telling him "to be one with the rock." This shot required a somewhat different technique than the other flying shots. Instead of being attached at the waist to a pipe, this time he was attached (very firmly!) from the knees down to a teeter-totter which was then raised to my father's eye level. Since all Leonard's close-ups were shot from the waist up, it became impossible to see the mechanism which gave him the appearance of floating. Again, he endured his discomfort with good cheer. (Later in the movie, I asked him what the difference was between a Leonard Nimoy *Star Trek* movie and a Bill Shatner *Star Trek* movie. He replied with a laugh, "In a Bill Shatner movie there's a lot more running and jumping.")

In spite of my father and Leonard's cooperative spirit, there were certain limitations to what they could safely accomplish in the flying sequence. Because neither could do a fall without wearing safety equipment, it was then necessary to hire stuntmen for all shots filmed without harnesses or other equipment. In the case of *Star Trek V,* most of the stunts were performed by a few men: Greg Barnett, who doubled Leonard; Donny Pulford, who doubled my father; and Tom Huff, who later doubled DeForest Kelley. They were led by a stunt coordinator, who would also be responsible for obtaining some second unit footage once we reached the Paradise City location in Ridgecrest.

This second unit director/stunt coordinator was Glenn Wilder, who has been in the business for twenty-eight years. It was his responsibility to choreograph the stunts while ensuring maximum safety for all those involved.

Glenn's first task was to coordinate Greg Barnett's dive from the top of the fake wall into an airbag. The stunt was designed to bridge the gap between Leonard's diving close-up and shots of Leonard flying through the air, which would later be filmed on stage using a special process. Greg performed his task easily and with a minimum of difficulty, even though he had to jump several times before he got it right for the cameras. With the completion of Greg's dive, the team was assured they had all footage necessary to assemble Leonard's flying sequence.

Close-up shots of Kirk falling through the air would later be filmed on stage, although the team still needed a realistic wide shot of Kirk falling off El Capitan. In order to get this wide shot, someone would actually have to jump off the real El Capitan. This job was awarded, not to one of the stunt doubles, but to Kenny Bates, a man who specializes in such dangerous falls.

"I wasn't there to see Kenny fall," my father said. "But I heard that he yelled the whole way down. When I saw the footage, I couldn't help but be glad I wasn't the one who did the stunt. He was really incredible. Kenny's fall was the key element in making the sequence look realistic."

The first day of shooting ended successfully. They had gotten all the required shots, including the technically difficult ones of Leonard flying and Greg diving off the fake wall. But the next day proved that a fall off El Capitan (fake or otherwise) was not to be the only dangerous stunt pulled at Yosemite.

IT'S LOCATION, NOT VACATION

In the script, when Spock says, "Captain, I do not think you realize the gravity of your situation," Kirk accidentally loosens some rocks and then watches them fall to the valley floor 3,000 feet below. In order to lend an air of realism to this shot, and to capture the scene in all its grandeur, my father wanted the entire sequence filmed from his point of view. In other words, the camera had to be pointing down at him as he literally hung from a cliff 3,000 feet high. The place he chose for this feat was Glacier Point, a magnificent vantage point from which one could view many of Yosemite's granite peaks thrusting up from the valley floor.

We arrived at the scheduled site just as the sun was rising, watching in awe as the rays of light illuminated the towering pinnacles. However, the location's incredible beauty did not necessarily inspire confidence in my father's idea. Some of the production team felt the shot was unnecessarily dangerous, since the realism it sought to capture could also be achieved using the optical process.

"Sometimes it's just not worth it to do something dangerous because special effects can take care of it," Ralph commented as we watched preparations for the scene progress. "I wanted to do this in a matte shot . . . I don't think I've sweated as much on a movie as I have today." At this point, Ralph motioned towards the cliff. "I mean, look at this. I'd hate to think of how many people would be out of work if he hurt himself."

Despite the objections, my father felt that there was simply no replacement for actually hanging off the cliff. "I know what I want to do is dangerous," he said. "But I also know that if I get what I want, the shot will be spectacular. The audience can always tell if something is fake or not, and a shot of Kirk really hanging off a mountain is irreplaceable. My desire for this shot is overriding my tremendous fear of heights. I just keep reminding myself not to look down!"

In order to obtain the shot without truly jeopardizing his or anyone else's safety, several precautions were taken. The grips, who were responsible for building most of the necessary camera rigging, constructed a platform upon which a camera and crane would rest. This camera was remote-controlled so that no cameramen would actually have to bend over the cliff to get the shot. My father was roped into the mountain with a cable which could support eight tons of weight. Glenn and the other stuntmen stood close by, as did a mountain climber, Dale Bard, who was asked to help choreograph all of my father's climbs.

Dale, a young, energetic man, has made countless climbs up El Capitan and other Yosemite landmarks. He has even spent many a night sleeping on small platforms nailed into the mountains, high above the valley floor. He jumped around the cliff area, nimble as a monkey, so accustomed to the heights that he appeared oblivious to any danger. He and the others made sure that my father was roped in safely so that no accidents could occur. Even so, I was tremendously fearful as I watched the scene progress. I was not comforted by the fact that the area was known to experience earthquakes fairly frequently. All we needed was one strong rumble and anyone on the platform or near the cliff edge would go tumbling.

My fears didn't dissipate quickly, especially when the action had to be repeated several times in order to assure the shot would come out correctly. Andy was concerned that the shadows from the clouds were making it difficult to see the valley floor, a problem of great significance since it would then be difficult to perceive the depth of the shot on film. In addition, in order to make sure no one on the valley floor would be hurt by falling rocks, they had to use foam pebbles tied together so they wouldn't tumble down the cliff.

My father was concerned that these fake pebbles didn't move realistically. However, in spite of all the concerns, the shot proceeded smoothly. Everyone, especially my father, breathed a sigh of relief when it was over. "I think we got something very exciting," he told me afterwards. "The entire episode—the danger, the cost, the fear—will have been worth it if this works out the way I think it will."

But his excitement didn't last. That night at the Ahwanee, we screened the day's work. These first "dailies," as they're called, were of Kirk climbing the fake wall and Spock flying into frame. My father watched the film expectantly, but was dismayed to find certain glaring mistakes. The fake wall looked shiny, and one could see a tree standing on the right side of frame, thus destroying the illusion that Kirk is thousands of feet above the ground.

He was crushed by this discovery. "That night I learned about the enormous detail involved in making a film," he commented afterwards. "Everyone was around to help me, but there was no substitute for my eye. It wasn't perfection and I'm aiming for perfection. At the same time, I know it can be fixed later, probably by blowing the picture up just enough to get rid of the tree. All the same, it made me realize that no one was directing this film but me, and that I had the ultimate responsibility to make sure everything looked right."

He was equally disappointed with the following set of dailies. Instead of seeing the valley floor 3,000 feet below, all that was really visible was an unclear picture of some granite walls. Since no birds were flying by the walls, and the crew had been prevented from allowing some real pebbles to tumble down the cliff, there was no reference point with which to judge the distance. The shadows on the valley floor contributed to the problem so that it became impossible to differentiate between shapes or gauge the distance to the valley floor below.

We watched the film in silence, fully aware that these problems meant the entire sequence of film was unusable. Not only had my father spent a valuable day trying to achieve the shot, but he had literally risked his life for something he would never incorporate into the film. He was bitterly disappointed by this terrible discovery, again realizing that in spite of his detailed preparation, certain elements would always remain beyond his control.

"We had no way of coercing the clouds into cooperation," he said. "And we couldn't force any birds to fly by the camera. All we could do was our best under the circumstances. Unfortunately, it just didn't work."

This failure was mitigated by the fact that Bob Carmichael had taken plenty of usable shots when he had filmed the climbing sequence. "We knew we always had the safety net of the second unit's work," he commented. "So it wasn't a complete disaster. But what it did do was point out once again that I have the ultimate responsibility for achieving the day's work. So what the incident did was make me more anxious to achieve the scheduled work on time, on budget, and without any mistakes. I took this responsibility very seriously, knowing how much money, time, and effort was at stake."

This sense of responsibility carried into the remainder of the Yosemite filming, where each shot was carried out in an efficient and economical manner. Indeed, the rest of the Yosemite schedule seemed easy in comparison. One of the remaining scenes involved Sulu and Chekov, who had to tramp through the underbrush until they were rescued by Uhura. The scene was relatively simple, and only took a small portion of the day to film. They also quickly disposed of another shot where Sulu and Chekov walk through the woods saying, "if you've seen one national park, you've seen them all," and the camera pans up to reveal Mount Rushmore, complete with a new black female president sculpted next to the other presidents. This shot was also easy to film, since the Mount Rushmore background would be added into the shot later by using a process known as "matte painting."

The final shots filmed at Yosemite involved Dr. McCoy as he watches Kirk climbing up El Capitan from their campfire site. Although DeForest, or "De" as he was affectionately called, still felt slightly weak from his illness, he appeared ready and willing to perform his scenes. They quickly disposed of these shots, since the next major logistical problem was fast approaching: the opening sequence between Sybok and J'onn was scheduled to be filmed at sunset that day, at the Cuddy Back location in Ridgecrest.

Achieving this sunset shot meant the entire crew would have to travel from Yosemite all the way to the Mojave desert in half a day. Most of the personnel could travel by plane, thus cutting travel time down significantly. However, the larger, bulkier equipment such as wardrobe and cameras could only be transported by truck. Some of these trucks actually left in the dead of night in order to make it in time to the Cuddy Back location. The entire move had been smoothly orchestrated by the production and transportation departments, and everything was timed to arrive just as it would be needed. So even while my father quickly wrapped up the remaining shots and was then whisked off to the airport, he was excitedly anticipating the next phase of the adventure—Ridgecrest, where all the Nimbus Three exterior shots would be achieved. What he didn't count on, however, was another lesson in the unpredictability of movie making.

He arrived in Ridgecrest late that afternoon, and immediately drove to the Cuddy Back location site to await the arrival of the camera equipment and wardrobe. The scheduled shots involved Sybok's ride towards J'onn, and the subsequent mind meld sequence between Sybok and J'onn. My father wanted to film both shots against the setting sun, with dust clouds obscuring the light so that Nimbus Three would look desolate yet eerie. The Cuddy Back location, a vast, arid landscape where the earth was cracked with dryness, was the perfect site to shoot these two scenes. He and the crew, including such key personnel as Nilo, Andy, and Dodie, eagerly awaited the cameras, and their opportunity to realize the vision they had planned so long ago.

They waited and waited, but no trucks appeared on the horizon. The only one able to begin working was Mike Woods, who was responsible for creating the dust cloud effect. He had abandoned any idea of burning tires or any similar substance to create the dust clouds, and was now relying on several vans to drive about the location and kick up the dust. While he was coordinating his drivers, my father and the others continued to sit around and wonder where the equipment trucks were, continually eyeing the setting sun with a sense of anxiety.

Finally, two hours later, the camera truck arrived. When asked where he had been, the driver informed us that he had been driving all night to get to Ridgecrest on time. When he had finally arrived, no one was around to tell him where to go, so he went to the hotel and fell asleep. When he was finally told where the location site was, it was already late afternoon.

But even with the arrival of the camera truck they couldn't

begin work. For one thing, the stuntman scheduled to double Sybok in the opening riding sequence was nowhere to be found. To make matters worse, no one knew where the wardrobe truck was, or the truck carrying the tree which was supposed to appear next to J'onn in the mind meld sequence. It seemed as though every truck carrying key equipment was scattered between Ridgecrest and Yosemite.

While the situation carried its own peculiar brand of humor, the underlying consequences were not amusing. The sun was quickly setting, and my father's only opportunity to achieve the opening sequence was fading as rapidly as the light.

The situation forced my father to make some emergency decisions. He told Nilo to go into the nearby "woods," which were all the way up in the surrounding mountains, in order to find a suitable substitute tree. Nilo persuaded a ranger, whose job had formerly been only to ensure the preservation of Cuddy Back's federally protected land, to accompany him. When they got to the woods, the ranger discovered he only had a hatchet, unsuitable for cutting the size branches needed for the tree. Nilo then had to send the ranger back for a saw. As he saw the ranger disappearing, leaving him all alone in the desert, Nilo asked, "What if I see a rattlesnake?" The ranger turned around and said, "Make a lot of noise." While he waited for the ranger's return, Nilo found himself humming Philippino folk songs out loud to the sky, desert rodents, and any rattlesnakes that happened to pass by.

When Nilo and the ranger finally returned, my father looked at the branches and requested they be painted white. But when he saw the results, they were so obviously different from the original tree that he decided to wait and do the mind meld scene the next day with the real tree. In the meantime, the search for the tree continued.

Finally, it was discovered the tree had been mistakenly delivered to the Paradise City location at Owens Dry Lake Bed. But discovering its whereabouts didn't get them any closer to the start of filming. The sun was still setting, and no stuntman or wardrobe had yet appeared to complete the riding shot. My father grew desperate, and decided to improvise.

Being an accomplished horseman himself, he decided he would ride the horse towards the camera. He instructed Dodie to find a piece of burlap which would pass as a cape and throw it over his shoulders. Since no buttons were available, they took a piece of rawhide and tied it around his throat to keep the material in place. All Nimbosians were supposed to wear gas masks to protect themselves from the harsh winds and dust, but unfortunately all prop gas masks were on board the wardrobe truck as well. They then had to resort to painting a standard surgical mask, which all the crew members were using as protection against the dust and wind, a dull black color. They quickly threw all this apparatus together, and he was ready to do the shot. As Harve put it, "I used to do this in college when I was seventeen. The director had to double as a stuntman in a burlap costume."

Just as they were ready to go, however, the stuntman and wardrobe appeared. It turned out that the stuntman had been in Ridgecrest all along, standing around at the hotel for two hours. Apparently some kind of miscommunication prevented them from being driven out to the location site. And the wardrobe truck, it turned out, had met with disaster—a complete engine breakdown. Joe Markham, who later drove out to the site along with other wardrobe personnel, told me what happened.

"The trailer carrying the wardrobe had broken down, with all the clothes for the first shot. Just as we, who came out later, reached the stalled vehicle, the van that was coming from the set to the wardrobe trailer arrived at the same time. We grabbed the clothes for the first shot and took the van back to the set." They arrived just in time to dress the stuntman, run him out a distance, and film him galloping back towards the camera.

In spite of an entire day of mishaps, everything finally came together for one glorious moment. The wind, which had been blowing in exactly the wrong direction all afternoon, decided to cooperate and blow the dust across the camera frame instead of away from it. The stuntman was dressed in the proper costume, complete with gas mask, the sun flaring red behind him. All forces combined to create the image which my father had seen in his dreams and planned for months with the other members of the team: A horseman, his silhouette illuminated by the setting sun, rides in slow motion towards the camera. Shrouded by a cape, his face mysteriously hidden in shadow, he is an eerie, terrifying force of the unknown.

When we saw dailies of the scene, everyone burst into applause. My father turned around and pointed at Andy Lazlo, who was sitting right behind him, as if to say, "You knew all along, didn't you?" Andy simply beamed. A potential disaster had not only been averted, but had turned into a dramatic moment for the film. That evening, everyone left the screening room with a smile.

But in spite of the day's success, my father's anxiety did not lessen. "The first day pointed out to me once again that, on a certain level, things were beyond my control. I knew we had a strict timetable within which to complete all the necessary shots. I felt tremendous anxiety about this schedule, knowing that the studio and the rest of the team was looking to me to pull it all off. I didn't sleep much those first days in Ridgecrest. I just kept thinking, 'Pace, pace, I've got to keep up the pace.' I don't think anyone was pushing me harder than I was pushing myself. And I knew I'd have to press the importance of pace on the crew if we were to finish on time."

Unfortunately, he faced difficult circumstances under which to communicate this message. The next day's work took place at Cuddy Back, where the crew was forced to work under a punishing sun in temperatures over 100 degrees. To make matters worse, the vans were out in full force, kicking up enough dust to choke everyone under their brown haze. The first-aid man, who was also equipped with number twenty-five sunscreen and emergency snakebite kits, dispensed white surgical masks to everyone so we could breathe through the dust. The situation was wretchedly uncomfortable, and it took a great deal of effort to remain cooperative and relatively cheerful.

Despite the difficult circumstances, my father wanted to squeeze the entire mind meld sequence in before the sun started dipping towards the horizon. Since he also wanted a shot of Sybok laughing with the sun setting behind him, as well as a shot of a lone rider galloping towards Paradise City, he knew he didn't have much time to accomplish the scheduled work. He pressed the crew hard, anxious that the sun would set before he could complete his goal.

Despite his good intentions, his anxiety eventually took its toll on the crew. Harve approached him during the middle of the day to make a suggestion, and my father was unnecessarily gruff in answering him. Later, he commanded Mike Woods to get a generator ready, whereupon Mike responded, "Bill, please let me help you." I knew my father was trying to stay calm, but new problems kept cropping up, which only added to his distress.

Because the wind was constantly changing directions, it was extremely difficult to predict how long the dust would hang in the air during a take. Often they would be ready to shoot, just as the wind would shift and blow all the dust away from camera. This problem became particularly evident when filming J'onn's opening shot as he runs towards the tree. Mike Woods was relying on the vans to kick up the dust, as well as a huge airplane engine which had been transported out to the desert for just this purpose. The crew would get blasted by a huge cloud of dust every time they were ready to film, most of the time watching in dismay as the dust clouds would float towards camera and then leisurely blow past it. My father's distress gradually mounted as he watched several unsuccessful attempts, until finally he exploded and started yelling. In a half-joking gesture of frustration, he even flung himself down on the ground and pounded the cracked earth.

Unfortunately, his dramatic gesture didn't solve anything. The dust difficulties had eaten up valuable time, and the crew subsequently found themselves struggling to fit the riding shot in before the sun dipped below the horizon. As the rider began galloping towards camera, my father told the cameramen to roll, even though one of the long lens cameras couldn't yet find the rider in its sight. As a result of not waiting, the long lens camera lost the shot. Andy turned to him and said, "You can't do this. You can't roll while we're not ready." My father struggled with his growing sense of anxiety as he watched the sun finally sink below the desert mountains. They had gotten the necessary shots, but at some cost to his own psyche and the patience of the crew.

Later, Harve took him aside and told him, "I'm your confidant, not your supernumerary." My father finally admitted he'd gone too far, and apologized. Ralph also had a talk with him. I asked what had transpired between them during the conversation.

"Basically what happened was Bill crossed the line . . . he was pushing too hard," Ralph said. "I told him, 'Your passion for the picture is both a blessing and a curse. The passion is what excites the crew, they like working for you . . . you make them feel good, you have a good time with them. But the downside is, you create panic. You're trying to do their jobs. Let them do their jobs. Let Mike Woods decide where the fan is going to go. You tell him the way you want the wind to be in the camera, and let him figure out where to put it. Forget it. You get all worked up about it and it creates problems. Then you've got four cameras going; four operators, four lenses, four systems, four different exposures, and it just can't all happen in a second . . . if we come back from location and it doesn't look like location, then what have we accomplished? Nothing . . . we have to show the vistas. We have to show that we were here. If it takes longer, if it puts us over schedule a day or two, let's do it. Because that's what makes the movie great.' "

After talking to Ralph, my father realized he was right. "I was used to a TV schedule where everything goes boom, boom, boom, one scene right after another with no time between," he said. "I knew I had to adjust to the different pace now that I was directing a feature."

Although he vowed to become more easygoing, the next couple of days didn't give him much chance to do so. The crew moved to Trona Peaks, a vast, eerie landscape where twisted pinnacles rose from the bone-dry earth, reminders of a more primitive time when the surrounding land was a lush, tropical lake and these formations developed under water. Now the land had been converted into federally protected parkland, and the *Star Trek* crew again found themselves carefully picking their way across designated pathways so as not to injure any important sites.

They were there to film several crucial scenes: the daytime arrival of Kirk, McCoy, Spock, and Sybok on the God planet; Sybok leading his army towards Paradise; and Sybok's army advancing through the desert dunes. Not only was there a great deal of material to cover in a short amount of time, but each shot presented its own set of difficulties. The terrain was slippery and dangerous, making the arrival scene hazardous for both the actors and the crew. The site where Sybok's entrance to Paradise City was to be filmed was separated from the other locations by a rough, unpaved road which made travel difficult. And the army shots required a large group of extras who all had to be dressed in ragtag clothing, as well as several complicated "A" and mid-range make-ups, all of which had to be ready on time.

In order to meet the intended schedule, everything had to run smoothly, corresponding to the timetable carefully laid out by the production team. Knowing that timing was crucial, it was difficult for my father to sit quietly by and not monitor everyone's progress throughout the day. It became nearly impossible, however, when certain things began to go wrong.

"My day started at five-thirty AM," he explained later that night. "We were driving to Trona, when we saw a truck broken down on the road. I asked what happened, and the driver said he had a flat tire and to please report it. He said he was carrying the extras' wardrobe. We arrive on the set at six AM, when I reported to the transportation department that the truck had broken down. They said they already knew about it and that it would be fixed, and not to worry since no principal actors' wardrobe was on the truck.

"I then went into make-up and sat down so that one of the make-up artists could work on my face. While I was sitting there, he said, 'I'll do the stippling on your beard later.' This statement startled me because all the characters were sup-

121

posed to be cleanshaven and neatly uniformed when they arrive at the God planet, not dirty and unshaven as they appear in the rest of the scenes we were filming that day. We had changed the original order of the shots around so that the cleanshaven shot was first, not last as it had originally been planned. The problem was, no one had communicated this change to the make-up department, so they had made Larry up for the unshaven shot first. After we realized the mistake, we were able to catch Larry before too much else had been done. . . . then I found out that the principals' wardrobe *was* on the truck which had broken down, and by eight AM, it still hadn't arrived on the set. At that point I thought, 'I've always known directing was communicating to the actor. I never realized directing was also communicating to drivers and to everyone else.'

"Finally, all the wardrobe and make-up problems get solved. We all arrive on the set, dressed and ready for work. Our first shot of the day, the arrival at the God planet, took place at the same peak where I had first envisioned the shot on our scouting trip. I called it the nine AM shot, because I saw on the scouting trip that I would have to get the shot by nine AM in order to have the sun coming up from behind the peak at just the right place. I had several cameras going at once, in order to get a variety of angles and widths on the shot. The problem was, we were up on this hill and it was difficult to communicate what I wanted. I realized I hadn't done this very well, so I found myself screaming directions; wide on one camera, tight on another, a different angle on another, that sort of thing. So all this is going on while the actors are waiting around in the hot sun, including Dee, who was still recovering from his illness.

"Then, while we're up on the ridge shooting the scene, I look over to the place where we're going to film the actors when the earth starts rumbling and quaking as the amphitheater forms. In order to create a feeling of height for this amphitheater, we were going to build a tower where we could place the camera. So I look over to where the tower is supposed to be being built, and I don't see any tower. I've just had this lecture from Ralph about how I shouldn't push every-one so hard, so I keep my mouth shut and don't say anything. But by ten AM I still don't see any tower, so I think, 'screw it,' and I go tell the first assistant director, Doug Wise, that no tower has been built. He goes to make sure it gets started, and I don't think about it anymore, figuring it's being built.

"So I shoot all the other shots we had scheduled, and by twelve PM I go back to the tower site. There's still no tower, so I wait an hour for the tower to be built and the camera to be hauled up. After an hour, it's still not done, and that's when I lost it. 'Why wasn't the tower built?' I was going around yelling, feeling humiliated that on a thirty-some-odd million dollar movie I have to think of these things. It turns out there was some miscommunication and that we were getting a Titan crane for the shot and that the tower didn't need to be built immediately.

"So finally we get it worked out and the tower gets built. Now we need dolly tracks for the shots inside the amphitheater since we needed a way to roll the camera and the platform upon which it rests across the ground easily. The grips say it'll take forty-five minutes to build these tracks. I don't want to wait around for forty-five minutes with nothing to do, so I go with Andy to the site where the army is waiting to grab some army shots. It turns out the tracks only took twenty minutes, so we lost time traveling back and forth. Luckily, we get all the amphitheater shots without a problem.

"Now it's three PM and Larry has forty-five minutes to get his unshaven make-up on and his dirty wardrobe on so we can film his entrance to Paradise City. The shot involved him riding up to a crest, motioning to Paradise City far off in the distance, and saying, 'Behold—Paradise!' to his ragtag army. The next cut is a shot of the city in the distance, with a lone rider, who later we find out is Caithlin Dar, galloping towards the city gates. The problem with the shot was, the rider was way off in the distance, maybe a mile away. By the time she would reposition to do the shot again, several precious minutes would tick by. So now it's four PM and we still have to do the big army shots before the sun goes down at five-ish. We do Larry's line, and he says, 'Can I have another shot at it?' and I look at the setting sun and say, 'No!'

"The site for this particular shot was separated from the rest of the locations by a length of rough terrain. A small group of us had gone out there to do the shot, and we were dropped off by the driver who then drove away and left us there. So now the shot is over, and we look around, only to find ourselves out in the middle of nowhere with nothing in sight except a pickup truck and a ranger nearby. So I jump on the pickup truck and say to everyone, 'get in!' Everyone piles on the truck and we go crashing over the desert floor, until someone yells 'Stop!' We look out and see the van, which had dropped us off, stuck in the desert road which is the only path back to the other location. We try to get the van out of the way, but it won't budge. I take one look at the setting sun and say 'Run!' Everyone says, 'No, no, you can't!' but I insist. We're standing there arguing, when the pickup truck, which had found another road around to where we were, arrives. We jump back in the truck and roar off to the army location.

"We arrived at the army location just as the sun was about four fingers above the horizon. I had instructed Glenn Wilder to get some second unit footage of the army shuffling through the desert while I was doing the other shots. Unknown to me, there had been a miscommunication which resulted in Glenn not getting a camera to shoot his assignment. So these poor extras, who had been standing around in the hot sun for over two hours, had done nothing by the time I arrived. They had no water, and one of them had even collapsed from the heat. So here I come roaring up to the location in my pickup truck, complete with a megaphone from which I start yelling instructions to these poor bedraggled extras. Much to their credit, they were incredibly cooperative. Glenn had done a wonderful job rehearsing them, so they knew exactly what to do. I positioned groups of them behind several dunes . . . each group had a number, which I would call out and they would then appear from behind their dune and run forward. Because almost no sunlight was left, all the shots were backlit, so we couldn't see any of the make-ups we had spent hundreds of thousands of dollars on. We just barely managed to get all the shots we needed before the sun went down . . . I just kept thinking, 'In TV you wouldn't do this. In a seven-day shoot you wouldn't do this. Thirty million goddamn dollars and look what's happening.' "

The crew returned to the hotel in Ridgecrest that night in a crumpled heap. The hotel, with its clean rooms, comfortable dining room, and clear blue swimming pool, seemed like heaven compared to the grimy location site. Some crew members simply collapsed in their rooms and ordered room service. Others jumped in the pool, or ate in the large dining room so they could watch the world series on the room's wide screen television. Because Ridgecrest is a small community (most of its inhabitants work at a nearby naval base), there's very little in the way of evening entertainment. One of the few restaurants open at night was a Mexican place close to the hotel. My father, Harve, Ralph, Nilo and I chose this place to relax and review the events of the day.

The restaurant was quiet, clean, and decorated in authentic south-of-the-border style. The first thing we did was order some drinks. As we sat waiting for them, I wondered aloud why so many things seemed to have been miscommunicated that day. The others ventured an explanation. "The problem is coordination," said Ralph. "Ideally there are several communications. I or someone will realize something needs to be done. Then I'll tell Doug and Doug will tell the drivers. The problem is these nonunion drivers are not experienced. They won't be thinking ahead. Like, if the first unit wardrobe is in with a bunch of trucks, it should go first. Stuff like that. But these people don't think that way." I felt compelled to point out that some of the drivers had worked, as they put it, "heroic hours," sometimes barely even sleeping before going back on shift. Everyone agreed they were trying hard, but that the regular drivers' experience would have made a difference.

"There is a changing of the guard going on with the Teamsters," my father explained. "They get paid a lot of money to drive the trucks and then guard them. Now everyone is saying that movies cost too much money, and one of the expenses is the drivers. The Teamsters are saying that it's things like the expensive actors which are driving up the costs. So there is this dispute going on. But while some people may think the Teamsters are getting paid too much, the advantage is they are very familiar with industry proceedings. They know to do certain things automatically, whereas people who haven't worked in the business don't.''

We continued this line of discussion as the waitress brought our drinks and then our meals. It was now relatively late in the evening, and the restaurant began to empty out, growing quieter as each group walked out the door. After we finished, we asked for the bill and waited quietly until the waitress brought it to us. Suddenly out of nowhere, a woman catapulted herself into my father's lap and began hugging him frantically, virtually strangling him as she wrapped her arms about his neck. He was so surprised he let out a yelp, and his chair tipped over backwards. Both of them landed on the floor. The woman was so startled that she quickly got up and left. The rest of us just stared in open-mouthed amazement. My father calmly got up, dusted himself off, and sat down in his chair. We all began to giggle. The incident reminded me of the three teenage girls in Disneyland who had followed us so zealously through the park. Maybe things hadn't changed so much in twenty years!

As we got up to leave, I marveled at the enduring power of STAR TREK—still able to elicit such an enthusiastic response after so many years. When we walked through the door into the soft desert night, I looked at the black velvet sky above, and the twinkling stars seemed to wink an amused confirmation of my thoughts. In spite of the day's problems, they too believed STAR TREK was doing just fine.

That night ended the first phase of the Ridgecrest schedule. For the next few days, the crew would be working at the Paradise location to film all the daytime scenes. The schedule would then make a radical shift and they would be forced to undergo a grueling week of night shooting both at Paradise City and back at Trona Peaks, where the Rockman would make his first appearance.

The crew, all veteran filmmakers, did not look forward to night shooting in the desert. They knew temperatures often dipped below freezing during the fall months, and were familiar with the inevitable physical exhaustion resulting from all-night vigils. This particular shoot was made even more complicated because of the amount of physical stunts involved, as well as the large amount of extras that needed to be dressed and told what to do. These challenges produced the expected reaction from my father.

"My concern is to get everything done on time without anything going wrong," he said. "We don't have time to make any mistakes. We have to get in and out of Paradise City, then on to Trona Peaks as quickly as possible. In spite of my talks with Harve and Ralph, I'm still very concerned about the schedule. We have a lot to do in a short amount of time."

The exhausting schedule quickly made itself apparent. Our next day started before the sun had even risen above the horizon. We all piled sleepily into the vans at five-thirty AM, then groggily endured a forty-five-minute ride out to Owens Dry Lake Bed where the Paradise City set had been built.

Once a thriving repository of water, Owens Lake had been slowly drained by the thirsty population of Southern California. Now only a dry, dusty lake bed remained. As the sun slowly rose over the horizon, it illuminated this land so that we could see its wide, lonely expanse. And in the middle of this area stood the small, delapidated town of Paradise. Even from a distance we could see Herman had done a wonderful job creating that futuristic ghost town my father had first envisioned. The buildings were worn and tired, torn curtains hung from the windows, and even a chain link door stood at the entrance to the saloon. Our excitement grew as we approached the set, already anticipating the day's work.

We arrived at the town and tumbled out of the van. The first thing to greet my eyes was the very odd sight of Nimbosian soldiers and aliens eating oatmeal and drinking orange juice. Their call had been even earlier than ours, since each one had to be dressed and ready to go by the time we arrived. Dodie and the rest of the wardrobe department had done a heroic job in getting them all ready. Each Nimbosian had been given a complete, suitably ragged outfit, and had then been photographed and assigned a bag in which to place the costume at the end of the day. In this manner, Dodie and the other wardrobe personnel were able to keep track of all articles of clothing going out and coming in. The army, consisting mostly of Ridgecrest townspeople who had managed to get some time off from work, waved a friendly hello to my father as he walked by. He grinned at them and moved towards the center of the town, where the day's action would take place.

As the crew and cast began to gather, the town took on a strange, carnival-like quality. Grips, electricians, cameramen, hair stylists, wardrobe personnel, aliens, Nimbosians, and assorted others milled about, spilling out of doorways and hidden alleys into the streets. Outside the main gates stood Nimbosian horses, now painted blue instead of their former, more subdued gold color. Wranglers, wearing cowboy hats and spitting chewing tobacco, stood close by their animals to ensure their safety. Stationed just beyond the wranglers, the white Paramount trucks stood like sentinels, guarding the entrance to the location site. With the studio name emblazoned boldly on their sides, they resembled circus wagons transporting wandering Gypsy tribes. All this was taking place in the middle of nowhere, with the desert surrounding us on all sides of the city gates. Paradise truly seemed like another planet the Federation might care to explore someday.

In the middle of this confusion stood my father, megaphone in hand. He was trying to coordinate all the shots for the day, including Caithlin's entrance into the town, and the army's subsequent takeover of the city. In spite of the massive amount of people to direct, he anticipated the day's work would go smoothly.

His confidence was partially due to the extras, who were incredibly cooperative; most of them were obviously thrilled to be working with Captain Kirk. While filming Caithlin's entrance, he was having a good time working with this enthusiastic crowd. He told the extras, "If you ever wanted to be actors, this is it. Because it's your attitude which is making the shot. So the attitude is, you really don't care—oh, it's a new rider, you're only mildly interested." The extras took his words to heart, and each gave a stellar performance. They were then able to quickly move on to the next scene.

The only tense moment occurred outside the city gates as they prepared to film the army's run into the town. The scene involved several shots of the army's feet, so my father began to examine all the extras' shoes before the camera rolled. All feet were supposed to be wrapped in rags so their twentieth-century sneakers wouldn't be noticed. Just as they were ready to roll, he noticed some unwrapped shoes at the end of the line.

"What's this?" he demanded, pointing at an unfortunate soldier's feet. "Are these your shoes? I thought all these people's feet are supposed to be wrapped in burlap. Why hasn't this been done? You call these legwraps? It's not what I saw at the studio, guys." His words struck such concern into the hearts of Nilo and the wardrobe personnel that they immediately dropped to their knees and began a "shoe patrol" for any unwrapped sneakers. Nilo was crawling along on the dusty ground, when he pounced upon an unwrapped pair and told Joe Markham to wrap them in burlap immediately. Since the crew had only been together for a short time, Joe did not yet know who Nilo was. Later he approached my father and said, "For an assistant director, that guy is really pushy." Everyone got a good laugh when the confusion was cleared up.

After the shoe emergency was solved, it was time for the army to run towards the gates. Glenn Wilder demonstrated the pace at which the extras should run, and christened it "The Sybok Shuffle." My father found this very amusing. "See that pace?" he joked with the extras. "Do that. More athletic of course. You guys ready? This is your moment in the sun, if you know what I mean." The "shuffle" went off without a hitch, and they were ready to move onto the actual battle, which begins once the army crashes through the city gates.

Glenn had choreographed several stunts, using Greg Barnett, Donny Pulford, and several other stuntmen who would work during the Paradise location scenes. One of these stunt-men included R. A. Rondell, who comes from a family of stuntmen, and who was the stunt coordinator on "T. J. Hooker." It was a small reunion for "T. J. Hooker" personnel, since Donny Pulford was my father's stunt double on the show for much of the time.

Thanks to these veterans' expertise, the remainder of the day's work went smoothly and quickly. My father was so pleased with the results that day, that when Andy said, "Isn't it a shame you can only use this for about four seconds?" he jokingly responded, "Oh no, I'll cut back and forth to it. Even in the middle of the movie I'll cut back to it."

The daytime sequences were disposed of so quickly that we moved onto the night shooting before anyone could catch their breath. Paradise may have resembled a carnival during the day, but at night it took on the eerie, mysterious quality of a deserted town. Illuminated by the city's neon lights, the surrounding desert looked more like the surface of the moon than anywhere on earth. This eerie feeling was further emphasized by the presence of the shuttlecraft, which had been transported from the studio to the location site for just one scene. How odd it was to see a twenty-third-century flying machine inside the walls of a futuristic ghost town! Our strange surroundings prompted Andy to say, "If this is Paradise, can you imagine what Hell is like?" We all laughed, but his words rang true. We were truly beyond anything recognizable by earth standards.

In spite of our imaginative surroundings, the crew had some nuts and bolts work to accomplish. In a couple of nights, they had to film the entire nighttime battle scene, including several fighting sequences; a scene where Spock applies the Vulcan nerve pinch to a horse, causing it to fall; and the arrival of the shuttle craft. Although each shot involved a series of difficulties, the falling horse stunt caused the most concern.

Because he was a part of the Teamsters Union, the wrangler originally assigned to the movie, Corky Randall, had been prevented from working on the show or using his horses. Consequently, another wrangler was asked to train a young, inexperienced horse. Although, as the wrangler put it, the horse was "green," they succeeded in getting the needed footage. The horse reared on cue, then slowly tumbled to the ground as Spock gave it the Vulcan nerve pinch.

While the crew struggled to stay on schedule, several interesting incidents took place that livened up the sometimes dreary routine of filming. For one thing, the Cat Lady sign outside the saloon crashed to the ground without warning, breaking into several pieces. Luckily, no one was hurt, but the accident caused a delay as the crew then had to replace it with a back-up sign. Another alarming moment occurred when all the generators for the set lights failed, causing a two-hour delay while the electricians searched for an answer.

An amusing incident occurred after Leonard and my father filmed the landing party's ride toward the front gates. Instead of being driven back to the set with my father, Leonard was accidentally left out on the desert with the other stuntmen as they walked their horses back to the wranglers. Since he wore a hooded cape, no one realized the mistake until one stuntman said, "Greg?" to Leonard, thinking he was in fact his stunt double, Greg Barnett. To the stuntman's dismay, Leonard answered, "No, Leonard." All the poor stuntman could do was answer, "Oh," and keep walking.

Another humorous moment came when Kenny Myers was driving back to Los Angeles for his wedding the next day. Unfortunately, he took a wrong turn and ended up in Death Valley. Since he had run out of gas, he was forced to stay the night in an out-of-the-way hotel, and just barely made his own wedding.

Meal breaks were another source of interesting location experiences. After six hours of filming, union rules required that the cast and crew be given a rest and some food. Any violation of this schedule meant we went into meal penalty, which allowed the crew to be paid extra. Since economy was the name of the game, these breaks were almost always timed to the minute so that no violations would occur. Thus, we would find ourselves eating breakfast at six PM, and lunch at twelve midnight—always at large tables laid out in the middle of the desert. It was possible to gaze at the moon while eating a tunafish sandwich or chocolate cake.

One night my father and I were munching on hamburgers and salad along with the stuntmen, who were all joking as usual. As we looked at the empty desert surrounding us, we began guessing what kind of animals lived out there and what they were doing at that particular moment. Maybe there were wolves or coyotes out there, wondering what we stupid humans were doing in the middle of the desert. The mention of coyotes triggered a thought from my father. "I thought of a great idea for the sound the Rockman makes," he informed us as we ate. "One night at home I heard this unearthly howling. I couldn't figure out what the sound was, until it finally dawned on me that it was a cat being eaten alive by a coyote. It was this weird, tortured scream that sounded like nothing else. I thought it would be great for the movie." His statement was met with blank stares by the rest of the group. "I had a girlfriend that used to make sounds like that," one of them finally said. We all burst out laughing. "Yeah, you married her," his friend joked, and we laughed even harder, the sounds ringing out among the vast, empty space of the desert, probably scaring off any coyotes that happened to be around. I guess the night shoot was beginning to get to us all.

Although my father's suggestion triggered a humorous moment, it brought up a serious matter for consideration. We were moving into the final phase of location shooting, which would take place at Trona Peaks. There, some of the most crucial moments in the film, including the God planet sequence, would be shot. Because the movie relied heavily on that sequence to "sell" the final moments of the picture, it was vital that this portion of filming go off without a hitch. Any mistake at this point could seriously undermine the entire film.

My father felt tremendous pressure to accomplish this task successfully. To further complicate matters, he had only one night to film shots initially scheduled for two. Not only did he have to film the Rockman sequence in a few short hours, but Kirk's climb up the mountain, and his run to the shuttlecraft along with Spock and McCoy, also had to be filmed before daylight. As the crew wrapped up work at the Paradise City location, my father struggled with these new concerns. Would he have enough time to accomplish all his tasks? Would the Rockman suit work as planned and would it look realistic on film? Was it scary enough to sell the final moments? These questions remained unanswered as we moved into the final phase of location shooting.

Because my father was so concerned about the upcoming evening's work, he, Andy, and Nilo left the hotel early in order to examine the site before sundown. Most of the Rockman shots would take place high up on a pinnacle, where the monster was supposed to suddenly appear in back of Kirk as he is desperately climbing to safety. Filled with both concern and anticipation, my father, Nilo, and Andy eagerly climbed up this peak in order to plan the evening's shots. Because these formations were actually centuries of calcium carbonate buildup, the terrain was sharp and slippery, as difficult to climb as a coral reef.

Despite the danger, all three managed to reach the top unscathed. Getting an entire crew up there, however, would be an entirely different matter. After examining the planned camera angle, Andy, calculating the difficulty involved in getting a camera, crew, and cast up the mountain safely, shook his head and said, "This is madness."

The statement did not discourage my father. "I knew what we were doing was difficult, especially getting everyone up there without injury," he said. "But I also knew that Andy's lighting, coupled with the mysteriousness of the location, would make the Rockman shots look spectacular. These shots were crucial to the film, and I knew we could get them if everything went smoothly."

In order for his plan to work, however, nothing could go wrong that night. The schedule was literally planned down to the minute so they could fit everything in before the sun rose. Quickly disposing of some less complicated shots, they were ready to climb the mountain before ten PM, giving my father two luxurious hours in which to get all the Rockman footage

133

before a twelve midnight lunch break. Because the terrain was so slippery, the cameramen were literally roped together as they climbed up the mountain, their expensive equipment on their backs. Everyone else carefully made their way up the peak, lest they slip and tumble backwards onto the unfortunates climbing behind them. Despite the danger, no injuries occurred, and the crew quickly readied themselves for the Rockman shots.

Getting the Rockman into position was a complicated procedure in itself. The latex suit did not allow much freedom of movement, nor did it allow any air inside to cool the stuntman's skin. The suit had been outfitted with an air cooling system, which would pump cold air in from outside and then circulate it around the suit so the stuntman would not overheat. Despite this precaution, the stuntman could only last a few minutes once the head mask was on. Because my father had wanted a smoking effect for the monster, the suit had also been outfitted with a system which would pump cigarette smoke through the costume and out all the cracks of the suit.

Unfortunately, the amount of smoke which could be pumped through the suit was limited, so that every couple of minutes the special effects team would have to replenish it. All these factors meant that the crew would have a limited amount of time in which to get each take, and they would be forced to wait for several minutes after each try.

Despite the complications, my father was in a confident mood. "I was thinking, 'It's ten PM and I've got two whole hours in which to film the Rockman appearing from behind a boulder. No problem—I've got it. And I've got the rest of the night in the bag because all we had left was to film Kirk, Spock, and McCoy running towards the shuttlecraft, and then Kirk running out of the shuttlecraft when the monster appears.' I was thinking that the worst of the location, and the worst of the filming, was almost behind me." He was in a confident, jovial mood as we stood on this pinnacle, Andy's reddish lights eerily illuminating the craggy peak so that it truly seemed we had entered the underworld. The surrounding desert, silent in its all-encompassing darkness, stood in strange juxtaposition to my father's laughing voice. It suddenly struck me how strangely isolated we were on top of this mountain, a lonely camera crew in the middle of nowhere. My father's voice suddenly seemed reassuring, comforting in its familiarity.

There was a mild breeze blowing as we gazed at the valley below, a gentle contradiction to the frenetic activity taking place on the pinnacle. When the filming began, however, this breeze began to gather force, changing direction so that it forced all the smoke from the Rockman's suit away from camera. Since the smoke's function was to obscure the harsh lines of the suit, the wind was preventing the crew from achieving the desired effect for the shot. Because each try meant several minutes would tick by as the crew replenished the smoke or gave the stuntman air, much of the two hours was eaten up trying to get the smoke going the right way. Before they knew what was happening, time was almost up and they still hadn't gotten the shot.

As the time before the required break drew closer, my father became increasingly frantic. "Here I was thinking the sequence would be no problem," he said. "Then suddenly I found myself desperately trying to get the shot before we had to move on. I knew it was my only chance to get the shot while on location, since we still had to do the shuttlecraft scenes before the sun rose. And the smoke wasn't blowing the right way, the stuntman was having problems moving into position, the suit kept running out of smoke. Everything was going wrong. I knew if I didn't get it right then, I wasn't going to get it." His anxiety level increased until he almost panicked, snapping at one of the crew members who tried to make a suggestion. It seemed like the entire evening would be a loss.

Finally, time ran out. They had managed to get some required footage, but none of it was up to the standard they had envisioned. Suddenly they not only found themselves strapped for time to finish the other shots, but the entire ending of the movie was in jeopardy. "I knew we could try and do something about the Rockman sequence once we got back to the studio," he commented. "We could go in close or do an optical or something to save it. But what we couldn't do was get back to the location to grab the remaining shots. So my first priority was to get the crew moving down to the valley and over to where the shuttlecraft was waiting for us.''

In order to motivate the crew, he had to act quickly and forcefully. ''I wanted to give them the speech from *Henry the Fifth* which starts, 'Once more unto the breach, dear friends, once more,' which is Henry's exhortation to his soldiers to try harder,'' he explained. ''Only under the pressure of the moment, I couldn't remember the speech. So instead I said, 'You've been knocking yourselves out, running for me this whole time on location. But now I'm asking you to do one more thing. Run faster, just this one more time. Because if you don't, we're not going to make it.' And they did. They ran for me. I mean, we literally ran down the mountain to the shuttlecraft site. And we managed to just barely get in all shots. In fact, on the last shot of Kirk running out of the shuttlecraft as the Rockman chases him, you can see the horizon just beginning to lighten.''

Disaster had been just barely averted. But a new, gaping hole in the plan had appeared. When we saw the Trona footage at dailies, one thing became glaringly apparent: The Rockman footage simply did not work. Not only was the smoke blowing the wrong way, but the immobility of the suit gave the Rockman a stiff, unnatural look (as Harve put it, the monster looked more like a Lobsterman than a Rockman). Although somewhat relieved that they wouldn't have to use footage they had never been happy with, the team now had to brainstorm an alternative plan.

What was this creature supposed to look like? Was it humanoid in shape, or simply a mass of throbbing energy? They rechristened the creature ''The Rock Blob'' for lack of a better name. And so, at the eleventh hour, the team found a new, urgently pressing problem foisted upon them.

My father had done his best. He had managed to complete a grueling, uncomfortable location schedule on time and on budget. Although this accomplishment boosted his confidence, he looked ahead to the remaining weeks of studio work with mixed feelings. "We've got to keep this up," he said to me as we prepared to leave Ridgecrest. "It's going to be very difficult to do. We've given ourselves an onerous burden." Not only did he have to make sure the studio filming stayed on schedule, but now he had to find a solution to the Rock Blob problem as soon as possible.

The location shots at Ridgecrest were already history as he climbed aboard the plane back to Los Angeles. As the desert grew smaller and smaller behind him, finally fading into a dusty memory, he turned his face towards home and the Paramount lot, where a new phase of the adventure was about to begin.

5

BACK TO PARAMOUNT

The crew returned home exhausted, but there would be no real rest for any of them until principal photography ended. As soon as my father landed in Los Angeles, he immediately went to Paramount to prepare for the next day's work.

"I was so anxious to have everything go right from then on, I couldn't resist walking the sets," he said. "I wanted to have everything perfectly organized for the next day's filming. The problem was, I was exhausted from the lack of sleep and the stress of location. I kept thinking of this story I had heard about Jack Lord while he was filming his series, 'Stony Burke.' Apparently he missed a night's sleep once, and never recovered from it. The rest of the time was a downhill fight into that valley of fatigue. That story was constantly on my mind that first day back. I was worried the same thing would happen to me, which was something I couldn't afford. I knew I had to be sharp and focused, ready for the challenges this next phase would bring."

He had a lot to think about. The bulk of shooting still lay ahead, in such interesting locations as the shuttlecraft landing bay, the *Enterprise* bridge, the Klingon Bird of Prey, the *Enterprise* observation room, a Nimbosian barroom, a mock forest, and the God planet. The schedule presented an enormous challenge to the entire crew, but the brunt of this concern fell on my father, who was still preoccupied with schedule and budgetary concerns. Although he anticipated the challenge of the coming weeks, he also dreaded the inevitable complications they would most certainly bring. Unfortunately, his fears did not prove groundless. Almost immediately, a seemingly endless succession of problems began to occur.

The first scheduled shots were on the shuttlecraft landing bay set, an enormous, sleekly designed stage built especially for *Star Trek V.* Herman very carefully followed drawings from other *Star Trek* books so that the landing bay would closely resemble fans' expectations of the interior.

"There has been a lot of speculation about what [the landing bay] looks like in a lot of books," he said. "We followed the drawings in those books of what the shuttle bay should look like. I think that's a nice thing to do to give to the fans."

But this stage came complete with its own unique set of problems. Unknown to most people, there was a hollow vault underneath it where most of Paramount's valuable antique furniture was stored. Because of the hollow vault underneath, the floors would not support a tremendous amount of weight. Consequently, no cranes could enter the stage to help move the shuttlecrafts into position. This unfortunate limitation resulted in inumerable delays while the crew struggled with the problem of how to transport the shuttlecrafts. The production lost a full seven hours one morning as they attempted to place the shuttlecrafts in their desired positions. In addition, the set proved very difficult to light, which further delayed their progress. The crew found themselves almost a whole day behind before they had even shot anything.

Everyone breathed a sigh of relief when these problems were finally solved; however, new ones soon cropped up to replace them. For the crash scene, or "hot landing," as it was called, the shuttlecraft was supposed to hurtle forward until a netting popped up to stop it. In order to make the scene look realistic, sparks were to fly out from under the craft as it screeched forward. These ideas were imaginative, but they proved more difficult to realize than anyone had anticipated. Not only were the sparks running out before the sequence ended, but the crew was having problems pushing the craft in the right direction. On one take, these problems culminated in a near disaster as the shuttlecraft almost crashed into a wall. In order to avoid future mishaps, the crew then wired the shuttlecraft until the cables reached almost outside the stage doors. This straightened out the shuttlecraft's trajectory, but it also used up more valuable time. They finished up the landing bay shots as quickly as possible, and pushed on to the next scheduled sequence of sorts.

Since the shuttlecrafts were standing ready and available, the crew's next task was to film all scenes taking place aboard the shuttlecraft *Galileo*. This included the scenes before and after the crash, as well as a fight sequence between Kirk and Sybok once they leave the shuttlecraft. Since the interior of the shuttlecraft could barely accommodate all key personnel inside its cramped walls, the shooting of these scenes presented a challenge. Having anticipated this problem, my father had preplanned his shots in order to avoid wasting time with last-minute solutions. However, no amount of planning could have prevented what was in store for him.

The first shots involved dialogue between Kirk and Sybok where Kirk warns his captor that the Klingons are quickly approaching. Throughout this dialogue, the *Enterprise* can be seen in the background through the shuttlecraft *Galileo*'s front window. Of course, everyone wanted this background picture of the *Enterprise* to appear as realistic as possible. In order to achieve this effect, it was decided the best method to use would be the rear projection process. This meant that Bran would prepare a reel of film of the *Enterprise* floating in space, which would then be projected onto the rear of a screen positioned at the *Galileo*'s window. In this way, the *Enterprise* would appear to be floating just outside the shuttlecraft's window.

To guard against any delays, Bran transported two of his rear projection machines to the set just in case one broke down. It seemed that everything was well planned and would go off without a hitch. Unfortunately, problems began to occur almost from the very beginning. As my father would begin his dialogue, Bran would start the rear projection machine and the image of the *Enterprise* would then appear through the window. This image was supposed to last until all dialogue was finished. However, the reel of film was only thirty seconds long, far too short for the amount of dialogue in the scene. The actors then found themselves in the awkward situation of having to rush their lines before this reel, or "plate material" as it is called, could run out. Often they would get almost to the end of their lines, only to have the image suddenly disappear from the window. It was an unfortunate miscalculation, and cost my father, the actors, and the crew a great deal of time.

To make matters worse, Bran's rear projection machine would periodically break down. Since the camera and rear projection machine both run film at twenty-four frames-per-second, this malfunction affected the synchronization of the rear projected image with the camera's shutter gate. For rear projection to work, the camera's shutter has to open at the same time that a frame of the film appears on the rear projection screen. Any miscalculation usually results in the rear projected image appearing on screen while the camera's shutter gate is closed. If this happens, the camera cannot pick up the rear projected image, and the rear projection screen will appear blank when viewing the film. In order to avoid this problem, everytime Doug Wise would say "Roll!" Bran would then say "Synch!" to let everyone know that the machines were synchronized. My father was then free to say "Action!" and the scene would begin.

Unfortunately, every time the scene would start, they would inevitably be forced to stop a few moments later because they no longer had "synch." Everyone cast a suspicious eye at Bran, who up until this time had done nothing to prove his expertise except talk. He insisted that there was a wiring problem somewhere on the set which kept blowing out his equipment, thus causing the "synch" problem.

"No one believed him," my father later told me. "We'd look around this huge stage and say, 'Oh sure, it's a wiring problem. Yeah, sure.' " Bran continued blaming it on the faulty wiring, especially after his second machine blew out.

The production was held up for an entire day while Bran, the electricians, and everyone else, searched for a culprit. Finally, after hours of searching, they found the problem. A wire on the panavision camera had frayed, and was electrifying all the steel beams on the stage. Bran had been right, after all.

After solving the "synch" dilemma, it seemed as if their problems were over. Much to my father's distress, however, such was not the case. The next shot involved Kirk, Spock, and McCoy traveling on the *Galileo* towards the *Enterprise* after they've been called away from shore leave. As inspiration for Kirk's line, "All I need is a tall ship and a star to steer her by," my father wanted a reflection of the *Enterprise* and the moon to be seen from the *Galileo*'s window. In order to achieve this effect, they relied on a large photograph called a "translight" to represent the reflection. Usually a translight is made by taking a 35 millimeter mock-up, then making a huge eight-by-ten inch negative from this mock-up and blowing it up. Yet another miscommunication resulted in the thirty-five millimeter mock-up, instead of the eight-by-ten negative, being blown up into the translight. This mistake resulted in the translight appearing cumbersome and unrealistically bright. The discovery of this error came too late to rectify, and caused some dissension among the troops that day. Sparks from the shuttlecraft were not the only ones flying around as Andy, Bran, and my father all expressed their frustration over the series of events that had taken place.

Matters were made worse when David Nicksay appeared on the set to announce the project was now a full three days behind schedule. My father worried that if they fell behind an entire week, the studio might be forced to cut some script out of the picture in order to save time.

Because of the time pressures, they quickly attempted to complete all shuttlecraft shots, including the fight sequence between Sybok and Kirk. This battle was carefully choreographed by Glenn Wilder, whose main challenge was to try and give Sybok the appearance of superior strength for which Vulcans were famous. In order to achieve this effect, wires were attached to my father so he was lifted into the air as Sybok slammed him against the shuttlecraft.

However, when viewing the scene in dailies, my father, Harve, and Ralph nevertheless noticed that the wires were visible upon close inspection. Although this discovery troubled them, they decided the problem could be addressed in the editing room by giving the sequence only momentary attention. There was no more time to devote to the problem, since far more pressing concerns loomed on the horizon. The next sequence was rapidly approaching, and before he could catch his breath, my father found himself back on the *Enterprise* bridge, commanding yet another *Star Trek* adventure.

Because the bridge is perhaps the most universally recognized *Star Trek* set, and serves as "home" for the *Enterprise* crew, special attention was given to its design. Since the bridge sets from prior *Star Trek* movies had all been scrapped, Herman had the opportunity to start from scratch. He used this chance to improve on certain aspects of the former designs.

"I was fortunate because the *Enterprise* was destroyed in *Star Trek III*," he told me. "The set itself was eleven, maybe close to twelve years old. It wasn't in very good physical condition, and when it was designed it looked great but was not as easy to shoot as it might have been. The walls were attached to the floor, so if you wanted to take out a wall unit you couldn't do it unless you also pulled out a floor plug."

In rebuilding the set, Herman gave the bridge a circular design, and made each wall removable without disturbing the platform beneath the set. In this fashion, the crew could shoot in a 360 degree radius without having to dismantle an entire portion of the bridge.

John Dwyer made further overhauls by decorating the bridge in a sleek, yet comfortable way. New additions included mauve carpeting, new console chairs specially ordered from Norway, and a new captain's chair.

"The old chair was flat up the back and had two aluminum panels that locked on your leg, with buttons on them," he said. "It was a real hindrance to the actors. Not only did you have to remember your lines and your moves, you had to get out of this thing . . . so we constructed one that was easy to get out of and looked semi-comfortable." Such attention to detail added warmth and texture to the new set.

Part of Herman's design included a console with twenty-nine television monitors, which would relay visual information to the *Enterprise* crew as they embarked on their journey. A significant portion of preproduction time was spent discussing what should appear inside those monitors during the various phases of the adventure. After much discussion, the team agreed on the look these films or "graphics" should have. It then fell to associate producer Brooke Breton to coordinate the creation of these graphics, no small task since all twenty-nine monitors had to have some sort of visual image going at all times.

Brooke then worked closely with several groups, each responsible for a different type of graphic. For standard, less complicated graphics, Brooke and the art department cut gels to represent an image, then shot these cutouts with an animation camera. They also used another technique called "polar motion gags," the same process used in some beer billboards to make the water look like it's running.

For the more complicated graphics, such as when the *Enterprise* is approaching the Great Barrier, Brooke went to an outside company for help. She then spent many weeks with them, supervising the creation of this more elaborate visual material. Once these jobs were complete, Brooke would also be responsible for coordinating the playback of these graphics on the actual set. The creation of this material was a good example of how much time, effort, and attention to detail is invested in each aspect of the production.

Brooke, Herman, and John Dwyer were not the only ones preparing for the bridge sequences in minute detail. My father had been busy planning his work on the *Enterprise* set for weeks before the start of principal photography, aware that certain problems would inevitably arise. For one, most of the *Enterprise* sequences required the entire bridge crew, four hostages, and various lower-ranked personnel to be present on the set. This meant my father would have to coordinate at least fifteen persons' movements within very cramped confines. To complicate matters further, he was warned that the monitors might reflect the camera in their glass view screens, which could ruin an entire shot.

Part of his planning involved the decision to use a "steady-cam," a camera which is literally harnessed to a camera operator to facilitate his movement about the set. By doing this, my father hoped to accomplish his desired shots quickly and with a minimum of reflection problems. Although the steadycam rental fee is high, he felt he could actually save money by cutting down on film time if he used the steadycam judiciously and effectively.

His theory proved correct. Not only was he able to move the camera around with ease, but he completed each day's agenda so quickly that they began to make up lost time. It seemed as though everything was finally going right.

The cast and crew sensed the burden lifting, and the bridge set took on a festive mood. A game began to circulate, the object being to attach as many clothespins as possible to someone without being noticed. After someone had been on the bridge, it was not unusual to see him walk by with five or six clothespins pinned to his back a few minutes later. Visitors would stay for a short time, innocently unaware of the game's existence. When they turned to leave, the crew would all giggle at the inevitable clothespins attached to their collars, skirt bottoms, or sweaters. No one was exempt from attack except one person . . . throughout the entire shoot, no one ever dared pin Captain Kirk. His collar remained untouched.

I too was having a great deal of fun, not just because of the game, but because my sister, Melanie, was present on the bridge, playing the part of a young Yeoman. It brought a smile to my face to see both my father and sister in Starfleet uniform. The next generation of Star Trek had truly arrived. Melanie became quite adept at the clothespin game, and managed to score several direct hits without being discovered. And I could always count on her to entertain me. She and Rex Holman took to singing and dancing the can-can in between takes. I was truly sorry when her part was over and I no longer had a playmate. She left me to fend off the clothespins all by myself.

In spite of the good times, one debacle did occur. My father came to work one morning in a cheerful mood, ready to accomplish another full day of work. To his horror, he was informed that there were scratches on the previous day's work, most likely rendering it completely useless. It seemed as though the hard-won advance in the schedule would now be lost. In viewing the dailies, my father realized the significance of the mishap.

"Here I was congratulating myself for making up this time," he said. "Then I saw the dailies that all went out the window. There was a huge scratch on the right side of the screen. There was no way we could use the film. That meant I would have to reshoot the entire sequence, which would put us nearly four days behind—close to the dreaded one week mark. The possibility of a real disaster was imminent."

The crew searched for an answer as to why the scratch occurred. "They thought it might have been a problem with the camera, but no one really knew," he said. "So we tried to fix all the possible reasons why the scratch would have appeared. The next day we came back, thinking that although we might have to reshoot the previous day's work, the problem was now solved. While on the set, Leonard says, 'Oh, you have the same magazine in the camera.' Everyone thought he was making a sick joke, laughing about the idea that the same thing would happen again. We thought that the last thing that would happen was a repeat of the day before. But sure enough, I came back the next day and there were more scratches on the film. I just threw up my hands and went into the make-up trailer, where everyone was sitting in stony silence. They all knew what had happened. It was a very serious moment. I had now lost any time I had managed to gain, and was again worrying about the schedule. It seemed like there had been so many problems with which to contend."

There was a somber mood that day while watching dailies. No one could understand why the same thing had happened for the second time in a row. It seemed they would have to reshoot two days of work, when Bran suddenly sat up in his seat and said, "I may be able to do something about this." Since the scratches were all on the right side of the screen, he proposed blowing up the film enough to get rid of the offending material. When he announced he could get the results back within a day, everyone looked at him in amazement. "Bran became the hero of the moment," my father said. "Not only had he found a solution, but he got us the material back incredibly quickly. He really came through." Although they were worried the composition of the shots would be altered, my father gladly sacrificed this concern in favor of gaining back his two days of work. Suddenly, the production was back on track and on time. A feeling of euphoria swept through the ranks. It seemed *Star Trek V* refused to be daunted by technical problems.

The crew's morale remained high, even though it was time to face those most dreaded of Federation enemies, the Klingons. There may have been many battles between Kirk and the Klingons over the years, but my father was actually looking forward to capturing his enemies on film. Part of his excitement was due to the enormous preparation that had taken place prior to the actual filming date.

Again, a large portion of the time had been spent designing the perfect Klingon bridge, which was largely based on old drawings and plans from previous *Star Trek* movies. Herman had improved on prior Klingon designs, though, by adding a long neck to the set. This neck was originally designed to appear only briefly as the bridge doors open and close when Klaa appears. Instead, my father decided to take advantage of the wonderfully textured corridor Herman had built and leave the doors open, which made the set seem much larger, much more a part of an actual ship. And Andy, by lighting the bridge in dramatic tones, gave the entire set the dark, clanking feeling of a submarine. My father had also decided to use the steadycam again, which would not only save time, but would give the sequences additional energy and movement.

The two actors playing Captain Klaa and Vixis, Todd Bryant and Spice Williams, had spent a great deal of time preparing

147

for their parts as well. Playing a Klingon meant, of course, that they had to learn the Klingon language. The task of teaching them this complicated tongue fell to Marc Okrand, the founding father of Klingonese. For *Star Trek III*, Mark had invented an entire alphabet and vocabulary for the Klingons, eventually codifying his efforts in *The Klingon Dictionary*. He spent many hours teaching this language to Todd and Spice. He started by showing them the Klingon alphabet, and then had them memorize all their lines in English and in Klingon. Both became so fluent they were eventually able to spit out their lines in either tongue upon request.

But learning a new language was only part of their preparation. Both actors had to endure a three-hour make-up job each morning in order to appear sufficiently "Klingon." The process started with a bald cap being placed over their hair. A forehead appliance piece was then fastened to their skin using a strong adhesive glue. Both the appliance piece and their skin were then painted with make-up which was a combination of acrylic mixed with adhesive. Each then donned a hairpiece and then put on their costumes to complete the picture. Although their wardrobe was based on Klingon designs from prior movies, both Todd and Spice had to have uniforms individually cut from leather in order to achieve that snug fit for which the Klingon physique is best suited. Woe to the Klingon who had to use the restroom after his costume was on since he would then undergo an equally elaborate ordeal to get it off.

In spite of these discomforts, both Todd and Spice were pleasant, professional additions to the cast. Their dedication and enthusiasm for their work gave the Klingon sequences an added energy and zeal. For my father, the Klingon sequences proved to be some of the most enjoyable work on the movie. He laughed and joked throughout the entire day, thrilled with the actors' performances, the imaginative set, and the smoothness with which all technical facets of production came off. He later told me, "I've just had a day of which all moviemakers dream."

The rest of the team agreed. After viewing the material in

dailies, everyone burst into applause. They had done their job well. Not only had they achieved some fantastically colorful shots, but they had performed their tasks with skillful efficiency, actually picking up crucial time. For the first time during production, *Star Trek V* was almost ahead of schedule.

The crew applied their newfound efficiency to the next phase of the shooting schedule, the interior scenes of the Nimbosian barroom. The barroom was actually two different sets, one where the drinking, dancing, and fighting takes place, the other where Caithlin introduces herself to Talbot and General Korrd. Since the latter required a less elaborate production, the team decided it would be filmed first.

Preparations for this scene had also taken place some time before. Each actor had been made-up and fitted in their individual costume many times. Charles Cooper, the actor playing Korrd, had to undergo a make-up process very similar to Todd and Spice's, only his make-up was finished with a layer of KY jelly in order to give him a slick, oily look. Because Charles's costume was so heavy and constricting, he had a cooling system similar to the one used for the Rockman suit built into it. It was not unusual to see him anchored to his chair by the rubber hose and generator that was plugged into his suit. Cynthia Gouw, the actress playing Caithlin Dar, had to shave half her eyebrows and put up with a hair appliance on her head that she and Donna nicknamed ''Winkie.'' And David Warner had to look as unkempt as possible to give St. John Talbot that deteriorated look.

But the actors' make-up and costumes were not the only elements preplanned for this scene. My father had also suggested that running water should course through the pipes in the background of the room as the three characters talk. The idea was to make Talbot and Korrd appear even more decadent and destructive than their appearance implies, since they were using Nimbus's precious water to make their own alcohol. Unfortunately, it was belatedly discovered that the running water interfered with the sound of the actors' dialogue so it was turned off. The necessary impression of dilapidated physical and moral character would have to come from the actors' performances instead.

In spite of the actors' wonderful performances, the scene is actually most interesting not because of what happened during its filming, but of what didn't happen. Because of concerns regarding pace and time, most of this scene was cut out of the movie. It was an unfortunate, albeit necessary, cut, since the dialogue contained a great deal of humor. Because it is such a good example of the kind of material that gets weeded out during the editing process, the original dialogue is reprinted here. This was also the scene that all the actresses auditioning for the part of Caithlin Dar read for my father and Harve:

INT. BACK ROOM

The stranger lowers the breathing device from her face and is revealed to be a young woman. A Romulan. Her name is CAITHLIN DAR and she stands on the threshold of the room, trying to adjust her eyes to the murky surroundings. She's a little nervous and a long way from home.

The back room is a storage area for unwanted odds and ends. A ceiling fan swishes overhead pushing hot air around. TWO MEN are sprawled in chairs at opposite ends of a table. They're too busy drinking to notice Caithlin's entrance.

CAITHLIN
Gentlemen, I'm Caithlin Dar.

The man seated closest to Caithlin slowly swivels his head in her direction. He wearily extracts himself from his chair and comes forward. He's a Terran (specifically, an Englishman) named ST. JOHN TALBOT. Thin and dissipated, alcoholic, Talbot is a veteran of the diplomatic corps. He pats down his unruly hair and straightens his soiled suit. He gives Caithlin a tired smile and extends a limp hand.

TALBOT
Ah, yes. Our new Romulan representative. Welcome to Paradise City, Miss Dar, capital of the so-called "Planet of Galactic

Peace." I'm St. John Talbot, the Federation representative here on Nimbus Three and my charming companion is the Klingon consul, Korrd.

Caithlin regards the hulking figure at the other end of the table. KORRD is an old, overweight Klingon, a once great warrior now past his prime. He doesn't rise to greet Caithlin. Instead, he takes a swig from a flagon and emits an earth-shaking belch.

CAITHLIN

I expect that's Klingon for hello.

Reacting to Korrd's stench, Caithlin holds her breathing device in front of her mouth.

TALBOT

He doesn't speak English.

CAITHLIN

And I don't speak Klingon.

TALBOT

I'm relieved to hear that. Please sit down, Miss Dar. Can I offer you a drink?

Without warning, Korrd drunkenly lets loose with a barrage in his native tongue. (It is subtitled in English for those who don't speak Klingon.)

KORRD

(Romulan women belong on their backs!)

CAITHLIN

What did he say?

TALBOT

He says he hopes you'll enjoy your tour of duty here. Might I ask, Miss Dar, what terrible thing you did to get yourself banished to this armpit of the galaxy?

151

CAPTAIN'S LOG

> CAITHLIN

I volunteered.

> TALBOT
> (Spewing grog)

Volunteered?

Talbot turns to Korrd and translates her answer into Klingon. Korrd chortles derisively.

> CAITHLIN

Nimbus Three is a great experiment. Twenty years ago, when our three governments agreed to develop this planet together, a new age was born.

> TALBOT

Your new age died a quick death. The great drought put an end to it. And the settlers we conned into coming here—the dregs of the galaxy. They immediately took to fighting amongst themselves. We forbade them weapons—they fashioned their own.

> CAITHLIN

Then it appears I've arrived just in time. The policies the three of us agree on will have far-reaching results . . .

> TALBOT

My dear girl, we're not here to agree. We're here to disagree. This "great experiment" as you call it was instigated to satisfy a bunch of bleeding hearts whining for "galactic peace." It was intended to fail.

> CAITHLIN

I'm afraid I don't share that view.

> TALBOT

(pleased) There, you see? We're disagreeing already.

> CAITHLIN

I'm here to open discussions for a solution to these problems.

BACK TO PARAMOUNT

Korrd comes to life. He roars with laughter and spits back a disgusting mouthful of Klingon. Talbot winces.

> CAITHLIN
> (losing patience) What did he say? I want his exact words.

> TALBOT
> He said the only thing he'd like you to open is your blouse. He's heard Romulan women are different.

Caithlin's embarrassment turns to anger.

> CAITHLIN
> You tell Consul Korrd—never mind. I'll tell him myself in the only Klingon I know.

Caithlin lets loose with a Klingon epithet. No translation necessary. Sputtering with rage, Korrd hurls his flagon aside and clambers to his feet.

> KORRD
> (in perfect English) Screw you, too!

> CAITHLIN
> He does speak English!

> TALBOT
> (surprised) Sly old bugger!

Further argument is interrupted by shouts from outside and the whine of a warning klaxon.

The dialogue was later trimmed to contain only the most necessary exposition, since it became apparent the approaching battle sequence was slowed by the conversational tone of the scene.

However, the rest of the barroom sequence remained intact. In fact, the scene where Caithlin enters the bar with her hood over her face actually took place during one of the more colorful and interesting days of production. In order for the sequence to work, several different departments had coordinated their efforts. For example, all sorts of intergalactic beings were present, including several aliens, courtesy of Kenny Myer's make-up magic. All were dressed in Nilo and Dodie's accumulations from Western Costume, including two ladies who were wearing chain mail as a tribute to their "alternative life style," as Dodie tactfully put it. John Dwyer had done a wonderful job decorating the room, adding interesting touches such as chairs soldered together from junkyard pieces of metal. He even placed a flask from the original series on top of the bar.

Propmasters Don and Kurt Hulett, who had been responsible for coordinating all props during the production, also got into the act. They brought many of the strangely shaped bottles and glasses that were piled behind the bar, not to mention keeping track of all incoming and outgoing phasers, communicators, tricorders, and other Starfleet equipment. The combined efforts of all concerned resulted in a look for Nimbus Three that was both amusing and intriguing—Paradise City made the trip from Ridgecrest to Paramount without losing any of its initial inspiration.

The bar sequence's crowning achievement, however, was the creation of the Cat Lady, played by Linda Fetters. Not only did she sport feline facial features, striped skin, and a tail, but Linda had the dubious distinction of being the first Cat Lady with three breasts. Again, Kenny Myers was responsible for creating the look of this most unusual alien. He had actually spent many weeks testing different patterns of striping on a willing model, who had to stand for hours at a time while Kenny and his team experimented with markings from such exotic animals as zebras and Bengal tigers. Because the striping would cover the entire body area, they were forced to work around some extremely delicate areas. "My wife used to get jealous," he laughed, "until she came along with me a few times to sessions like these. Then she realized that, after a while, it's just like working under a car." After much experimentation, Kenny finally settled on the Bengal tiger striping as his guideline.

But there was more to the Cat Lady than mere animal markings. While the striping experiments were under way, Kenny took a body mold of Linda's chest area so he could begin sculpting her third breast onto the mold. Once the sculpting was complete, he made an appliance piece which would be glued onto Linda's body when the time came. He also made an appliance piece for her face to lend her features a feline quality. In order to give her eyes that same realism, special contact lenses were custom-made for her to wear. Unfortunately, the lenses were so uncomfortable that normal vision was almost impossible, and Linda could only wear them for brief periods. A special suction cup was also needed to pry them loose. The outfit's final touches included a tail and a wig, painstakingly prepared by Kenny's wife, Karen. The entire look would take almost six hours to assemble, which meant Linda needed a four AM call to be ready by ten AM.

On the day of production, my father greeted Linda and the rest of the cast and crew with a sense of excitement. "I had seen a large portion of the barroom sequence in my head for months," he told me. "I knew I wanted certain things, like the Cat Lady dancing on the top of the bar, the aliens playing pool, and the aliens fighting while the commercial is playing in the background. But in order for me to get what I wanted, I had to contend with a number of things. For one, Linda had a limited amount of time she could keep the contact lenses on. That meant if I didn't get it right away, we'd have to wait while we got her off the bar, took out the lenses, and then back in them again after she rested. Also, once the 'pool table' was filled with water, it would be too heavy to move, so we were locked into its placement from the very beginning. I also wanted to make sure and keep the scene alive while Caithlin makes her entrance and then walks to the back room. As it turned out, once I'd composed the shot I realized it didn't look quite right, but I didn't know why. I had to think quickly, because I didn't want Linda to suffer needlessly. She couldn't see at all, and at one point the camera knocked into her. A funny moment occurred when she said, 'I really can't see.' Glenn Wilder then responded, 'In that case, what are you doing Friday night?' It was a very funny moment, and I laughed in spite of my urgent need to figure out the shot. Finally, I solved the problem by going in tight on the bartender before I began the pan up to Linda. All in all, I was very pleased with the way it turned out.''

Once they had accomplished the shot, the crew cleared the room so they could film the Cat Lady attacking Captain Kirk in the empty barroom. Again, the scene involved several complicated elements, including the stunt itself. My father anticipated needing a trampoline so that Linda could jump from behind the bar onto his back. She easily sailed over the bar and landed hissing and clawing on him as they twirled around. ''I thought a long time ago that the sound of the commercial playing in the background would be an interesting contrast to the sounds of a life and death struggle between Kirk and the Cat Lady,'' he said. ''So I wanted the tape to start playing as we bumped into the jukebox during our fight. Unfortunately, the video playback operator who normally ran the commercial had called in sick, and someone who wasn't as familiar with the equipment replaced him. We then spent a long time trying to coordinate the playback with the bump into the jukebox. Since I only had one day to complete all the barroom scenes, this naturally made me quite anxious. But eventually it turned out all right and we got the shot.''

Once the initial fight was captured on film, the crew next moved to the shot where Kirk throws the Cat Lady into the pool. In order to lend an air of realism to the shot, Linda was hooked to wires at her wrists and feet so she would be lifted into the air as Kirk threw her forward. Although she was an experienced stuntwoman, my father was worried the sequence might prove too dangerous. ''I had originally chosen Linda for her voluptuous figure, not her stunt skills,'' he told me. ''I had been worried she'd get banged around while floating in the air, especially because she would be dangling near the ceiling until they could lower her to the ground. As it turns out, not only was she a first-class athlete, but she was a real trooper. She was able to keep her body sideways the whole time so she didn't get hurt. And through the whole ordeal, she didn't complain once. She was a true professional.'' Everyone was so impressed with her attitude and abilities that they burst into applause upon completion of the shot. Linda's cooperation had gone a long way toward making the day a success.

After these technically complicated shots, the rest of the barroom scenes were easy in comparison. The crew quickly disposed of all the shots where Sybok enters and takes the three representatives hostage. Because they had perfected their rhythm, the crew now found themselves easily accomplishing all required tasks so that they were soon ready to make the next move. As the day drew to a close, they began hauling cameras and equipment to the set where many of the movie's most dramatic moments would occur . . . the observation room aboard the U.S.S. *Enterprise.*

Of all the scenes in the film, the observation room actually remained staying closest to my father's initial vision. From the very beginning, he had wanted a grand, yet intimate setting where Sybok could unleash the inner demons in McCoy and Spock's minds. He had always seen the sequence as a departure into the realm of the unconscious, so he knew the room would have to open up and reveal different scenes as each character's secret pain was explored.

In order to achieve this effect, he, Herman, and Nilo worked closely together to develop a set which would fulfill all necessary functions. ''We decided the observation room should resemble a nautical men's club,'' my father told me. ''Its large bay windows would remind us of the grandeur of space, yet its furniture and interior would give an intimate feel. Herman used a lot of wood, which he felt would be very rare by the twenty-third century, to give the appearance of richness and warmth. It was very important to have this feeling of intimacy, since the mind meld sequences would be very deep, personal experiences. In order to play these sequences the way I wanted, we designed the observation room so that it had two extensions, one on either side of the set. On one side, we built a hospital room for the scene with McCoy's father. On the other, we built a cave where Spock's birth would take place. This meant we could shift between reality and the interior mind meld scenes without cutting away or dissolving. This was a key factor in making the scenes interesting and dramatic.''

Dr. McCoy's sequence had actually been based on my father's personal experience. "When my father died he had tears on his face," he explained to me. "Since he had just had a stroke, he couldn't talk, so no one knew why he was crying. That image of tears running down his face has always stuck in my mind. I wanted to create a scene which drew from that image, even going so far as to add a shadow—the Shadow of Death—over the actor's face as he takes his last breath. This was a very personal, very emotional scene for me. It then became very important that it play the way I imagined it."

But my father faced certain obstacles before he could see his vision become a reality. When DeForest Kelly first read the script, he objected to the content of his mind meld sequence. He felt that McCoy's "pulling the plug" might be too controversial an act for some *Star Trek* fans to accept. My father then had to convince him otherwise.

"After De read the script, he didn't want to do the scene," my father said. "So I took him to lunch and tried to convince him it would work. I said, 'De, this is the best scene you've had to play in a long time.' He's such a wonderful actor, and I really felt he hadn't had a chance recently to show what he was capable of doing. Finally, after much talking, I convinced him to do it. His one stipulation was that we add an explanation of why McCoy committed the euthanasia. We added a short bit of dialogue where Sybok asks, 'Why did you do it?' and McCoy answers 'To preserve his dignity.' With these new lines, De felt that McCoy's motivations were clearer and more understandable. Once we solved De's objections, we were then closer to getting the scene I had envisioned."

In fact, the death scene proved to be one of the more emotional moments in the film. In order to perfect the hallucinatory quality of the sequence, a screen, or a "scrim" as it is called, was placed in front of the hospital bed. When the time came for McCoy to turn and face his pain, the lights behind the scrim went up to reveal his dying father. The close-ups were then obtained by removing the scrim and going in close with the camera. During the close-ups, DeForest whispered his lines to the actor, Bill Quinn, who played his father. Bill, who as it turns out had known my stepmother's mother from his days in radio, was an accomplished and professional addition to the cast. Working together, he and DeForest created an emotionally powerful moment. When the sequence was over, I could see that my father was visibly moved.

"It's the strangest thing," he said after they had finished for the day, "but I have played that scene over and over in my head for months. It came out almost exactly the way I had imagined it. What an incredible feeling for me . . . my father, the dialogue, the performances—it was all there."

This intensity of feeling carried my father through the next sequence of Spock witnessing his birth and subsequent rejection by both his parents. My father had originally envisioned the scene in a dark cave, where the mysterious birth rites of Vulcans take place, hidden from the outside world. As the scene played, we would see Spock's feelings of betrayal revealed as the "secret pain" he had kept from even his closest friends. My father hoped this would provide additional motivation for some of the film's events, particularly the scene in the shuttle bay where Spock seems to turn against Kirk and the *Enterprise*.

However, he faced the same type of obstacle with Leonard as he had with DeForest. "Leonard felt that Spock had already dealt with the rejection issue in prior movies," my father said. "He felt that Sybok would get nowhere by showing him a pain he had already resolved. In order to deal with this objection, we decided to add another sequence to the mind meld after Spock witnesses his birth. In this mind meld, Sybok and Spock both appear as young boys, and we discover that Spock begged to accompany Sybok when his brother was banished. Spock's secret pain was that he stayed on Vulcan to pursue 'the Vulcan way,' instead of going with his brother. This satisfied Leonard's objection."

Although they had now settled on a concept for the sequence, capturing it on film proved more difficult than anticipated. For the birth scene, they were using two small twins under nine months of age. Since union rules impose a strict schedule for all children, the production was extremely limited in the amount of time they could get the babies in front of the camera (problems of this sort are why movies and television shows always use twins, so they can increase the amount of camera time they have with the children). For nine months and under, the maximum amount of time in front of a camera was about twenty minutes. The crew had to struggle to fit the shot into the required time frame so that no union rules would be violated. Although it was difficult to get the placement of the baby correct so that its shadow would appear on the wall, they finally succeeded just as time was running out. Once again, it seemed no task was impossible for the crew of *Star Trek V.*

The remainder of the observation room scenes were captured with a minimum of difficulty. The one problem occurred with the starfield, which was being rear-projected onto a huge screen outside the bay windows of the set. Since they were using low light levels to make the scenes more dramatic, the camera's lens was opened very wide to allow the maximum amount of light inside. Unfortunately, the wider the lens aperture, the less depth-of-field could be achieved. This meant that the stars would appear out of focus on film, a problem which Andy had previously warned would inevitably occur.

"There was really nothing we could do about it," my father said. "Short depth-of-field is just a fact of life when using this kind of light and background. We thought it would really be obvious, but when we saw the film in dailies, we realized it looked romantic to have slightly blurry stars. Of course, we were very relieved to see that the problem hadn't really affected the quality of the film."

As they neared completion on all the observation room shots, the crew had succeeded in pushing the production ahead of schedule. Everyone's spirits were high, and the clothespin game reappeared in full force. This time crew members grew more ambitious, and began pinning large metal clips to each other. While the battle raged on, it was discovered Larry Luckenbill was about to have a birthday. The crew then got him a birthday cake, complete with Trona Peak decorations on

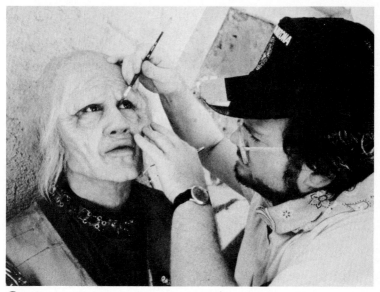

Special effects makeup artist Kenny Myers transforms a human into a Nimbosian.

My father directs the landing of the shuttlecraft on the God planet.

The Cat Lady dances as Caithlin Dar makes her way through the bar.

My father guides Walter Koenig and Larry Luckinbill through their mind meld.

Father and daughter share a funny moment when my sister, Melanie, played the young yeoman.

"The Wires of Torture"

Scotty is determined to outdo the Klingons once again.

My father faces his enemies, the Klingons, as he directs Todd Bryant and Spice Williams.

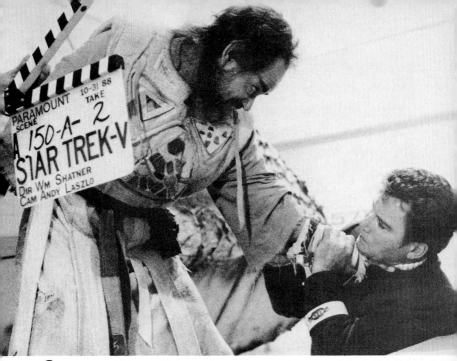

Sybok overpowers Kirk as the scene begins.

Uhura tries to tell Scotty of her hidden feelings.

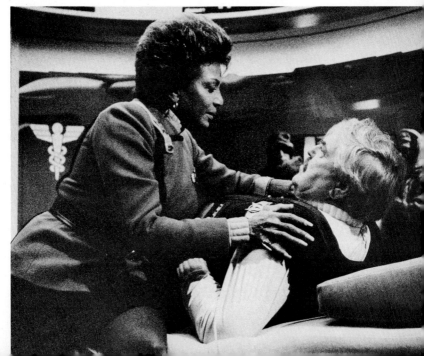

Production designer Herman Zimmerman and art director/
costume designer Nilo Rodis on the God planet stage.

Cinematographer Andy Laszlo toasts his director at the end
of principal photography.

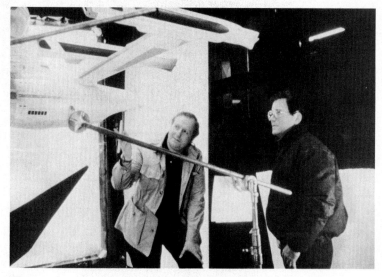

Bran Ferren explains the magic of motion control photography.

Captain James T. Kirk leads the *Enterprise* crew on its newest mission.

A journey of wonder toward the God planet.

Old friends team up once again.

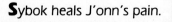

Sybok heals J'onn's pain.

it, and sang "happy birthday" to him right on the set. It was a lovely way to finish one of the more interesting and dramatic phases of production.

The growing ease and confidence with which the entire crew functioned had also carried over to my father. Gone were the anxious moments where he wondered if he would indeed have time to complete each day's work. Gone were his energized attempts to hustle the crew along, or oversee each aspect of production. It seemed as though his own growth had coincided with the movie's progress.

"I was learning a great deal without realizing it," he later told me. "Each day that went by provided me with a new perspective on what I was doing. And thanks to an incredibly talented group of people, I was able to use that knowledge practically." In fact, he had learned so quickly that Mel and Ralph told him if he continued at the present pace, they would not have all the sets ready for him on time!

My father carried his growing sense of confidence onto the next stage the team would be filming . . . the God planet set. Although they had captured many of the needed shots on location, it was necessary to complete the God sequence on stage since it called for a rock cathedral to form as God appears. Constructing such a cathedral on location would be next to impossible, so the team relied on Herman and his ingenuity to construct a simulated one on stage. Herman and his crew were forced to work at a Herculean pace to strike the landing bay set and erect this cathedral on time.

This unusual setting would be the site of much activity over the next few days. Not only did they have to film the actors talking to God, but the crew also had to film the fight between evil Sybok and good Sybok, as well as the explosion of the cathedral itself. In addition, since they had failed to capture the Rockman sequences at Trona, they now had to refilm Kirk's climb up the mountain and his subsequent confrontation with the yet-to-be-defined Rock Blob.

Initially, the God planet set had caused my father great anxiety, since they had planned for the special effects to be filmed live, using the rear and front screen projection processes. However, some weeks before filming on the set was scheduled to begin, Bran informed him that using the optical process in post-production to achieve the desired effects would be more efficient. Although this relieved my father's worries about using rear and front screen projection, it introduced a whole new set of problems.

For one thing, they would no longer be able to see (and react to) the effect as they were filming. They would also have to wait several months before finding out exactly what the effect would look like. And there was no guarantee the effect would turn out the way they wanted.

There was another important element they now had to contend with as well. Since most of the shots involved close-ups of the actors' faces as they looked into the "God column," it was crucial to estimate the correct light level the special effect would produce on their faces. This "reactive lighting," as it is called, must match the intensity of the effect itself, otherwise the actors' close-ups would not appear realistic when compared to the effect itself. In addition, since the column would later be "painted" next to the actors, incorrect reactive lighting would also result in a mismatch of the shots involving the column and the actors standing next to it.

Because of these problems, they spent much time figuring out a way to get the light levels at the correct intensity. Finally, they decided to use a special lighting machine that Bran had suggested might solve the dilemma. The crew set this round, odd-looking mechanism in the middle of the cathedral, in the same place where the special effect would later be added. They then placed a television set on top of the machine which, during the actors' performances, would run the film of George Murdock playing God. My father hoped to make the actors' job easier by giving them this film as a reference point for their dialogue. The strange setup reminded me of some futuristic version of God, something which MTV or Andy Warhol might have thought appropriate.

Once they solved the reactive lighting problems, the team quickly shot the needed close-ups. Although it was uncomfortable for the actors to stare at such a bright light, this sequence did not involve some of the more elaborate technical requirements that later ones, such as the explosion of the cathedral, did. However, it did contain its own set of difficulties.

One of the more complicated elements of this scene occurred when Kirk is hit by a bolt of lightning and is thrown backwards to the ground. Of course, the production could not risk using my father for the stunt, since he could not afford an injury. For that reason, Donny Pulford was elected to do it. He was hooked to a cable which was then jerked backwards at the correct moment, which in turn yanked him back as well. Although he landed hard on the ground, he was on his feet a few moments later, receiving applause from an appreciative crew.

The next sequence of shots involved the fight between the two Syboks. In order for the fight to appear realistic, my father had very carefully choreographed all the movements of Larry and his double. His goal was to obscure the double's face as much as possible, to give the appearance that Sybok was fighting himself. This meant using fighting positions that hid the front portion of the double's face. The actors were forced to twirl around and around many times as the camera recorded their fight.

Because an optical of the column would have to be added into the shot later, a special Vista Vision camera was used to film the sequence. This camera, which uses film with eight perforations instead of the usual four, allows a larger than normal negative to be developed. This larger negative makes it easier for the optical to be "painted" on the film at a later date. However, this camera is much larger and more cumbersome than an ordinary camera, uses up film faster, and takes longer to reload. It became especially frustrating to my father as the cameramen had to continually load the Vista Vision cameras every time they ran out of film. When the sequence was finally finished, we reviewed the results in a special Vista Vision screening room, which was really nothing more than a cold, ancient room hidden in one of the buildings. To my father's dismay, it was discovered there were scratches on this Vista Vision film. The team was afraid they would have to reshoot the entire sequence, when they noticed that the effect of these scratches was to blur the edges of the two figures together. It appeared as though they had created the effect on purpose! Everyone breathed an amused sigh of relief, and they decided to use the original footage and save themselves the expense of reshooting.

After the Vista Vision crisis was solved, they moved on to the most complicated God planet sequence, the collapse of the cathedral. In order for the sequence to proceed correctly, several different elements had to be coordinated. Herman had precut and rigged the bottom of two peaks so that they would fall on cue. Mike Woods and his crew were responsible for shooting off the smoke when the rocks of the cathedral crashed to the ground. And Bran and his group were once more in charge of the reactive lighting. They placed their lighting machine in the center of the cathedral so that lightning would appear to flash as the cathedral collapsed.

As the various groups prepared for the shot, the air of tension on the set was palpable. A single mistake meant the entire set would have to be re-rigged at tremendous time and cost. When the signal was given, everyone went into action. The boulders fell on cue, the smoke hissed perfectly, and the reactive lighting went off without a hitch. The crew burst into applause. They had all gotten it on the first try.

They repeated the process for the explosion which occurs as Kirk, Spock, and McCoy watch from behind a boulder. This time, Mike Woods had rigged the set so that a huge fireball would burst from the ground. When he received his cue, he triggered the explosions and we heard a loud "boom." A huge, billowing cloud of flame flew from the ground into the rafters of the stage. It was a rather frightening moment because we realized the power of the explosion and its ability to cause damage. However, every precaution had been taken to ensure the safety of the cast and crew, and no injuries occurred. Once again, the crew burst into applause. The production was powering full steam ahead.

The next shots seemed tame by comparison. While on location, the crew had been unable to obtain all the required footage for the Trona sequence. Since going back was impossible, they now had to simulate Trona Peaks on the Paramount lot.

In order to match the peaks at Trona, Herman had constructed miniature versions of the mountains which he placed next to each other in descending order of size. Andy then matched the lighting to the night shots at Trona, and Mike Woods obscured the area with smoke. When seen through the camera lens, it was impossible to differentiate between this simulated Trona mountain range and the real Trona Peaks. The crew was then able to film all the shots they had been unable to obtain while on location.

This included a shot of the mountain where the Rockman had formerly stood. Bran would later add an optical of the Rock Blob so that the creature would appear next to Kirk as Kirk is struggling up the mountain. Although they had not finalized any ideas for the Rock Blob, my father, Harve, Nilo, and Bran felt the creature should look somewhat amorphous in shape. They began to play with the idea of a throbbing energy mass which takes cobra-like form as it rears up to confront Kirk. My father was very excited by this idea.

Erecting this simulated mountain peak also enabled the crew to film the shots involving the Klingon Bird of Prey's rescue of Kirk. Since bringing a huge battleship onto the set would be impossible, the ship's appearance next to Kirk was done by a special process known as "blue screen." This involved transporting a huge, blue screen onto the stage and placing it behind the simulated mountain peak. The shot of Kirk turning around to face the Bird of Prey was then filmed using this blue background, which would later be replaced by the actual shot of the Bird of Prey, so that the battleship would appear to be hovering over Kirk. Although the finished sequence would be spectacular, filming the blue screen shot was actually fairly mundane work.

This relative lull in the schedule allowed the crew to indulge in one of their favorite pastimes—perfecting the clothespin game. By this time, some of the more ambitious members were tying carrots to metal clips, and then pinning these clips to their unfortunate comrades. One particularly adept player managed to clip one of the woman crew members, who then spent several minutes walking around the set with a carrot dangling down her back.

Another entertaining moment was provided by Jeff Dawn, who had already achieved fame in Ridgecrest by jumping into a jacuzzi while still wearing his cowboy boots. Since Danny Bronson had been constantly hiding his make-up case, Jeff decided to get revenge and play a practical joke on his friend. He took a tire off Danny's car and hauled it up to the rafters of the set. It took Danny awhile, but he finally found his missing tire, still dangling from the God planet ceiling. The incident reminded me of the story my father told me about Leonard's bicycle. It seemed like some things never changed!

Yet another amusing episode occurred after Larry Luckinbill had complained that the trailers for the principal actors all looked so similar he couldn't tell them apart. The next day, one of the second assistant directors brought in several huge banners and pinned them all over Larry's trailer. When Larry arrived, he was greeted by signs such as "Larry Luckinbill," "He Lives," and "The Journey Ends Here." It was moments like that which relieved the boredom that inevitably crept into the day.

Once the God planet sequences were finished, the crew had completed the majority of their work. The next several days were spent grabbing "odds and ends" which were in themselves quite important. One of these scenes was where Scotty wakes up in sick bay and hastily escapes from Uhura's embrace. It was a fun scene to watch and was completed with a minimum of difficulty. Another interesting scene was the escape through the ship's bowels, where Scotty directs Kirk, Spock, and McCoy to the turbo shaft. Because of the piping on the floor, the shot was actually more difficult to obtain than appeared. Since the camera would be in front of the actors as they stepped over these pipes, each pipe was designed to open and then immediately close again as the camera truck rolled by. In this manner, it would appear no camera had been following the actors as they walked forward. However, timing

these openings and closings proved more difficult than anticipated, and many takes went by before they could get the pipes
closed without the camera picking up their movement.

One of the major triumphs that took place during this period
was obtaining the flying footage in the turbo shaft. "When I
first envisioned the turbo shaft scene, I thought it might be
impossible to get the material," my father said. "I knew it
would be incredibly difficult not only to build such a set, but
to rig it properly and safely so we could get the flying effect to
look realistic. In the back of my mind, I was always ready to
cut this sequence from the movie if I had to. Ironically, it
proved one of the easier moments to get. Herman had designed
an incredible set, and Mike Woods did an amazing job rigging
it with the flying apparatus. Glenn Wilder spent a few days
with his stuntmen flying up and down the shaft, so that when
we got there he had already ironed out all the kinks. I couldn't
believe how smoothly it went, and it was all because the team
had time to work on the set before we actually filmed on it."

Although the sequence proved easier to get than he had
anticipated, there were still some difficulties involved. The
apparatus was constructed in a similar fashion to the Yosemite
flying equipment, only in this case, the actors were attached
to the rig from their backs instead of their abdomens. The rig
was then attached to the space between the wall panels, and
was run up and down the length of the shaft. Greg Barnett
dubbed the entire apparatus "The House of Pain," since the
fiberglass trunk molds which supported the actors' weight
contained no padding of any kind. He and the other stuntmen
endured five days of discomfort while Glenn picked up extra
footage for the production's use. When my father, Leonard,
and DeForest arrived to film their close-ups, they suffered
through the ordeal like true professionals, although my father
winced with pain as he was finally lowered to the ground.

While this difficult sequence was being filmed, David Loughery commented on the similarity between the turbo shaft and
a certain fairground game. The set reminded him of the traditional lumberjack's contest where the object is to sledgehammer a disk as high up a scale as possible. My father thought

this idea was so funny that he instructed Kurt Hulett to make a huge plastic sledgehammer. One day in between takes, he filmed various crew members taking a crack at an imaginary scale. This film was later intercut with some of the turbo shaft flying footage, so it appeared that each crew member was sending the actors flying upwards as the scale was hit. This footage, as well as other funny material collected throughout the production, was later shown on a blooper reel at the wrap party.

As filming on the turbo shaft sequence drew to a close, my father and Leonard had finally perfected their flying technique, an ability which proved useful during the next phase of shooting; an outdoor set, where they would complete the flying sequence of Spock rescuing Kirk from his fall of El Capitan. Originally, my father had planned the sequence so that Spock would lead Kirk on an elaborate trip through the forest while Kirk was still hanging upside down. However, budgetary constraints altered his vision.

"When I first envisioned this scene, I thought of Spock flying through the air, holding Kirk by the foot," my father explained. "We were going to build two huge towers at Yosemite, and string a cable between them from which Leonard and I would be suspended. I was going to include a fun shot from Kirk's point of view, where the camera would be filming upside down as they flew along. Then a log would suddenly appear in front of them, and the camera would jump over it as Spock pulls Kirk over the log. But when we saw all those wire tests, we realized it would be very difficult to hide the apparatus well enough to make the sequence look realistic. Also, we began to get the figures back for how much building the towers would cost us. It turned out to be way too expensive, so we dropped the idea."

The team was then forced to come up with an alternative plan. "We decided to do a much simpler version of the whole thing here at Paramount," he told me. "Since our wire tests had proved frustrating, we hired the man who did all the rigging for *The Boy Who Could Fly*. He suggested tipping the entire set sideways, so the wires would be horizontal instead of vertical. This would make it much more difficult to spot them. Herman and his crew then built a set where the trees and boulders were attached to a platform, and this platform was tilted on its side. Mike Woods' team then attached cables across the set from which Leonard and I would be suspended. So we found ourselves flying again only a short time after the turbo shaft sequence had been completed."

It proved an uncomfortable undertaking. Donny Pulford and Greg Barnett again spent much time ironing out any possible kinks in the equipment. This time they dubbed the set "The Wires of Torture," since they were suspended by tight, inflexible harnesses for many hours. When my father finally climbed into the apparatus and was hung from the cables, he commented, "I feel like a slab of beef." He and Leonard spent the next several hours swinging back and forth across the cables. When it was all over, Leonard asked my father, "Aren't you going to tell me how brave I was?" My father responded with a laugh, "No one's talking about it—it's a well-kept secret." They both then limped off to their respective trailers where they enjoyed a harness-free lunch.

But their flying days were not over yet. After they finished with the outdoor set, they went inside to complete some "blue screen" shots of the flying sequence. While my father and Leonard were again suspended upside down, a blue screen was placed behind them. This screen would later be replaced by footage of the mountain speeding by the camera. When the two images were combined, my father and Leonard would appear to be falling next to the mountain. By using this technique, the team could obtain close-up shots of both actors without putting them in any danger. All they had to do was endure the discomfort of being in the harness and hanging upside down for several minutes at a time.

As with the Bird of Prey blue screen shot, the process was very slow and tedious. Because there was a lot of sitting around on the set, the crew was able to complete their crowning achievement in the history of the clothespin game. Once Leonard was back on the ground, they attached a metal clip to his back which had fifteen balloons tied to it.

Leonard realized what was happening and decided to give my father a laugh. Standing poker-faced, in front of him, he said, "I'm ready for the next shot." My father took one look at Leonard and the fifteen balloons floating behind him and burst into hysterical laughter. It took a few minutes before everyone calmed down enough to finish the shot.

Once the flying sequence had been completed, only one sequence remained to be filmed—the campfire scene. The team decided that this particular scene would be filmed right on the Paramount lot. Herman then performed his usual magic, constructing a forest setting on the same stage where the God planet had existed just a short time ago. The set looked almost like a real forest, with one exception. None of the trees had tops on them. "We couldn't get the trees finished on time," my father explained. "So I knew I would be forced to film the shot tighter than I would have liked. Still, I was very pleased with the way the whole thing came out. I knew it would be a great way to end the production."

The scene emphasized many of the themes which have made *Star Trek* so endearing to the public. "This sequence sets up many of the important ideas in the movie, family and death, for example," he commented. "It also has a great deal of humor, which sets the tone between the three of us. One of the bigger challenges of this scene for me is that it's five minutes long, which is very lengthy in movie terms. I'm trying to use a lot of different angles to give it some punch, but with just three different people sitting around a campfire, it's hard."

My father felt a sense of completion before he had even begun filming the scene. "I had the strangest feeling today," he told me. "So far in this movie, every time there's been a new setup I've studied my script, and spent a lot of time thinking about how I want to approach the scene. But today, I realized this is the last scene. I don't have anything to think about. I have the feeling the movie is over. I've rehearsed with the actors, I know the setup. I've done all my work. This is really the end of it—the culmination of all those months of planning, all the time spent in preproduction, the frenetic attempts to complete filming on schedule and on time, the struggle to see my vision become a reality. This is the moment where it all stops.''

In spite of any sadness this realization may have brought him, actually filming the sequence was a very happy experience. Since it was near Christmastime, holiday cheer abounded on the set. One of the grips even appeared one morning wearing a Santa suit, sporting a red cap complete with antlers. The actors spent more time laughing and joking than actually working. Leonard even hummed tunes like "Home on the Range" in between takes. When it came time for him to play the lute, there were many cracks about his atonal approach to the instrument.

"I know you played this thing on the series," my father joked. "But I think you're out of practice." They laughed even harder at DeForest's attempts to sing "Row Your Boat." He never joined in at the right moment.

"I've heard of tone deaf before," my father said, "but tone deaf and arrhythmic, too?" It seemed appropriate the three of them should end the production with such good feelings between them.

When filming on the sequence was over, they broke out the champagne and an elaborate cake. While everyone toasted to the success of the movie, Andy presented my father with the slate that had been used throughout production.

Although it was a bittersweet moment, it was comforting to know all their efforts would soon produce tangible results. Within a few short months, the movie would be appearing on theater screens across the country. Soon everyone who saw the movie would know what energy, dedication, and determination had gone into making the newest chapter of the *Star Trek* saga become a reality.

A few days later, the cast and crew celebrated together one last time at a beautiful wrap party. At a lovely restaurant in the San Fernando Valley, they were able to celebrate their efforts and say goodbye to their friends all at the same time. They ate from an elaborate buffet, and danced the night away on the large dance floor. When the blooper reel was played on large television monitors on either side of the room, everyone laughed heartily at the moments which had made *Star Trek V* unique. It was a lovely way to show appreciation to the people who had worked so hard on the film.

Although he celebrated along with everyone else, my father still had a lot on his mind. As he twirled my lovely stepmother across the dance floor, I knew he was thinking about the new tasks which would confront him in the weeks to come. Principal photography may have been completed, but there was still a great deal of work to be done before the picture would be ready for the viewing public. My father and several core members of the team still had to edit the film and add sound effects, music, and all the special effects to the film. In fact, almost as much work lay in front of him as he had just completed.

For my father, the adventure was not yet over.

6

INTERVIEWS

While the end of principal photography merely marked the close of one phase of my father's work on *Star Trek V,* for all the other actors it was the end of their involvement with the film. Before they scattered across the country, however, I had a chance to talk to each cast member, to ask how *Star Trek* had affected their past and how it is shaping their present lives. Since my own life has been so dramatically influenced by *Star Trek,* I wanted to know if they, too, felt *Star Trek*'s power as much as I had.

I began with Leonard Nimoy. Throughout the years, I have always wondered how he approached playing Spock, and whether he ever felt frustrated by the public's overwhelming identification of him with the Vulcan character.

Q: *Your career is now going through a change. At the same time, Spock, who had died, has been brought back to life, reeducated and is now coming into his own again. Do those things relate to how you are now performing as Spock?*

A: I think they do. Even if you don't make a conscious decision to let them, I don't think you can help but find— particularly when you've been living with a character that's traveled along with you side-by-side for twenty-two years— that they do. When I came in to have meetings with Bill and Harve Bennett and David Loughery on this script, my feeling was that Spock, having gone through that process which included dying and coming back, and as you put it, "reeducated," had come back better than ever. And something about me feels comfortable with that right now. There are a lot of personal things that have happened to me, work things that have happened to me, that have given me a new perspective on myself. And I think there is a definite relationship between that and what has happened to Spock.

Q: *How different is your image of Spock today than twenty-two years ago?*

A: In the sixties he was a little bit more brittle than he is now. He was more a character in search of himself at that time than the integrated character he has become. I think that has to do with two things: One, the series of stories we've put him through, and two, what's happened in my life, my personal life. I think he's a little smoother around the edges now.

Q: *Do you like him better now?*

A: I've always enjoyed playing the character. I've always enjoyed the opportunities this character has given me to study mankind in an interesting kind of way; to stay outside, to pretend as if the character is outside the mainstream of the emotional experience, though he really is in touch with it and understands it all. Now I'm enjoying him in a different way.

Q: *Spock seems more in touch with his sense of humor. Is that you or is it the script?*

A: I think that in this particular script there was a very definite effort, and I think quite a successful one, to find that humor. It also happens that I'm more receptive to it than I may have been earlier—looking for it, enjoying that, wanting to be in touch with that. Whereas, when I first started playing Spock, I was much more interested in the severity of the character, the containment of the character, the sensibilities of the character. We've done all that, or a lot of that. Now I'm more open to the idea of a Spock who has that little bit of a twinkle.

Q: *As Spock has now come into his own, will you play him with his feelings a bit more up front?*

A: I think it's still fun to let a little out and reign it back in again. I enjoy doing that and I think the audience will enjoy that. We are playing Spock for an audience, we mustn't forget that. I don't think the audience wants to see that get entirely lost, because that's a fun part of watching the character.

Q: The Voyage Home *was a comedy. That mood has partially carried over to this film. Partially your input?*

A: Yes. When we started working on *The Voyage Home* we—Harve Bennett and myself—were asked to come up with a concept for the movie. We immediately agreed on two things: that we wanted to lighten up and we wanted to go back in time, to do a time travel story. We had played three very severe stories. In the first *Star Trek* motion picture, humor was completely forbidden. There was some in the second. It was jaunty. It was Nick Meyer who was jaunty. There was less in the third because I was very much concerned, very much interested in the passion of these characters for saving their friend. I felt that I wanted to focus on that intensity rather than the humor, though there was a moment of laughter here and there. Having done that, I wanted to lighten up. I thought, okay, done. Spock's alive. Let's have some fun. We worked very hard to put it in there. I really enjoyed working very hard to put it in there. I really enjoyed working the humor in that picture.

Q: *Where did the idea of the whales come from in* IV?

A: It was a long process. We knew we wanted to come back to the twentieth century, so we asked "Why are we coming back? Is it an accident or is it a time warp? Are we looking for a person?" I read a book called *Biophelia* by a Harvard biologist. He wrote that by the end of the twentieth century, we'd be losing as much as 10,000 species per year off the planet. So I thought, "That's interesting. Suppose we didn't know what all those species are. So there's an awful lot of species we're losing. What does that mean to society?" That gave me "we're coming back to find something that's extinct." I thought whales would be great fun cinematically, as well as being a very current concern.

Q: *What's your biggest challenge in this particular film?*

A: There are a couple of interesting challenges. It is

Spock's brother who is kind of the motor that runs our operation, gets us going, gets us involved. The challenge in that is, on the one hand, I know that Sybok can be a very impassioned and therefore not a very predictable or necessarily reliable individual. On the other hand, he is my brother. I've got to give him some room, some leash to run on, and maybe even support him or help him in some way while trying not to be disloyal to the captain or to earth or the crew. So I guess it's a question of balancing loyalties and friendships against my compassion for this man who asks for our help. It's a delicate dilemma.

Q: *What's the most refreshing thing in this film?*

A: The physicality of it. I think this is the most physical of the movies we've done and I think that reflects Bill's energy, Bill's sense of what is fun for him, which he always enjoyed doing during the series, and which the movies have more or less gotten away from. I'm just talking sheer physical running and jumping. We haven't done much of that so that's fresh.

Q: *How do you feel about the subject matter of this film?*

A: For me the subject matter has to do with the brother thing, the rest of it is what it is. I'm not on a search for Sha Ka Rhee or infinity or the final frontier. My brother is. He infects other people with that idea. I think that Spock remains curious but not really sold. Even Kirk begins to believe that maybe it can happen. I don't want to say that Spock is cynical, but he is preoccupied with what is happening to his brother. If Sha Ka Rhee is there, fine, it's there. If not, it isn't. Sybok for me is the focal point.

Q: *Spock re-experiencing his separation from Sybok?*

A: Even after re-experiencing their separation, Spock says, "I'm not the outcast, the lad you left behind so many years ago . . . I've worked that out." Let's deal with what's now, and what's now is this brother of mine who is obsessed with this idea, and I can't simply drop my loyalty here to carry on with him. If these people want to go, I'll go with them, and help them if possible. But I was essentially saying, if you force me to choose sides, I have to choose this side, because this is real to me.

Q: *So having chosen that side and lost his brother permanently . . . ?*

A: I think there's a great sense of loss. I wouldn't describe it as pain. I think the loss of Sybok—the pain of that loss is something Spock dealt with years ago, as part of that process that he's worked through. I think if Spock and Sybok had more to say to each other in that speech where Spock says, "You're my brother, but you do not know me," I think Spock would say much more like, "although you're my brother, I've gone through far more, and far more personal experiences, with these people. I've gone through more brotherly experiences with these people. I have spent more time with these people. I have been helped, given back my life by these people. Things that never happened between Sybok and Spock. Therefore, although in blood and name we have a relationship, the relationship with Kirk and the rest in a way is more real, more valid." And therefore when it's over, when this whole story is over, I think Spock has to feel he made the right decision.

Q: *Did you make those sorts of observations in the story meetings?*

A: I had one major concern, in that when Sybok does his magic with Spock, as he has done with all his other people and now McCoy, and they all chose to go with him, my concern was that, no, Spock can't do that . . . Sybok tries to play his magic on Spock using information that [he] has . . . [but] Sybok does not have all the necessary information, and that's why I said that Spock has to say, "Sybok, you haven't got it. You don't understand what you're dealing with here. You may be able to do what you do with people whose feelings are not resolved. But mine are resolved. I have died, come back, been reeducated, gone through that whole process." At the end of *Star Trek IV,* Spock is able to say to his father, with a twinkle in his eye, "Tell mother I feel fine." It's an inside joke that even the father doesn't get, so Spock has lost his fear of his father. He's grown up. He's a totally grown-up individual person. He's able to stand toe-to-toe with his father and when his father says, "Your associates are decent people, you've chosen well," and Spock says, "Well, these are my friends."

177

It's like "You don't get it, dad," in a nice way . . . carrying that into *Star Trek V*, I think that Spock has a kind of sadness that Sybok doesn't understand all of this, doesn't get it, thinks that he can still step into Spock's life and automatically pick up as the older brother, but it just doesn't work that way.

Q: *Do you come to work for this picture with a different feeling than the last two, where you were also directing?*

A: Absolutely. I don't think that I could sit here and have this conversation with you if I were directing this movie. When I direct, I'm very heavily involved all day long and thinking constantly about the work. When I'm acting, not quite so. But when I'm doing both it's just impossible. Particularly for me because the Spock character requires two hours of make-up. Average straight make-up might require a half hour. So I have to figure I'm putting in an hour and a half a day more than any other person and it's very draining, very demanding. I'm very glad that I did it, but I'm very glad that it's Bill doing this one.

Q: *Do you have any thoughts of becoming a triple threat, like Mel Brooks, say (writer-director-actor)?*

A: Not really. I had wanted to direct for a long time. This seemed to be an opportunity to do that, and particularly to start out with material I know about and understand. There's also a help in acting in the film as a character that I knew, particularly in *Star Trek III*, where I had not very much on-camera time. So there were only a few days that I had to work as an actor out of a fifty-day schedule. In *Star Trek IV*, it seemed to me I was on camera about half the shooting schedule, so I had some days off, but again, playing a character that you've played before and lived with for twenty years is a lot easier than starting out to make a film where you're playing an entirely new character and directing a movie. That's awful tough. People do it. Woody Allen has done it brilliantly. [So has] Clint Eastwood. I admire them. It's hard work.

Q: *Why did you become an actor?*

A: I got bitten by the bug real bad. At first, I was just drifting into it but then the bug hit me. I started acting in children's plays when I was eight, but that was just accidental. I was in a local settlement house where there was a theater and there were plays. When I went home they put me in plays. And I was okay at it. I could remember my lines and I got past the stage fright that everybody starts out with. I was dependable and could sing, carry a tune, so I was in children's musicals. But when I was a teenager I started getting into adult drama and I was quite taken with it. I became obsessed with the idea of being a part of theater life.

Q: *What was your first exciting role?*

A: It was a play written by Clifford Odets, *Golden Boy*. That was William Holden's first big star role—the movie of it. Also a play by Odets called *Awake and Sing,* a story about a family during the depression in the thirties. It hit very close to home for me. It was the first time I was ever involved with material that really had something to do with me and my life.

Q: *And you've never lost that desire, except it's expanded?*

A: I have a broader interest now. My interests were extremely narrow in the beginning. I just wanted to act, act, act, act. In the late fifties, early sixties, I started teaching acting and I became much more interested in directing as a possibility.

Q: *How do you teach acting?*

A: Well, there are certain techniques and crafts. The ability to create a real, private moment in front of an audience. To act as if there is no audience at all. To act as if you are somebody else. To create differences from one character to the next, so you can bring something to each.

Q: *Do you find people assume that you are like the character of Spock?*

A: People wonder. People can't help but wonder what a person's really like when he's playing [someone with] such a strange emotional life. They must wonder, "What is this person really like? How much of him is Spock, and how much is me?"

Q: *Do you call upon certain aspects of your own character to play Spock?*

A: I think that's what an actor does.

Q: *Have you found Spock has limited you in the past?*

A: I don't think so . . . there are bound to be people in our industry who see you in that. The same thing is true of a cinematographer or editors . . . [you] look for someone who's done the kind of film you're doing . . . it can be helpful because people can understand what you do and they can find it useful . . . it works both ways.

Q: *Do you think that directing offers you an opportunity to stretch your artistic abilities more than acting does?*

A: Yes . . . you're covering all the territory. You're working visually. You're working with the camera, you're working with the set design, you're working with casting, you're working with the writing of the script. You have a lot more input in the overall project than an actor does. An actor is only introduced at a specific point during the process, just like a wardrobe person makes a contribution, the editor makes a contribution, the cameraman makes a contribution, the writer makes a contribution. The director is working in all those territories.

Q: *Would you direct another* Star Trek?

A: I don't think so. I've done two. That's enough.

Q: *Do you want to direct or act in the future?*

A: I want to do both.

Q: *What kind of roles do you want, a scientist, or a bad guy, or . . . ?*

A: I want to play a seventeen-year-old kid [he laughs].

DeForest Kelley was next. Throughout the years, I have always felt "De" Kelley was one of the nicest, warmest people I have ever met. The caring and compassion he brings to the character of Dr. McCoy is ever-present in his own personality. I wondered how the success of playing Dr. McCoy had shaped his life over the years, and what his real feelings about *Star Trek* were. I had the opportunity to ask him these questions in between takes of the last campfire scene, on the "Yosemite" stage.

Q: *What did you think of the script for* Star Trek V?

A: I think that *V* is interesting in that it's entirely different from any of the others, which is refreshing. *Four* was a wonderful motion picture, and you think, what are you going to do after *IV?* My feeling about [films] is that you can never tell about them until they're strung together and scored and you look at it. Very seldom do you ever hear anyone come back from dailies and say that the dailies look terrible. You don't know until you see the final product. But in examining the script I thought that it had an awful lot of things going for it, and if it comes together the way we all hope it will, I think it's going to have a little bit of something for all the *Star Trek* fans, and hopefully that thirty-five percent of the audience that we picked up in *IV* will enjoy it. We have a great deal of the humor of *IV* once again, there's conflict, adventure, and some powerful drama.

Q: *We learn things about McCoy that we've never learned before. Did you agree with those things in the script?*

A: I was concerned . . . I had to give the whole thing a lot of consideration. My discussions with David Loughery and Harve Bennett—we came to some conclusions concerning McCoy's character in this picture. Some things that had been done we tried to shape in a way so that those who know and love McCoy would have a better understanding. It was a matter of straightening certain situations out with him. I think it's likely to become a very controversial role, and one that is going to be very agreeable to some people and very disagreeable to others. You can't please everyone.

Q: *Is McCoy different at the end of this movie?*

A: I don't think so . . . I think that the public will have a greater insight into these three characters and their relationships to each other and how they generally feel about each other, which I don't really think has been shown on screen before. It's always been the three of them going about their work in a very workmanlike manner . . . in this film they're going to get down to some more human basics.

Q: *Will McCoy and Spock get along better?*

A: I think so. I think that relationship will always be one of great irritability with McCoy at times. You sometimes get the feeling that in his smooth way, Spock is really trying to annoy McCoy. We each think we've got the other's number, so to speak. I don't think we'll ever truly get away from that, but I think that McCoy is looking at him with more of a feeling of "I've got your number too. You're not bothering me so much."

Q: *Can you summarize how do you feel about this movie?*

A: I think it has all the earmarks of a real entertaining movie. I really do. I have the highest hopes for it. Bill has worked awfully hard on it, and he's done a tremendous job. I don't know how he did it. It would kill me.

Q: *You don't have a desire to direct?*

A: None whatsoever.

Q: *Did you ever?*

A: No. I did a little bit during the series. I think we were all looking at it as a way to make some kind of move. But that never materialized; didn't materialize for Bill or Leonard. At that time neither one of them were ready to direct. I did have thoughts about it during that period, but it went right out the window. Then when I saw all the problems involved with Leonard directing, the long hours, the frustration, I just thought "I don't need that." [He laughs] There are a lot of things I don't need.

Q: *Are you happy with the way it all turned out?*

A: Oh sure.

Q: *Do you ever get sick of playing McCoy?*

A: Oh, sometimes, and then again I look at it and I think— I'm sure Bill does, too, and Leonard—"Gee, what a pain in the ass," you know. And then I look at it in another way and think how privileged we are to be part of this show and to be what and who we are together, and what comes with it, and the fact that *Star Trek,* unlike anything else, has a lot of class. A lot of class. It is so highly regarded in so many areas, all over the world, and you think, "What do you want out of this business? Do you want adulation?" Christ, how much can you have? You know, it gets to the point where you don't need any. What do you need? What do you want? Sure, we all would like to find something to just turn us over in the right kind of a role. But I'm even more or less getting away from that. I'm looking at it and thinking, "Christ, we have great opportunities to do a lot of things on this show."

Q: *Do you see it going in a new direction?*

A: I think it would be interesting to take a new direction . . . that would utilize us in an intelligent way, and remain cognizant always of the fact that we are getting older, but utilizing that age.

Q: *But haven't they done that?*

A: They have. You know, it started with my giving Bill a pair of glasses, and something, you know, is always being referred to. When McCoy on the ladder says to Jim, "I'll never make this," whatever it is. So those little things are put in there, because if we don't do that, the critics are going to pounce on us. When they can't find something to pick on in the story, they are going to start talking about pot bellies, wrinkles, and that sort of thing. We have to kind of fend for ourselves in these things, you know. I think it's working out wonderfully, really, for all of us. I mean, what more could anybody expect out of a show like that?

Q: *And your own career? Because I remember one day you were talking to me on the observation room set about you— after* Star Trek. *You weren't working as much, but you thought it was your fault because you hadn't pursued it.*

A: Yes. Bill and I and Leonard, as close as we are, we have a feeling. I know the three of us have a feeling we're related when we see each other. We don't see each other a great deal on a social basis. But you don't need that. When you do see each other, that feeling, that deep feeling, is there. But unlike Bill and Leonard, I've never had that kind of drive in my career. I know this is a hackneyed statement, but I am, I guess, a lazy actor. I have not pursued my career to the extent I could have.

Q: *Is there a reason for that?*

A: I don't know exactly what it is. I started my career on this lot, under contract as a young player. In the glory days. And I've done a lot of things in my life. I've done a lot of bad things, and I've done a lot of good things. If I had not done what I had done in the past, and just gone into *Star Trek*—if I had done several TV shows, and then gotten *Star Trek*—I would be most frustrated. But I have touched a little bit of

183

fame before this, and I've left it, and picked it up again. I don't know, I guess inside of me I keep saying, "What do you really want?"

Q: *Have you come up with any answers?*

A: Peace. [He laughs]

Q: *I think you've got that. I think going down in history as Dr. McCoy isn't such a bad thing.*

A: Well, I don't know. None of us is six feet under yet. You never know what's going to happen to any of us. [He laughs again]

One of the things I remember best about growing up around the *Star Trek* crew is Nichelle Nicholls' bright smile. Even if she was sick, or tired, she would always flash that smile when I saw her. She has always struck me as a bright, enthusiastic woman, someone with tremendous energy and drive. In between takes on the shuttle landing bay set, we sat on the shuttlecraft's pontoon and talked about how *Star Trek* had affected her life and how she has utilized that energy and drive to shape her career.

Q: *What is your opinion of the* Star Trek V *story?*

A: I think this is the perfect story to follow *IV,* with its humor and fun and the wonderful idea of saving the whales. Now we come to something dynamic and dramatic and exciting, and they very wisely kept some of the humor. We're on a very dangerous mission and it's no nonsense and high adventure again. But wisely they let some of the humor from *IV* overlap, so *IV* doesn't stand out like a sore thumb. Somebody made the comment we're back to business as usual. But we have some sense of humor and much more interplay of the characters, which is really nice, more so even than in *IV.* So it's really moving toward what *Star Trek* is all about. What we, the fans, have been waiting for. I'm very excited, not only about *V,* but about the prospects of the adventure continuing. Because if they can do this after *IV,* something as exciting as this, then they can continue this. It's just a matter of good writers and good story lines.

Q: *What did you first think of "Star Trek" when you originally got the part?*

A: Oh, I thought it was great. When I first did the TV series, I thought everything was coming up roses. I thought I'd do this and then go on and do a million other things. Maybe if we were lucky it would last five years or three years. Then I'd go and do other things, and somebody, someday would say, "Remember that show you used to do? We really liked that."

Q: *And?*

A: [She laughs] And the show just refused to die.

Q: *Is that something that troubled you?*

A: Well, there's such a thing called typecasting. I never used to believe that, but of course it's true. I never realized it because I have a lot of other talents, my singing, my writing, and other things I do. I became involved with NASA, and I had my own business, a consulting firm to aerospace education . . . I was so busy that I didn't realize I wasn't acting, you know. And that was setting a precedent. I was being typecast in the meantime. So I wasn't sitting around waiting for work. I was absolutely inundated with work and luckily I've always been very busy. But suddenly, you discover—and I enjoy and enjoyed at the time—the fans. I thought it was wonderful. What an exciting, lovely thing to have people who cared so much about it, they didn't want it to die. I still thought rather lightly about it. It was nice to get together once in a while, but then [that typecasting] became reality.

Q: *Is this a source of frustration on some level?*

A: Actually not; not the fandom and not the fact that the show has remained exciting. But the opposite of Hollywood—"The Industry" that sees you in one light—is not acknowledging your talents that got you to that point to begin with. And that can be frustrating.

Q: *If you could have ideally sketched it out, how would it be different?*

A: I probably would have done everything I did. There also was a point in time, right after "Star Trek," when a lot of black exploitation films were being done . . . and I got, to be quite fair to the industry, an awful lot of offers. Scripts sent to me to star in. And I did one . . . I played the role of a Madame . . . I put on twenty-five pounds to play the role. She was supposed to be a great, big gal, but I convinced them, and I was a size six . . . to come back down. [She laughs] It turned out very well for me, but then I was getting only those kind of roles, so I decided to wait. So I went back into musical comedy. I went back into singing, back into dancing . . . and I didn't attend to my film acting [or] television career . . . I thought, "It'll always be there." But you can't do that. And by that time, "Star Trek" was quickly becoming a legend. Then finally, of course, we started doing the films, and the die was cast. We were forever the "Star Trek" crew. No matter what we do, we'll always be Kirk, Spock, Uhura, Scotty, Chekov. And that's that. I take it as a great compliment. We created characters that simply will not die, whether we like it or not. [She laughs] And so the happy part is now doing the films.

Q: *Do you feel cheated somehow in your career?*

A: No, because life doesn't ever happen the way you think it will. You have to be ready for whatever it throws at you. If you sit and let yourself be daunted by what didn't happen, or what could happen or should have happened, you'll be a miserable, dried-up old prune somewhere, bitter and angry.

Q: *What else would you like to do, direct, produce . . . ?*

A: I have directed in theater, but I'm not qualified to direct in film because I haven't studied it . . . it's a specialty and a craft just like anything else. It's not a matter of just saying, "Oh, it's my turn to direct a *Star Trek* film." You have to know what you're doing. It takes a special talent. I think Leonard has done a brilliant job, and working with Bill has been a pleasure . . . when Leonard first was directing, I thought, "Oh, no. Now my co-star becomes God," you know, because the director becomes God. But it was fantastic. He was a delight, came in prepared and talented. All my fears vanished with him. I always knew Bill would have directorial talent because . . . [She laughs hard] he's always been directing us! But the funny thing about that is, so many times his ideas have been very good . . . In the series, if we had an insecure director, it scared the hell out of them. Good directors you could always help because they were very secure. They would not only discuss with him, but many times with most of us pertaining to our roles. But Bill had an edge on a lot of directors in that he's an actor. He knows the actor's plight, he knows our needs.

Q: *What would you say that plight is?*

A: The plight for the actor is you want to do your best. You're developing a character, you're putting your best foot forward, you hope to hell you're right. Many times you've got [your character] figured out and along comes another actor who's coming at it from a completely different point of view, and you go "Ooops." Or a director doesn't like your interpretation, so you say, "Ooops." There are so many frustrations. Everything that can go wrong does go wrong. An actor earns every penny he makes and then some.

Q: *Do you feel like you've been undercompensated for all these years?*

A: Yes, yes, yes. Yes. I would be lying if I didn't say so.

Q: *What made you want to become an actress?*

A: I was born.

Q: *But you were a dancer first?*

A: No, I was in theater. My first love was ballet, but I wanted to do it all. I came out of musical comedy primarily, as opposed to drama.

Q: *Is that how you see your future going? Do you want to create on your own?*

A: Exactly. I'm recording, I produce, I've written a couple of things, an operetta . . . So you just keep your creativity going. You have to. And if the industry doesn't do it for you, you have to do it yourself.

Q: *Do you feel like being black hurt you?*

A: No. I think at the point in time that Gene Roddenberry did "Star Trek," certainly I wasn't up for as many roles as white actresses were up for. But also, Gene cast me. He specifically meant to cast a female and a black. So I'm just glad I was better than the rest of the gals who went up for it and got it.

Q: *What about now?*

A: Now, when I got that part, I was the first black actress to play a major role in a series. It opened up a lot of doors for black actresses afterwards. Like Diahann Carroll doing "Julia," which was a part they originally talked to me about doing. But I couldn't do it because I couldn't get out of "Star Trek" . . . and I still can't! [She laughs]

Although I have never spent much time with Walter Koenig, I know him to be a man of varied talents. He has just written a science fiction novel of his own, called *Buck Alice and the Actor Robot,* and is starring in the motion picture *Moontrap.* In between takes on the *Enterprise* bridge, I asked him how he felt about the latest Star Trek adventure.

Q: *Do you think there is anything unique about* Star Trek V *in relation to the other* Star Trek *stories?*

A: Unique only in terms of degree. In magnitude . . . the story lends itself to some extraordinarily creative visuals . . . in terms of the story, *Star Trek* story, it deals with the three main protagonists, Kirk, Spock, and McCoy . . . even more specifically on them than in any of the other scripts. The story is really about those three characters. So in that regard, I think it is different. But then again, it's purely in terms of the intensity of the situation. I think there are some wonderful action sequences, planet sequences where there are battles, again, on a magnitude that we haven't seen before.

Q: *Do you think* Star Trek *says anything new?*

A: I think rather than breaking new ground, it has exploited and maintained ground we know is proven.

Q: *What about with the characters?*

A: The character of Spock, the towering intellect, the character of McCoy, the irascible charm, the character of Kirk, the charismatic, flamboyant, theatrical image. I think all three of those characters are very well defined, perhaps as well as any other time in the other *Star Trek* films.

Q: *Do you think people will like that?*

A: I think aficionados of those principal characters will be gratified, because not only do we intensify their relationships, we get some history of the characters that has not been offered before. I think that will help ensure an even greater sense of identification with the characters. We learn more about them, particularly Spock and McCoy.

Q: *What do you think the title says?*

A: Actually, *The Final Frontier* seems to suggest—and innumerable fans can attest to this—that this is the last picture . . . I'm constantly being asked "Is this the last of the *Star Trek* films?" And that may work well for us, psychologically. First of all, it is a controversial title because of that. There's a lot of talk, a lot of discussion as to whether or not that's the case. And I think there's a certain amount of relief when we say, "No, it doesn't have that meaning. It means something quite different. It means a place where we go rather than a place where *Star Trek* is going."

Q: *What do you think this film is saying?*

A: That ultimately you have to take responsibility for your life and for what occurs. I think that probably that's what this picture is about . . . My feeling is that the principal statement of the movie is: You can't rely on the supernatural and you can't rely on forces beyond your control to shape your own life. You have to take it into your own hands. That isn't to say you can't have faith, religious faith, etc. But not to throw off responsibility and let some other entity assume it for you. I think this story—and I try to couch it in the most positive way—has to do with the three main characters. The supporting group is really ancillary to the story. . . . If it's a story of family, it's a story about the family of the three top guys. Maybe that's supposed to be a microcosm of the greater family. Maybe it's supposed to represent a larger type family, the entire seven crew members that the audience has gotten to know, the entire *Enterprise,* the universal family. Maybe that's part of the design in the screenplay. If indeed that is the case, it's focused on the three main people, though.

Q: *Do you think the humor is intensified in this movie?*

A: No, I don't think it's intensified . . . I think you'd be very hard pressed to find a moment that is more charming, more fun, and more spontaneous than the bit in *Star Trek IV* between Spock and Kirk, when they're in the truck trying to decide whether they want pizza, or whatever it was. It was a genuine, fresh moment that even the critics pointed out.

Q: *What do you think your character will be remembered for?*

A: I don't have the faintest idea . . . In several episodes and in three out of the five films, Chekov has suffered some kind of physical trauma [he laughs] and I am frequently asked about that. "Why is Chekov always getting beat up?" . . . I would like to think of Chekov as a character that has some sense of fun, that perhaps is not as institutionalized an officer as some of the others. That there's some irreverence about him . . . and I don't know what else to say because the opportunities have been limited as to how the character has been developed.

Q: *You write, don't you?*

A: Yes. I have a novel coming out soon. It has a science fiction setting, but it has little to do with science fiction. It's about two people who are marginal characters at best. Then they have to deal with an apocalypse and they [he laughs] don't get much better . . . I'm also trying to option a play, *Two Boys in Autumn*. It's about Tom Sawyer and Huckleberry Finn meeting years later, each harboring a secret. I toured in this play with Mark Lenard. I play Tom Sawyer. His secret is he never got over Becky Thatcher. And he likes little girls. [He laughs] Huckleberry Finn's secret is that he committed a mercy killing—his wife—and still feels guilty about it . . . I also have a film coming out called *Moontrap*.

Q: *Do you ever resent* Star Trek?

A: When I compare myself to some actors, who have all the talent in the world but who have never managed to break through, I feel privileged.

As each new *Star Trek* film has begun, I have walked onto the set anticipating a friendly reunion with the cast. I pull the heavy stage door back, and start fumbling my way along in the dark. Inevitably, an unusual, distinctive sound leads me to safety—George Takei's deep, resonant laugh. The sound is as jovial as George himself, who invariably is a cheerful, pleasant reminder that *Star Trek* is alive and well. I had a chance to ask George how *Star Trek* has influenced his own journey.

Q: *What have you done since* Star Trek IV?

A: I did a whole slew of TV work. The one that took me out of town was "Miami Vice," which was shot in Miami. "Murder She Wrote" was shot here locally. "McGyver" I did right here at Paramount. I went to England last year to do *Aladdin,* a musical version of *Alladin and His Magic Lamp,* and I played the genie. That closed in January. It played in Reading, England. Then I was back for the month of February and the first week of March because I was nominated for a Grammy for my reading of the audio cassette of the novelization of *Star Trek IV: The Voyage Home.* That Grammy was won by Garrison Keillor, but amongst my other competitors were no less than Leonard Nimoy reading a thing called "Whales Alive," as well as Katharine Hepburn and Lauren Bacall. Then I went to the Philippines to do "Return to the River Kwai." Then in July I went to Edinburgh to rehearse the play *Undertow* by Shimon Wincelberg. It won the Scotsman First Award at the Edinburgh national festival, an annual theater festival that they've had since 1948. I played Captain Kimura, a Japanese soldier who's marooned on an island near the end of the Second World War with an American soldier. In "The River Kwai" I play the commandant of the prison camp, Captain Tanaka. He is in the traditional sense a bad guy, but I saw him as a supremely good soldier, dedicated to his cause. Based on a real character and real incidents, *The Bridge Over the River Kwai* was a fictional piece by Pierre Boulle based on real events at a real prison camp. The story of "Return to the River Kwai" is based upon factual, historical occurrences.

Q: *Any of George in the commandant?*

A: I wouldn't be as ruthless, cutthroat or singularly driven as the character that I play. I do think of myself as a workaholic and as goal oriented. But I also consider myself an artist whose work is dealing with the human sensibility.

Q: *How much of George is in Mr. Sulu?*

A: I think there's a good amount of George Takei in Mr. Sulu and there's a good amount of Sulu that's not in George Takei also. Like Sulu, George Takei is a very disciplined, organized professional. George Takei, like Sulu, is also something of an iconoclast and an eccentric, the kind of Sulu that has as his hobby, fencing, an ancient martial arts activity.

Q: *Do you fence?*

A: I used to. I took fencing lessons but now with my crazy travel schedule I don't. It's been a good ten years now. But I do fancy that kind of activity. Where Sulu and George Takei differ is that Sulu is very mechanically oriented. He's a professional at what he does in the technological area, whereas George Takei is an artist. If George opened the hood of his car, he wouldn't know what to touch or what to kick or what to spit at.

Q: *How did you prepare for* Star Trek V?

A: Well, in terms of physical preparation, I had to ride a horse, and I don't ride horses. So for a week I drove out to Newhall to take, every day, lessons. Corky Randall started me out very gently, with the horse walking about in circles. And within two days, he had that horse actually galloping and it was terrorizing! But by the end of that week it was really a lot of fun and I went horseback riding on my own through Griffith Park a few weeks ago. But Corky had me firing phaser rifles while I was galloping, standing in my saddle! Beyond that, in terms of the character, it doesn't require much because we've been living with these characters for twenty-three years, and so I knew Sulu well.

Q: *How much has Sulu changed?*

A: There has been that passage of time, and of course we've changed physically. We'd like to think that the characters have matured. We know that they've advanced in rank, and that they have gained experience over the years. However, in terms of the scripts we really haven't changed that much. I'm still there at the helm console. My duties are essentially the same as what Sulu was doing when we were on the first five-year mission.

Q: *What has been your experience with [my father] as director?*

A: Directing a film of this complexity with all the kinds of technical aspects as well as the logistical aspects, locating in Yosemite and Ridgecrest, plus working at night, brings a lot of tension and trauma. I know all the front office relationships that are involved. The front burner has about twenty kettles boiling away. It's something that can drive a lesser man to ranting and raving, bursts of emotion and temperament. What really impressed me about Bill on this was knowing the kinds of pressures and forces that he's got to confront. On the set he has been extraordinarily vibrant and joyous, keeping the spirit of the set up. Keeping up the kind of creative, energized atmosphere that's necessary to get a good picture made. That's what has been most impressive about working with Bill.

Q: *How do you feel about this script?*

A: It's going into a whole new different area. That's the thing about the *Star Trek* movies. Each movie has been different in tone, texture, feel, quality. And here again we're moving off into another area while retaining elements from all of the past films. A philosophic film that questions who we are. The subtexts are very pertinent and specific to our times today— the issues of hostage taking, cultism, the environment having been successfully respected—our enjoyment of Yosemite in the twenty-third century makes a powerful statement.

Q: *When you're acting, what do you seek in a role?*

A: I like a role that challenges me so that I can use some of my own life experiences as a human being in the character. There are very few opportunities like that. I also look for a project that makes a statement, that has import for the audience viewing it. To play a character that has admirable qualities or supremely pathetic qualities that we can all find in ourselves, the great human weaknesses or the great gifts that an individual can have.

Q: *Why do you act?*

A: My mother says I made my theatrical debut in the

maternity ward. I think it's something about the need to perform, to become someone other than ourselves, the need to communicate via that need. I think it's almost an inborn need, something that you cannot really help, the way I cannot help the fact that I am a Japanese who is also American. Those are givens.

Q: *I know you are also very active politically?*

A: I am a citizen of this city. I am a member of this community in which I live. And I am a participant in the political process that makes this city work the way it does. We live in a participatory democracy which calls for the assumption of responsibility on the part of those of us who live in it. I am an activist in the community and in my city. I do participate on both a voluntary and an appointed basis in a lot of civic areas. One that I'm really most proud of has been having served on the board of directors of the Southern California Rapid Transit District and to have been a participant in the shaping, forming, and planning, early on, of the metrorail project. I think that that's going to be the great shaper and backbone of what LA will look like in the twenty-first century. I left that in 1984. I'm currently on the board of directors and the executive committee of the L.A. Theater Center, which involves two of my passions, the preservation and restoration of our heritage.

Q: *You're also on the L.A. Monument Committee?*

A: Yes, we're calling it, for the time being, The West Coast Gateway Committee. I'm on the judging committee. Last weekend we made a final decision and now we must sell the project to the people. I think it will be as controversial as the Eiffel Tower. The architect calls it *Steel Clouds*. The inside will be museums, galleries, theaters, a park that will connect the El Pueblo state historic park, the birthplace of LA, with the civic center and Little Tokyo. We intend to have the first phase completed by 1992, the anniversary of Columbus's arrival in America.

Q: *Do you feel like people are continually acknowledging you as Sulu and nothing else, in spite of your other activities? Has Star Trek ever been a source of frustration for you?*

A: Well, the thing is, if I felt that way there's nothing I can do about it. It's a given. Some of my actor friends say, "Why don't you leave *Star Trek?*" And I say, "Thank you very much, but if I left *Star Trek,* I'd forever be known as the guy that left *Star Trek.*" So I don't get away from it. It's a given in my life and as long as it's there I'll use it and enjoy it. Life would be a terrible drudge if something that's a given is terrible. "Oh, it's limiting me, it's confining me." It's like my saying, "Well, I'm a Japanese-American, and that's terrible."

Q: *You use them both in a positive way.*

A: Absolutely. I consider them an asset . . . [For example], when I served on the RTD board, my colleagues were attorneys or retired businessmen or people like that. If I have a particular view on an issue that I want to go public on, all I need to do is go and tell one of the reporters and I'll get it printed . . . there's also the flip side. It can be a liability. When I ran for city council, that's when "Star Trek" was still running in syndication. As a candidate there's this dumb thing called "the equal time rule." It's perennially brought up for examination, but it's not yet been acted on. What it says is, if any candidate appears on television, the other candidates have to have equal time. The inequality in it is that I can be a candidate running against half a dozen other people, and I am on the air say, seventeen minutes wearing this costume, and saying someone else's lines . . .

Q: *And that counts?*

A: But my opponents can each [have] access to say, "My name is Bob Smith and this is the way I feel about education," or "My name is Mary Jones and I feel this way about taxation." They can talk as themselves . . . The other side of that is, if the station chooses not to give a half-dozen seventeen minutes of their time, then their option is to pull the show that I appear on . . . Now I'd like to think that if I'm elected, I can speak for my other community, the entertainment community. But if I should get elected at the cost of my colleagues . . . I may be willing to forgo my residuals. But the other actors, writers, directors—my decision is imposing an economic penalty on them. So it would then be hypocritical to say I'm representing their interests when I've gotten in at their cost.

Q: *Is that what happened?*

A: I've been subsequently asked to consider running again for the [California State] Assembly, but I've decided that . . . after that experience, which gave me political credibility because I came in second with only a 3 percent difference from the guy that won . . . I really do enjoy my career. It's fun and it's fulfilling, and it gives me the opportunity to do these other things.

Q: *You think you might run again at some future date?*

A: I enjoy public service. I think it's an important thing that we do. But I think because of those problems my public service will be confined to appointed positions, advisory boards, things like that, rather than an elected position.

Q: *Is there a large crossover between entertainment people and political people?*

A: Well, being in the public arena in one capacity does give one some experience speaking publicly, in simplifying issues, and in articulating clearly to a large group of people . . . Also, if we're characterized in a heroic light in our professional acting career, it's certainly a persuasive image . . . So the opportunities for people in our business to cross over into the elected area are enhanced.

Q: *Well, I'd love to see you around. I'd vote for you.*

A: Thanks! [He laughs]

In one conversation I had with Jimmy Doohan, he mentioned that people often assume he speaks with a Scottish accent. I wondered how Jimmy felt about his incredibly successful identification with "Star Trek" and the character of Scotty. Was he proud, or did he feel frustrated about it? What other types of roles would he be interested in playing?

Q: *Would you like to comment on the message "Star Trek" brings to its audience?*

A: "Star Trek" is a morality play and a lot of people pick that up and I think that's probably one of the reasons why

"Star Trek" is as popular as it is. But I don't think it's the complete reason at all. As a matter of fact, I don't think anybody has really come up with the real reason why "Star Trek" has been as popular as it is. The only reason that I use is "Hey, it's got to be some kind of magic." You know, what else are you going to say because nobody even mentions a lot of the different things we had, like terrific scripts. I remember sitting around a table way back, five or six of us, and somebody was reading this script, and somebody was reading the script that followed it, and somebody was reading another script. People would say, "Wait until you read this one." Someone else would say, "Wait until you read this one." That was fabulous: actors don't normally get scripts like that, and we did on "Star Trek."

Q: *Do you have a favorite theme in* Star Trek V?

A: Well, I'm an engineer and all I care about is engineering really. Yet to get down to the brass tacks of engineering is really quite boring—for everybody, as far as I'm concerned. It's only when it breaks off into something else there for a second that I get to live a life other than the life of an engineer. That's when it's kind of fun.

Q: *Do you like Scotty?*

A: Oh yeah. Hell, I better. I'm so typecast now that I hardly do anything without a Scottish accent.

Q: *Is that very frustrating to you?*

A: Yeah, it's very frustrating and in fact, to me the height of the frustration came about fifteen years ago when I first realized that I was typecast. Then it was hard.

Q: *When did you first realize this?*

A: I was doing a movie in Spain in 1971, and I came back after six months over there and went to read for another part. I walked into the offices and the secretaries said, "Hello, Scotty," you know, and then the producer said . . . "Well, Mr. Scott." After the tenth time of not getting these jobs it was kind of like "Hey, this is tough, you know?" I would go up to people like John Conway . . . who had hired me thousands of times before because I was useful, and he would say, "Jimmy, you're known as Scotty." . . . I started in live television in New York . . . and I never played the same character twice . . . I did my hair the way the character was supposed to do it, and I did whatever the voice of the character had to do, because I'm not only good with accents, but I can change the tone of my voice in countless ways. So it really got bad . . . in 1972 and 1973, if it wasn't for personal appearances, which I started to do a hell of a lot, I would have been flat broke.

Q: *That's very ironic, isn't it?*

A: It was terrible, really. Then I got a play in San Francisco which I starred in with Rudy Solaris, and that ran for a year. So I met my wife and it was something to start with. Of course back in 1976 I did appearances at forty colleges, and in 1977 I did forty-two. And they just kept on going. Now my fee is so high the colleges can't afford me. So that's fine.

Q: *Do you feel like you've paid too high a price?*

A: Well, I'll tell you, it's become a different life. You know, I envisioned myself . . . [getting] large enough parts that I could of been like a Jack Nicholson, you know, kind of like a character actor . . . the only time I ever did leading roles was when I went back to Canada and the only reason why I went back there is I happened to stop at New York on my way home for Christmas, stopped in to the CVC offices. I spent about two hours there and came out with six months work . . . It was beautiful because it's more than an actor wants than to be working and working and working. It wasn't until the second year of "Star Trek" down here that I was making the kind of money that I was making in Toronto.

Q: *Do you feel that "Star Trek" may have helped you in a strange kind of way?*

A: Yes . . . as far as my career was concerned, it certainly has hurt me. But then again it has opened up something else.

Q: *I know you're interested in science. What kind of things have you done recently to satisfy your curiosity about it?*

A: Twice I've been to Lewis Research, the NASA Research base in Cleveland. I've seen two second blasts of rocket engines, and that's all they need to find out exactly what's going on. You sit and you watch that on film. I've also seen on film the zero g gravity experiments that go on, where they have a 500-foot chamber of concrete submerged into the ground and when they draw all the air out of that for the gravity experiments. They have to give the power company three weeks notice. The experiments are done at three in the morning. It's quite exciting. The first thing that they'll do is shoot up something which will stop just barely and then hang there for just a second at zero g and then it will plop down and the brakes to stop that pellet from going down—because it's traveling then at a tremendous rate of speed at 500 feet—is 20 feet of Styrofoam pellets. Those are the brakes. I also saw experiments with the new electric cars that will be coming out shortly. You know, [I] read in the paper recently that unless things change drastically in five or six years we have to go to electric cars.

Q: *Why are you doing this scientific research?*

A: Because I love to do it. I have been interested ever since. You know when they talk about Scotty reading technical journals? James Doohan has been doing that longer than Scotty's been alive. I was always very good in science at school . . . my father was a scientist and was the first man to invent high octane gasoline way back in 1924. He had three processes within two weeks time . . . I've been out to Ridgecrest—China Lake—about five times and twice to go to the labs at China Lake. It's the Naval Weapons Center. Of course I wasn't able to see the Department of Defense stuff, but there's many other things that they're doing out there. One man, a scientist, asked for a bit, like a drill bit, to bore a hole through a human hair and they got it for him.

Q: *Do you use any of the feelings you have visiting a place like that in playing Scotty?*

A: I'm sure that I transfer some of it to Scotty, but you see, that's the way I am anyway. I guess I do it automatically. When people ask me, how much is Scotty and how much is you, I tell them he's really 99 percent James Doohan and 1 percent accent.

Q: *Is Scotty any different in this movie than the last one?*

A: No, I don't think so. All they have to do is give Scotty

different things to do. That brings out different things. I don't really prepare at all. When I say that he's 99 percent James Doohan, [Scotty handles things] however James Doohan would handle them, because this is the closest that I ever come to playing myself.

Q: *Any challenges in this movie?*

A: No, not really. I'm working. I've been an actor for forty-three years. At the end of twenty years, you're supposed to be a complete actor. When I was about eighteen or nineteen, I started to feel that, because I'd been told that by my acting teacher. I said, "How long will it take?" And he said, "Well, depends on the type of work you get. It's about twenty years." And you know what? I started to feel that, a sort of sense comes over you where you think, "Hey, I don't care what they ask me to do, I can do it." That's the thrilling part of it. And a powerful feeling, knowing full well that at this moment in the scene, even though you still have to rehearse it, they're either going to be laughing about you making just one face or sound, or they're going to be crying. Or all the feelings in between. That's why when people ask me if I want to be a director, I say, "No way!" I'm satisfied being an actor. The rest of the time I'm terribly interested in seeing the country. My wife doesn't understand why I want another motor home. Within twenty months, I drove 52,000 miles in one. I take trips to places like Phoenix and Portland and Sacramento, etc., and sometimes I'll bring the whole family. I have six children all together. Four boys, two girls. Two boys are living with me in the San Fernando Valley.

Q: *How do you feel about the script for* Star Trek V?

A: I didn't care for it too much at first, but when we first read through it at Bill's place, I liked it a lot better. I think it's going to turn out very well. To me the best one we've done was *II: The Wrath of Khan. Four* was fabulous . . . but I prefer a good drama.

Q: *Tell me about your gas company commercials.*

A: I did two different versions, both shot at Raleigh . . . In January I have to do a bunch of radio commercials for them. The television one has now been established with my voice and face, and it will carry over. Who knows, I may do a bunch of newspaper and magazine ads too.

Q: *Didn't you recently do a TV show in Canada?*

A: "Danger Bay," it's a Disney Channel half-hour show. And I did six episodes of the new "Liars Club," which is just a game show in Vancouver. That's a great show, created by a friend of mine, Bill Armstrong. He used to be a writer/producer for the "Hollywood Squares."

Q: *What other things would you like to do? You'd make a great King Lear.*

A: Oh, God . . .

Q: *Would you like to do that?*

A: Yeah. As a matter of fact, I played Kent in *King Lear* with Maber Moore doing King Lear . . . Maber is a famous Canadian actor. He was just superb.

Q: *Do you agree with the way they shaped Scotty's character in* V?

A: The only objection I have to my character, and that's probably true of all actors, is that there's not enough to do . . . I think it's quite possible that he should be used not only as an engineer but as a human being.

Q: *Would you like to see that happen if they do another one?*

A: I think so. Of course, all the actors feel that way, but nevertheless that's the way I feel about it, you know. And that depends . . . Your father, Leonard, and Dee are the top stars, you know, what the heck. Right now, *Star Trek* has just become my way of life.

And what about the newest member of the cast, Larry Luckinbill?

I started with Larry Luckinbill. Throughout the filming, I was struck by his energy and enthusiasm for his part. How did he approach playing Sybok, and go about providing an emotional history for a character that had never existed in "Star Trek" lore? I had a chance to ask him about Sybok and his own life as we sat in his trailer during lunch break one day.

* * *

Q: *How did you get this job?*

A: I have no idea. Harve and Bill looked at the tape of *LBJ* and decided that the energy that I have was something they could use. There was a theatricality about the character of Sybok that they saw in what I did with LBJ. So this is Sybok as the 36th President from Texas in Space.

Q: *Were you aware of "Star Trek"?*

A: No. I had seen maybe one or two of the old series . . . it all came as a rather pleasant surprise to me. I went out and rented all the movies. But I really didn't know anything about "Star Trek" at all. I thought the movies, with the exception of the first one, were very good, increasingly good, which I like.

Q: *Can you describe Sybok to me?*

A: Sybok is tall, he's handsome . . . when we talked about the character, we talked about a number of things. We talked about Lenin. We talked about people who have gone off. We talked about Gene Scott, who's an evangelist. We talked about the charisma of a leader, any of the current third world leaders. And we came to the conclusion that really where the script heads with this—and it's a very deep thought and I accuse Harve of Mortimer Adlerism, [Adler], who wrote a book called *The Ten Philosophical Mistakes of the Twentieth Century*— it's a very deep survey of what we've tried to do as human beings and where we've ended up. What Sybok tries to do is to lead the unfortunate of the world to a better world, and his mistake or his misfortune is that he attempts to do it by stealing, lying, grabbing, forcing, and all that. And the same goes for Lenin, or Jimmy Swaggert, or whomever. They ultimately are culpable people because they will stop at nothing to achieve their ends.

Q: *What was your first impression of this story?*

A: I loved it. I thought it was [a kind of] spiritual resolution of this series of movies . . . it showed a more human Spock, an older, somewhat wiser and certainly funnier Kirk, it gave us a wonderful explanation of Dr. McCoy . . . and it all comes about in the pursuit of this Sybok rebel, who's trying to infect them and . . . take charge of the *Star Trek* bunch, which I like very much. I think that's the action of the script. He's trying to take them over, and they resist. In the earlier incarnation of the script, I liked it better when they didn't all resist quite so patently.

Q: *You don't get to take over the character of James Kirk, but you did have to deal with him as an actor and a director.*

A: I love Bill. I like his directing very much. I told him the other day [that] he's never said anything unhelpful to me. And when you consider the history of me and directors and the fact that I am very much an anti-authoritarian kind of person, I think that's remarkable, because I've never found directors particularly helpful. I find Bill helpful and it's not only because he's an actor and he understands, although to a large degree that's it, I think. He understands what the actor is trying to accomplish and he does trust actors. He trusts that you're there to do the job and he trusts that you're not there to f**k him up or counter his work. And to a remarkable degree he and I probably see eye to eye about acting itself. I'm not exactly his style of actor nor he mine, but I think that we both have a traditional background. We've played Shakespeare, we've done this, and there's a theatricality about it that's necessary, a kind of energy which is always there in his work and mine, too. I found it very disconcerting to be in a scene with him because here I am in a scene with the director and oddly enough, when the director stands in the scene, he's not your audience anymore. He's now some kind of character that you're supposed to be talking to. So maybe I relate less to him as Kirk than as the director. He's not Captain Kirk, he's the director of the film who comes to work dressed in a very strange suit . . . I look at him once in a while when he's standing there and I think, "I know he's not Kirk, he's really thinking about the camera angles and he's wondering if we're on our marks and he's thinking about 'is this shot the one that I really want?' " I know this is true because we talk about it all the time. That has been schizophrenic for me, and I know it is for him, because it's very difficult for him to do what he's trying to do. But I really think he's going to pull it off, although he may shortchange himself as a character in the film. I know I would feel that. But I really hope that this movie goes through the roof for him because I would like to see him work as a director, because the one thing about Bill is that he brings such joy to it. I'll never forget the day when everything went wrong. All day I think we got one shot in the shuttlecraft. We got down to do the shot, and he still took the time, wisely, to turn around and remind everybody of their job . . . and then went off into such a bizarre explanation to himself and to us about how everything had gone wrong, everything had screwed up, that we all started to laugh. He made it fun. As he said up in Ridgecrest once, ''We're all children here, and we're really here only to play act.'' That indicates real deep preparation.

Q: *Have you had any personal insights playing Sybok?*

A: Yes. Actually I kind of had one from the first day of dailies and today, just looking at the big speech [I give] to the crew, exhorting them to search for God . . . looking at my face and thinking ''No, Larry, you'll never be an aesthete.'' There's always something, to me, that will be essentially comic about my face . . . I could never really be Lenin without telling a joke.

Q: *Do you prefer playing comedy?*

A: I prefer playing dramatic, handsome, beautiful leading men, but unfortunately something else happens. I came to the movies wanting to be Montgomery Clift, because he fit my mood when I was in high school. I thought, ''Boy there's nothing better than to be sort of tragic and doomed and thin.'' But as it turned out, I'm sort of ribald and tending to put on weight here and there and sort of juicy and silly. As you get older you begin to realize that what girls like more than anything is a sense of humor in a man . . . If I had my druthers now, I'll wind up a cross somewhere between Gene Hackman and Jim Garner . . .

Q: *Why do you act?*

A: Just the money. [He laughs] I don't know, because I have thought of acting as a thirty-year detour. First I thought of it as a one-year detour, then a two-year detour, and so on. And after thirty years, you realize this ain't no detour. This is the way. You're on the road. But you think of it as a detour because it's not a fit occupation for a grown man and neither is anything to do with this business in a way, what you're doing or what Bill's doing or anything else . . . unless you accept the fact that playing, and playing for people to enjoy, is a worthy thing to do. And of course it is, but not when you look at it from the strictly business point of view of your parents, who want you to have something like a profession. You know, "Your brother's a doctor."

Q: *What do you hope the audience will see in this movie?*

A: I hope that what they see is a kind of light [thing] . . . something not too heavy, but that tends to show. If anyone takes a message from my character I think they should take away that "here's a guy with the best heart in the world but he just went about it in the wrong way and, as a result, he lost himself." He wanted very desperately to regain the trust and love of his brother in his later life . . . I think that could stand as a lot of grown men's epitaphs, that they wanted to make things right with their family. If they take away a sadness because that didn't happen, they'll take away the joy that at least they got together again, which I think is important.

Q: *Was reaching that point your biggest challenge?*

A: Absolutely. Reaching for that and trying to make it comprehensible to people. Make them feel it. The urgency of wanting to make up with Spock. It comes through as an older brother wanting to dominate him again, which is the way it would be.

Q: *What was the most refreshing thing in the movie?*

A: I have to say the assembling of this terrific crew and meeting George and DeForest and Nichelle and Jimmy and finding out what really silly people they are. And the crew. The first day we came in to do a really hard thing, [the] first shot [of] Sybok. Nobody knew what we were doing and we just sat in the make-up trailer and had fun. We played make-up and had a good time and I realized I was in the hands of people who had played make-up a lot and were willing to play and risk and dare to be silly. That was the first day of principal photography when I played bad Sybok and I didn't know who good Sybok was yet. I was on a blank set, talking to myself, and myself happened to be Bill reading me off camera.

Q: *What do you think the fight with the evil Sybok represents?*

A: The character coming to grips with . . . his real drives . . . the egotism that led him to think he was chosen to do this. Above all, led him to think that the end justifies the means. The end does not ever justify the means if the means are bad. The proof of the pudding is that he says, "Save yourselves. I will fight with me and destroy me!" That's still egocentric insanity if you really analyze it right down to the wire. But he doesn't have any choice. He will be consumed. It's Hitler in the bunker. The only wonderful difference is that Sybok isn't a burned out case, even at the end. He's still alive and kicking. And in *Star Trek VI* we'll see *Sybok: the Return.*

Q: *How does this project fit into your career?*

A: As I said to them when I was first interviewed, I've never really broken through on the big screen. I've always been kind of afraid. I've done lots of leads in little pictures, the off-Broadway kind of pictures—Paul Bartel, Jim Ivory, things like that. I've been awarded lots of things and been known as an actor's actor for a long time. I'd like to be known on the big screen, the public's actor. I'd like to really connect now with a bigger audience, and this is certainly a hell of a good opportunity to try that. The *Star Trek* system has lifted a lot of people and made them household words. My next movie I really want to play some kind of romantic character who gets the girl. I couldn't get God. I'm in a good spot right now. I'm over fifty and in a way that's a really good plateau with a slight upward incline to view the rest of your life and say what your next goals are. I've been through midlife crises six or seven times and come out the other end. Now I'm looking forward to actually coming to grips with the business as it really is and what I can accomplish in it. I really want to do that. I'm really grateful to *Star Trek V* and to Bill and Harve. People don't realize that after all these years of working and auditioning, to walk into a room and have your previous work speak for you, and to have a part offered to you with no audition, with no caveats—I'll never forget what Bill said, "What do we say to this marvelous actor?" And Harve said, "We'll be in touch with your agent." And man, I went home and cried. Not just because I was grateful, but how can anybody pick somebody out, just like that? And at the same time it was like, yeah, goddamn right they did!

7

POSTPRODUCTION

When my father returned to Paramount a few days after principal photography ended, a strange quiet had crept over the area where the *Star Trek V* crew had formerly made its home. Gone were the make-up trailers and the cheery morning smiles from Wes, Jeff, Donna, and Hazel. Gone were the busy grips, electricians, and assistant directors who would efficiently ready the set each morning. There were no more stuntmen laughing together in the cold morning air, no more actors intently studying their lines inside their trailers. *Star Trek V* seemed a mere memory, a ghostly whisper of days gone by. As he walked toward his office, my father couldn't help but feel a sense of loss at the absence of all that exciting activity.

His melancholy mood didn't last long. As soon as he opened the door, he was hit by a barrage of messages, appointments, and phone calls which required his attention. Most of them concerned the impending postproduction schedule, which was organized around several key events.

First, the editing of the movie had to be completed and finalized. Second, special sound effects and a musical score had to be created. Third, some dialogue had to be recorded, and other background noises added to the sound track. And fourth, the opticals had to be finished and added to the movie.

POSTPRODUCTION

There was still a long way to go before my father's job was finished.

The most important task was completion of the film editing, since most of the other jobs would require "locked film" before their material could be finalized. This meant my father and film editor, Peter Berger, would be working closely together for the next several weeks.

Peter had actually begun the editing process some time ago. As each phase of production was completed, Peter would sift through reel after reel of footage to make a rough assemblage of the film. Since each scene had been filmed in both wide and close angles, this meant Peter had to make some important choices on how to piece the film together. I asked him how he made those initial decisions.

"The process actually begins in dailies, when Bill is telling me which performances he likes," Peter said. "If there are, say, three takes on a close-up of Leonard, Bill might say, 'Gee, I like the first take best, or the first part of this, or the second part of that.' So that's your first guide, your first sort of road map of where he wants to go. You then have to see how that material works with where the scene is going storywise, and how all the performances work together. When I'm looking at dailies, I'm sort of deciding with the director, ruling out film as I'm running it, making notes as I go along . . . What I'm really doing is taking all that's been shot and making it into a workable story."

Peter began assembling the film on a "chem," a special machine which allowed him to run each reel of film individually while its picture played on a small screen in front of him. In this manner, he was able to make decisions about what material to include and then view the results of these decisions almost immediately. As he began this job, he kept a watchful eye over the pacing of each scene. It was critical to choose the right angles for each shot, the amount of time spent on each angle, and the proper emphasis of each plot point.

Certain things became apparent almost immediately. "For example, the back barroom scene never really worked correctly," Peter said. "We just kept whittling it down to make it helpful to the story instead of a hindrance." Other important decisions made during this phase were to shorten some of the army shots, remove the mind meld sequence between young Sybok and Spock, and eliminate all the Rockman footage.

"Our main objective during this period was to keep the pace of the movie going," my father commented. "This meant adding some things and getting rid of others. One of the more ironic things about editing occurred with the Trona footage. Even though we had struggled to get those shuttle shots in before sunrise, we had to cut them all out because they all had the Rockman climbing on top of the shuttle. Of course this was very difficult to do, since we had all worked so hard to get those shots done. But it was obvious we couldn't use them, so out they went. They were replaced by a sequence which had been reshot on the Paramount lot, where all shots of the shuttle no longer contained the Rockman. And there was now a blank spot in the film which Bran would later replace with the Rock Blob optical."

This was just one example of how the editing process shaped the film. Once my father and Peter finished their version of the film, they handed it to Harve so he could evaluate the material, so that he could perhaps make further changes to the pace and playing time of the film. Giving up control of the film caused my father tremendous anxiety.

"My version of the film was about two hours long," he told me. "That was too lengthy, since we had yet to add the opticals and end credits. So it was then up to Harve to cut some of this footage down to meet the apparent requirement of slightly under two hours. The problem was, I couldn't see where he could make any cuts. In my mind, each sequence was honed down to its bare essentials. I really couldn't imagine how it could be changed without damaging some important elements."

Harve faced a difficult challenge. He had to fit the film into the required time frame without damaging both the film's integrity and his friendship with my father. But he explained that there was only one issue with which he wanted to contend—the story.

"The problem of director expectations aren't unknown to Bill, Leonard, or anyone else," he said. "If a man shoots a picture, he's in love with every moment . . . But I have a different perspective. I say, 'I know you've worked hard for this, but it's irrelevant to the story.' " With this objective in mind, Harve's goal was to remove all unnecessary footage in the hopes of clarifying the story and meeting the timing requirements. By making these cuts he hoped to make "a terrifically good film a little bit better."

When he was finished, Harve played the results for my father in a studio screening room. Although he agreed with some of the changes, my father felt that many of the shots which had made the film unique had been lost. "As I was watching the film, I realized Harve had done a lot of things to the movie, some of which helped it and some of which I simply did not agree with," my father said. "A good example of how he helped it was the army sequence, in which I had included many stunts and long fighting sequences in my version. Harve had cut it down so that we only see the army overwhelming the town, which got to the point faster and was more ideologically consistent with Sybok's character. But I felt that some of the more important moments had been changed. For example, the opening sequence where Sybok's hooded figure comes riding into frame had been shortened dramatically. Also I noticed that the nine A.M. shot of the mountain at Trona was gone. I felt that these were two of the more important moments in the film, since they went a long way towards giving the movie an epic quality which it otherwise lacked. I realized at this point that Harve and I would have to work out a compromise position with which we could both live."

There then began a process of negotiation between the producer and director in which they decided what would remain in the film. "The negotiation consisted of me saying things to Harve like, 'I feel very strongly about this particular shot,' " my father said. "Of course, I tried to remain as reasonable as possible, because the last thing in the world I wanted was a complete breakdown of communication with my dear friend. And we agreed on certain things. We put Sybok's riding shot back in, as well as the nine AM shot, and kept certain cuts that he had made which we both thought helped the film. What was most surprising to me was the realization that legally the producer could take the film away from the director at this point. Mel Efros explained to me that after filming stops, the director no longer has the ultimate authority, that it is the producer who now takes over the film. I had no idea that this could happen. There have been instances of directors refusing to work on the final mix of the film because they have felt that their picture had been ruined. That's not what happened here, but it has happened on other films. And suddenly I realized that, to my great and undying satisfaction, Harve Bennett was sharing his legal authority with me. So we worked out a compromise where I got some of what I wanted, and he got some of what he wanted. I realized for the first time that it was no longer my film, which is what I had felt for three months during principal photography. It was now our film, in which several groups of people were collaborating to create the best picture possible.''

This collaborative process included deciding where music should be added to the film. This decision was made with the help of Jerry Goldsmith, the Academy Award-winning composer who created the music for *Star Trek: The Motion Picture*. Harve, my father, and Jerry all watched the movie on Peter's kem, discussing where the proper moments would be to place the music. Once these decisions had been made, a music editor recorded the exact length of each chosen scene. It was then up to Jerry to create music to enhance each of these scenes.

I visited Jerry at his home to find out how he works. When I arrived, Jerry led me to his study, where I was greeted by the sight of several computers, electronic keyboards, and other complicated musical equipment. Upon seeing this vast electronic array, I asked Jerry if this was how he generated his initial ideas. He explained he started the old-fashioned way, on the piano.

''I go home and look for a basic theme, a basic phonetic idea on the piano,'' he said. ''Then one thing leads to another." I motioned to the equipment. Did he use it to expand on all his music ideas? He answered that in the case of *Star Trek V,* not all the music would be electronically generated. "Twenty years ago, what we had electronically was very primitive," he informed me. "Now the [computers] have these microprocessors in them, and they all have memory, so that if you program a sound it stays there . . . I wouldn't want to do [*Star Trek*] all electronically, but I used a little bit of electronics on the first picture and I will on this picture, as well as an eighty-five-piece orchestra."

In addition to the electronically generated material, he explained that an important aspect of the music for *Star Trek* was to work with the emotional content of the material. "The idea is not to mimic what is on the screen, but try to get the pulse beating faster and the tears coming, or whatever the emotion is," he commented. "I think the interesting problem in *Star Trek* is that you're dealing with space, which is infinite and immense, and yet within that the characters maintain an intimacy." He pointed to one particular scene as an example.

"In the campfire scene, I wrote a new theme that opens the picture. We start with the *Star Trek* theme, and then we go into the whole Yosemite scene which is this very big, expansive, very beautiful, very broad scene. It gets bigger and bigger and then changes . . . later on in the campfire scene, Kirk says something about dying alone. I use that theme [then], to tie it all together. That one theme starts out in a big and broad way, and then comes down to something very quiet and intimate."

When I talked to him, Jerry had not yet composed all the music for *Star Trek V.* Nevertheless, he had some definite ideas about what he would be doing for certain scenes in the film. The Klingon music from *Star Trek: The Motion Picture* would be back to underscore all the Bird of Prey scenes. But for some of the more humorous moments in the movie, Jerry planned to leave well enough alone.

"I'm not planning to accentuate the comedy," he informed me. "If it plays fine, let it. Comedy has its own music. When Scotty bounces his head and knocks himself out, there's no music; it takes drama to the point of silliness, which is not the intention of this movie." Above all, he saw the God planet sequence as his biggest challenge. "You're dealing with a very touchy subject to begin with and you don't want to give it away until the very last second," he said. "But what the music will be like, I don't know yet." As I turned to leave, his Oscar glinted at me from the table on which it was displayed, assuring me that *Star Trek V*'s musical score was in good hands.

But while Jerry was busy composing, other aspects of the sound track needed attention as well. Since *Star Trek V* is a science fiction film, many of the sounds heard during the movie don't really exist which meant that someone would have to create them. In addition, since some of the dialogue was difficult to hear on the production track (particularly dialogue from the location filming), it would be necessary to rerecord this unusable material in a studio environment. It would also be necessary to repeat this process for some of the other sounds on the track, such as footsteps or clinking glasses.

Additionally, if an edited scene included both close-ups and wide shots, the sound track also had to be edited to match this new composition. Finally, someone had to put all the pieces of the puzzle together onto one usable track.

For *Star Trek V,* the task of overseeing all these aspects of production fell to supervising sound editor, Mark Mangini, who had worked on *Star Trek: The Motion Picture* and *Star Trek IV.* It was his job to hire the people for the various departments and oversee the "sonic approach to the film," as he put it. Mark spent many hours with Harve and my father discussing what sounds they wanted, and then transmitted this information to the various editors working on the film, whose job it would be to implement it in their individual areas of responsibility.

A large part of Mark's own work came in sound design, where he had to both oversee the work of the other sound design editors as well as participate in the creation of the material himself. Mark told me that he felt that this phase of postproduction afforded him a unique opportunity to stretch his imagination.

"Most people think that the sound that they hear in the

theater was recorded on the set," he commented. "Almost exactly the reverse is true. Just about everything you hear in these kinds of movies is completely fabricated. What we do is we create a sound for the devices and the gadgets and the computers and the spaceships and the overall environment . . . [for example], you can't go out and record the starship *Enterprise*. You can't record a photon torpedo. Someone has to invent those sounds, by using synthesizers or original acoustic recordings from out in the field. Then you massage and manipulate and mix them to create a whole new unusual sound that you've never heard before. So a photon torpedo might be a combination of things like an explosion, a synthesizer noise, a mix of strange oscillators . . . we might even add the slowed-down sound of a dog barking because that will give it the quality we're looking for, some strange acoustic quality that you can't place. The audience will say, 'Wow, that's weird,' but they won't know what it is."

Mark would often rely on sounds from prior *Star Trek* movies. "I have personally received [letters] from Trekkies who are concerned that the sound from feature to feature differs," he said. "There hasn't been a standard for the engine sounds, or turbolift sounds, or phaser sounds . . . it is incumbent upon me to try to respect our audience. Anything I can do to enhance the appeal of this movie in all my best interest [I will do it] . . . My ego isn't so big that I have to have only my sounds in the movie. If they love the old [Bird of Prey] de-cloaker, great! Then I can spend more time on the other sounds for this movie. So, I'm using de-cloaking from past movies, phasers from past movies, the *Enterprise* engine sounds, the Bird of Prey engine sounds, and the beam-up and beam-down sounds. So there is a consistency."

For the sounds unique to this movie, my father and Mark worked closely together to create something unusual. During the mind meld sequences, for example, my father wanted to use the sounds of the human body—heartbeats, breathing, blood pumping through the veins—to suggest the private, insular qualities of those moments. Mark later explained that he would use my father's suggestions to help guide his overall approach to the movie.

"We are using [those sounds] for the beginning of the picture," he said. "This is sort of a broad conceptual idea of your father's, that we draw analogies when we are trying to design sounds . . . if you look at the film as an entity, any given part of it should reflect something about its overall anatomy . . . so it's the heart [that] we use as a signature for the elements that reflect the soul of the movie . . . your father is trying to achieve this organic human spiritual feel [for the sound], which is what he's trying to inject into the movie."

In addition to the background noises that needed to be created, some of the sounds captured during filming also needed to be rerecorded. This process is known as "Foley," named after the man who invented it. In a small recording studio, an actor stands in front of a screen, where a black and white copy of the movie is playing. While watching this film, the actor will duplicate the background noises into a microphone. These sounds are recorded by editors sitting in a booth above the studio floor, and will later be incorporated into the movie so the background noises become clear and not muddled.

Sometimes the process is fairly straightforward. The editors may use clinking ice cubes to simulate the sound of someone drinking something with ice in it. But because the Foley editor sometimes uses materials totally unrelated to the original sound, the process can appear quite odd. For example, some of the sounds of horses clomping along were actually made by plastic cups. And in order to make the Klingons sound as rough as possible when they walked, Mark and the other Foley editors incorporated creaking leather and chains into the track. Because the Foley elements were so important to the overall sound of the film, the process was quite long and involved, and actually took several weeks to complete.

Mark was also responsible for coordinating the "ADR," or Automatic Digital Recording. ADR is an essential part of the film's sound engineering phase, since often it is difficult to understand or hear what the actors are saying on the production track of the film. The actual process occurs in a similar fashion to the Foley recordings. For example, if some dialogue needs to be rerecorded, it then becomes necessary to rent out a sound studio, call the actor down to the stage, watch the film on the screen, then recreate the performance for the sound editors in the booth. Although the actor is given a signal when to start talking, the ADR process is a very precise art which requires talent and patience to do correctly. I sat through many ADR sessions with my father, admiring the way he would coach the actors back into their roles, as well as their ability to recreate their performances without the benefit of make-up, costume, or atmosphere to guide them.

One of the more amusing and entertaining parts of ADR was recording all the background, or "Walla Walla" voices. The production track could not support the complexity of voice tones and dialogue my father wished to have in the crowd scenes, so it was necessary to have a group of actors who specialized in such background voices come in and record those parts. On the same stage that all the principals performed their ADR recordings, these actors sat in a circle around a microphone as each crowd scene was played on the screen in front of them. The group's director would then select a few actors at a time to improvise dialogue that would correspond to the extras' performances.

A particularly hilarious example of this method occurred while recording the background voices for the barroom scene. As each group of actors got up to perform their improvised dialogues, the studio took on the air of a comedy club where each act was funnier than the next. Three men got up and began a conversation where they were bargaining liters of water for the various women in the bar. When they were finished, two ladies approached the microphone and did a funny bit that matched up brilliantly with the performances of the "two women of alternative life-style" fighting in the corner. After them, four more men got up and began having a conversation in four different languages, Italian, Portuguese, Hebrew, and Latvian! By the time another actress did the Cat

Lady (humming in a half-human, half-feline tone of voice), my father was hysterical with laughter.

"I started out dreading this day because I thought it would be boring and long," he said. "But it's turned out to be one of the most fun times I've ever had on this movie. This is one of the most talented group of actors I've met in a long time."

When ADR was finally finished, it was time for the "final mix," where all the sounds recorded for the film would be combined into a single entity. At a nearby recording studio, my father, Harve, Ralph, Brooke, Peter, Jerry, and Mark all sat down in front of a large mixdown console and discussed how the various ADR, Foley, sound design, production track, and music elements should be combined together to form the perfect soundtrack for the movie. With the film showing in front of them, the studio engineers played back the different tracks at various levels so the group could hear all the possible choices. After much deliberation, they finally settled on a mix which they felt would bring maximum excitement, emotion, and tempo to the film.

Throughout this mixing process, it was apparent how much talent, dedication, and enthusiasm each member of Mark's team had contributed. But for my father, this process was a double-edged sword. As much as he enjoyed listening to the sound of the film taking shape, the final mix was one of the last stages in which he would be a participating member. As the process drew to a close, he knew his work was almost over.

For one member of the team, however, *Star Trek V* was still very much a full-time job. While the group at Paramount was busy with the sounds of the film, Bran Ferren was completing the special effects at his studio on the East Coast. He had three main areas of responsibility. First, he had to shoot all the optical effects for the movie, including the God column and Rock Blob effects at his studio in East Hampton. Second, he had to supervise the assemblage of all the optical material at his optical house in Manhattan. And third, he was responsible for obtaining shots of all the miniatures—the *Enterprise,* the Klingon Bird of Prey, and the shuttlecrafts—at his studio in Hoboken, New Jersey. Because we were curious how Bran worked his movie magic, my father and I decided to visit his workshops in person. When we arrived, Bran himself gave us the grand tour.

Our first stop was the miniatures studio in Hoboken, where the crew there was in the midst of filming the *Enterprise* flying sequences. We were both surprised to learn that the ship had been damaged to such an extent after being loaned to another studio for tour purposes that it had to be repainted and re-detailed. In fact, Bran informed us, each of the 30,000 panels of the ship had been individually hand-painted in various shades of gray to give it a realistic look.

As we gazed at the hull of the ship, Bran explained how the miniature process worked. In front of the *Enterprise* lay a large track, upon which a computer-controlled camera rested. This camera would film each shot of the *Enterprise,* a process which would be repeated as various elements were added. For example, a brief shot of the *Enterprise* flying through space actually contains many separate pieces of film. All the miniature shots use the blue-screen process, so the first shot would contain just the *Enterprise* and this blue background. The second shot would contain the ship lit the way it was supposed to look on the film. Since the *Enterprise* has twelve different sets of lights on it, the crew might then shoot these lights in two or three different combinations in order to control their intensity. In this manner, as many as five different pieces of film could be used just for one shot.

This process was repeated for the Bird of Prey shots, using a detailed model of the Klingon battle ship. As with the *Enterprise,* we had a chance to inspect the Bird of Prey in detail. Upon close examination of the miniature, I was startled to see a picture of Nilo staring at me from the bridge! Bran laughingly explained that some of the team members loved to play jokes such as these on their fellow workmates. In fact, when they'd first received the *Enterprise,* they found a plastic lizard in the hull.

Once these blue-screen shots of the miniatures had been obtained, the film was transported to Bran's optical house in

Manhattan. There, the blue screen would be replaced by moving starfield. Because the starfield film is also broken into several different elements, as many as thirty, forty, or even fifty pieces of film could be used for one scene.

Combining these pieces of film together was a huge job in itself, and had to be done on a machine called an "optical printer." Bran himself had designed their newest printer, whose special elements reduced the amount of time ordinarily required to combine the film.

Next, we moved on to his East Hampton studio, where the majority of the special effects photography was shot. Long Island seemed an odd place to house a special effects studio, but Bran said he preferred working in the country air to the cramped confines of Manhattan. When we arrived at our destination, we could both see why. Large houses stood on tree-lined streets, their backyards seemingly extending all the way to the ocean. The air was pristine and cold, and on all sides of the studio were trees and blue sky, with no traces of smog or traffic noise to spoil the quiet.

When my father and I entered the large studio, we were amazed at the amount of equipment which it housed. Cameras, computers, and other mysterious equipment filled each room we passed. Finally, we came to a large open area. In the back was a large water tank with several people busily working around it.

Bran informed us they were shooting the Great Barrier effects. By dropping different chemicals into the water tank, the crew was able to generate a number of amazing-looking chemical reactions. Filming these reactions would constitute the swirling masses of the Great Barrier clouds.

Near the tank stood a large Vista Vision camera and a beam splitter. In front of this equipment was a tall cylinder, extending almost to the ceiling. As we watched, the cylinder began to spin, creating the image of a large column of light. The beam splitter then projected George Murdock's image onto the cylinder, so that God appeared to be floating inside the column of light. This image would eventually constitute the God column effect. Bran also explained that he would repeat the process for all the God heads, using film of each face which had been preshot by my father during principal photography.

Bran had begun to seem like something of a wizard, and the next phase of our tour did not change this impression. Leading us down another corridor, he entered a room where several computers lined the walls. Pointing to one, he told us this particular computer could photograph objects so closely, that it was possible to see even the tiniest of details. To prove his point, Bran took a quarter and put it inside the compartment where the camera lens was housed. As we watched, he manipulated the computer so that its monitor showed first the printing on the quarter, then a single letter, then a speck of dust on the edge of the coin. He explained that he would use this process to film the entrance to the God planet, since the Bierstadt optical he was formerly planning had been cut out of the budget.

But rescuing the movie's initial concepts was not his only job. While he was busily supervising all his other tasks, Bran was also finalizing his ideas for the Rock Blob effect. He was using the sketches which Nilo had developed during the last stages of principal photography as his guide. It was Bran's job to take these sketches and transform them into reality, a feat made even more difficult because of the time pressures involved. Despite the scheduling demands, my father remained confident that the sequence would remain one of the more exciting and compelling moments in the film.

Bran next invited us to his home, where we were given a real treat. Bran's lovely girlfriend, Robin, conducts her catering business out of the house's industrial-size kitchen. A Cordon Bleu chef, Robin fed us to some of the best food we'd tasted in a long time. It was an incredibly hospitable way to end our adventure on the East Coast.

Out west, other members of the *Star Trek V* crew were putting the finishing touches on the film. Among them were Bill Taylor and Syd Dutton, the partners responsible for the matte paintings used in the film. It was their job to paint-in some of the backgrounds that were difficult or impossible to obtain on the stage or location, such as the shot of Mount

Rushmore with the black woman president's face, a shot which was later cut. In addition, they would paint a forest scene which would be used in the final shot of the movie.

For the movie's ending, my father had originally wanted a long pullback from the campfire which would then tilt up into the stars. When he was informed this pullback would be too expensive to implement, he was crushed. However, he discovered that virtually the same effect could be achieved using a dissolve into a matte painting. Bill and Syd then designed and shot a painting which so closely resembled the actual set that when the real film was dissolved into the matte painting, it was almost impossible to tell them apart.

In spite of the large numbers of people now working on all aspects of the film, the project still remained very much a personal experience for my father. He had spent months formulating the concept, then an equally intensive period of time with Harve Bennett and David Loughery shaping that concept into an acceptable story. Next had come the long preproduction process, where he set the costume, wardrobe, set, make-up, and other departments into motion. Once on location, he had expended tremendous energy, both physical and emotional, making each shot conform to the images he had dreamt of long before, a process that had continued during the rest of principal photography back on the Paramount lot. Once actual filming had wrapped, he spent an intensive few months shaping the editing and sound aspects of the film into their final forms.

Now, as the last of the optical and matte shots were incorporated into the film, he prepared for the final phase of his involvement with the movie—the preview screening process. Filled with both anticipation and dread, he knew the screening room at Paramount would soon be filled up with the people he most wished to please—the audience.

"This process is very important to me," he said in the last days before the screenings were scheduled. "It is these people who will tell me whether the movie was slow or exciting, inspirational or offensive. More than any studio executives, fellow crew-members, or friends, their opinions are the ones that matter." As the day of the first screening quickly approached, I knew my father was hoping for the best. And so was I.

Star Trek V: The Final Frontier was about to become a reality.

Reality, however, proved less than encouraging. After the first preview screening, the audience was asked to fill out questionnaires rating the film. Their responses shocked everyone. Only a small percentage of the audience had rated the film "excellent"—a category in which most of the "Star Trek" films had been placed. A discussion group was held after the film ended, in which approximately fifteen audience members talked about their reactions to the movie.

The "Star Trek" team listened with grim faces as the group listed their objections, the most strenuous of which dealt with the ending of the film. The audience did not understand why Korrd rescued Kirk. They were also unsure of Spock's role in the story since his loyalty seemed to waiver at times. In addition, problems with some of the (temporary) optical effects and uneven pacing were keeping the film from "selling" its audience.

Only two weeks were left before the film had to be locked for printing. Even less time remained to adjust the crucial moments of the movie. Harve's notable experience proved invaluable at this point, and he joined forces with my father to tackle the film's remaining problems.

First, they edited out five minutes from the film, which corrected the film's pacing problems and more clearly defined Sybok's role. They then adjusted the ending of the film, adding a voice-over of Spock saying "Captain Klaa, someone wishes to speak with you" after Spock demands cooperation from General Korrd. Harve also wrote, and my father shot, an additional scene on board the *Bird of Prey,* where Kirk confronts Korrd, Korrd exerts his supreme authority over Klaa, and Klaa apologizes for his unauthorized actions. This scene was the key element in explaining Kirk's rescue. Then, when Spock is revealed in the gunner's chair, the full impact of his heroic actions becomes clear. He convinced Korrd to help Kirk.

Kirk could not die because he was never alone—Spock never deserted him.

With these adjustments, and the addition of the final musical, sound, and optical effects, the team hoped they had remedied the problems that had confronted them. They would find out at a second preview screening. As the theater filled with eager viewers, I knew my father was anxiously awaiting this new audience's reaction, one that would tell him whether the team's last few weeks of effort had been successful.

The lights dimmed, the film began—and his worries were quickly dispelled. Laughing and cheering throughout, this group's reaction to *Star Trek V* was a far cry from the first audience's. After a resounding round of applause at the end, the group was once again asked to rate the film. This time, the responses proved what the "Star Trek" team had known all along: the film was a winner. As one member of the audience put it: "It doesn't matter where they go or what they do—as long as the 'Star Trek' crew is together, anything can happen."

For my father, this screening proved a vindication for all his efforts, hopes, and dreams. And *Star Trek V: The Final Frontier* proved once again that "Star Trek" was one of the most enduring legends of our time.